Early Praise for *Blood Drama*

"*Blood Drama* is very much a thriller, but it is a thriller with a romantic twist. Ian Nash combines innocence and recklessness in a way that endears him to the reader as much as it confounds the other characters in the novel. One can only imagine why he believes himself more capable of finding the bank robbers than the FBI, even to running his own sting, but he does. And when Ian begins to woo the beautiful Latina FBI agent officially in charge of the investigation, we see that his basic optimism about the future remains intact. Ian Nash is not an easily defeated man. He is a winner in spite of himself, and we love him for that."

— Sam Sattler, Book Chase

"I really enjoyed this novel, and I honestly hope it winds up being the first book in a series featuring the two main characters."

— Kristina Davis,
reviewer, Goodreads

"My keyword for Christopher Meeks is 'Authenticity.' As an award-winning dramatist, he knows theatre from the inside-out, and his frequent quotes from David Mamet add a savory sub-strata of wit and wisdom to *Blood Drama*. Mainly, though, he unfailingly entertains! Christopher Meeks synthesizes all with elan in this most recent narrative triumph."

— Gerald Locklin
author of *The Vampires Saved Civilization*

Other Books by Christopher Meeks

Love At Absolute Zero

The Brightest Moon of the Century

The Middle-Aged Man and the Sea and Other Stories

Months and Seasons and Other Stories

Who Lives? (A Drama)

Blood Drama

CHRISTOPHER MEEKS

White Whisker Books

Los Angeles

ISBN: 978-0-9836329-6-2

Library of Congress Control Number: 2013934558

Copyright © 2013 Christopher Meeks

First Edition

Editor: Lynn Hightower

Book design by Deborah Daly

Published by White Whisker Books, Los Angeles, 2013

PRINTED IN THE UNITED STATES OF AMERICA

*For my absolutely favorite librarian, Ann Pibel,
and to all librarians, including Michael Toman
at the South Pasadena Public Library.*

*This is also dedicated to Daniel Will-Harris, who convinced me
some years ago it was time to publish.*

Chapter One

"Coffee?" Ian said in the discomfort of Professor Cromley's office. The place looked like a small book depository with a view and a Mr. Coffee machine.

"Ian… Ian… Look, Ian. I'm—"

"I just thought we were meeting with—"

"We met."

"Without me? I don't understand."

"Coffee?" said the gray-bushy-haired man, pouring himself a cup. "Maybe some coffee would put you at ease."

"But the committee—"

"So I'll get to the point. We don't think you've shown enough progress in your dissertation."

"Two hundred pages?"

"You're taking the wrong approach on Mamet."

"It's still a work in progress."

"People are like gloves," Cromley said. "And sometimes they don't fit. It's not just the dissertation. It's your whole performance in the program."

Ian felt a rage building, but that wouldn't help. A better approach was needed. He calmed himself as best as he could, flattening the new blue silk tie he'd bought for the occasion against his blazer. "I'm sorry, sir," he said. "Maybe we've miscommunicated in the last few meetings. You'd given me certain dates, and I've kept to those dates."

"We debated long and hard, Ian," said the professor, sitting. The man looked toward Ian but not at Ian, as if delivering sad news to a war vet's spouse. "Your research isn't breaking new ground, and the recent problem with the class you taught—"

"I can't help low enrollment."

"I'm talking about your blow-up with that student—"

"Her rant against men—"

"No matter."

The rest of the meeting felt like a slow-motion crash. He was out of the program, as easy as lights out at the end of a play. He stared out Cromley's window at the wide view of campus, at modern buildings tucked into the green landscape, at trees still lush in October, their leaves blowing like moving fingers. The view was as if from Mt. Olympus. Was Cromley a god?

As Ian Nash drove his twelve-year-old Corolla the fifty miles north on Interstate 5 from the University of California Irvine campus back to his South Pasadena rental, he kept replaying the conversation. He was a glove? He didn't fit the program? If it don't fit, you must acquit, he thought. Ian had paid the tuition and taught. He attended the classes. Just because one undergraduate student was out of line was no reason to be thrown out of the program.

"Don't think of it as failing," Cromley had said. "Think of it as an opportunity to do something else."

That was outright snide. What would he do now for money? What would he do now for his life?

He was so consumed with these thoughts, he missed the Marmion Way turnoff on the Pasadena Freeway, which, if you weren't looking for it, came up so fast around a bend, you'd zoom by it as he did. Ian exited at Orange Grove, and, again so caught up in his thoughts, he drove without paying attention. He would need a job. What would he do for work without his degree? And what was to be learned here? After all, as David Mamet wrote in his book, *Three Uses of the Knife: On the Nature and Purpose of Drama*, "We have our ability to learn a lesson, which is our survival mechanism." The lesson was he needed money to live.

On Fair Oaks Boulevard in South Pasadena, moments after he decided he could use a coffee now, Ian noticed the logo of Carrie's Coffee on the Landwest Bank Building. He wondered would Professor Cromley call that a "deus ex machina," a coincidental ending? An ending to what? His morning? No, sometimes coincidences happened.

The gold-painted brick building stood out from its neighbor, the pharmacy. Carrie's Coffee paid well, he remembered one of his students saying in a directing seminar he'd taught. The small franchise had a health program and offered flexible hours. Amber, his former undergraduate student, made manager in no time at a Carrie's and loved the place. Perfect. He turned into the open lot. Ian would apply to Carrie's. He wasn't the kind of guy to mope around. He wouldn't let Cromley get the best of him.

Inside, Ian was surprised to see that Carrie's was part of the grand marble-floored bank lobby. Potted plants, mahogany wainscoting on the walls, and the same wood was used for the open teller area and the Carrie's counter. It gave the place a friendly feel. Tables and chairs were for the coffee drinkers, and comfortable leather seats were placed near the inset fireplace with burning gas logs. This would be a great place to work.

Ten minutes later, a Carrie's application before him, Ian sipped his coffee and shook his lucky Cross pen hard in a swift metronome motion to force all the blue to hit the tip. The pen hadn't been lucky for him with Cromley. Ian made incessant circles on the back of the application. He knocked the pen against his wrist and made circles again. The pen came back to life.

He glanced around. Bank business was brisk. A long line stretched all the way back to Carrie's tables. It was a Friday, after all. People were cashing paychecks or getting money for the weekend. There were more people working than he expected.

Ian returned his attention to his application and filled out most of it. "Salary desired" said one of the last spaces. As an undergraduate lecturer, he'd been making over forty dollars an hour, but he couldn't get that here. What was minimum wage these days? He didn't know. Was fifteen dollars an hour too much to ask for? He wrote it in, scratched it out and wrote in sixteen. Maybe it should be less, and he scratched out the whole space. Now it was too sloppy. He folded the application in half and put it in his blazer. He'd ask for another. He laid down the pen, took a sip of coffee, and looked around again. It was a great place to watch people as they came from all directions.

Ian spotted a woman with a white scarf come from the hallway and restrooms to the left of the teller area. She sashayed toward him like a model, wearing tight jeans and a killer push-up halter-top in green, and, despite her sunglasses, Ian knew their eyes connected because she smiled. He smiled. Definite connection. She then fiddled in her purse, standing at the end of the banking line near him. Today was working out after all. Another possibility: she could be Stella in *A Streetcar Named Desire.* She was gorgeous, had that sense of intelligence, and might be looking for kindness from strangers. Maybe she would be the one, his one, the one who'd make the last relationship fiasco with Pierra just a stumble on his path—not to mention the vitriol from his female student, the one who'd gotten him fired. How could he get her attention again? He cleared his throat. Nothing. Then he sneezed really hard. She and a few others in the line turned around. "Gesundheit," she said. Their eyes connected again.

"Thanks," he replied. She returned to her purse and pulled out a gun. She shouted, "This is a holdup. Everyone lie on the floor. Shut your eyes!"

The tellers and everyone dropped. So did the people at Carrie's. So did Ian. Only the music playing in the background, Rod Stewart's "Maggie May," kept going. Stewart said, "Oh, Maggie."

Ian's blood pounded so loudly in his ears, and his breath came with such difficulty, that he thought he might pass out. He shouldn't have come here. Coincidence again? He could hear Cromley quoting Mamet from Ian's dissertation: "It is difficult, finally, *not* to see our lives as a play with ourselves as hero." He didn't feel heroic in the least. Was this determinism at work? If he hadn't missed his exit, he would have been home and would have missed this. We are what we do.

Ian could hear footsteps near him, one set, then another. Accomplices? Ian didn't see any of the action because his cheek lay against the marble floor and his eyes were closed. Best to do what they wanted. He could hear movement in the teller area, then sounds of bank drawers opening.

Ian opened one eye. People lay around him like fallen man-nequins, unmoving. The hold-up woman's legs were like denim saplings. She wore tight boots with sharp heels.

A shot rang out, then another, and Ian squeezed both eyes so hard he'd hope it'd keep all bullets away. A man screamed in agony.

"Why'd you do *that*?" shouted the woman.

"He had a gun," her male accomplice yelled back.

Ian looked. Who got shot?

"Help… me," groaned a male voice.

Ian lifted his head. The woman pressed hard on the guard's shoulder to stop blood, which covered his shirt and her hand. She looked upset about it, ripping the guard's shirt to make a tourniquet. Two men were behind the tellers' counter bagging money. One of them, a tall burly guy with perspired underarms, had a ski mask on, but the other, a thinner man, had no mask, only a thin mustache, sun-glasses, and a baseball cap. No one else moved.

Ian quickly lay back down, but he was breathing faster. If he died, would anyone know to call his parents in Winnipeg? Would they care if he died? Did anything in his wallet say Winnipeg?

At least he was in his good blazer and pants. His mother had told him as a kid to always wear clean underwear in case he was found dead that day. Today might be the day, and he had not only clean underwear, but also a new silk tie from Macy's, one he bought for the committee. Maybe he shouldn't have worn good clothes and clean underwear. Maybe the grim reaper would stay away if he'd worn yesterday's boxers and a dolphin T-shirt from Tijuana.

"Zetta," shouted the gunman. "Leave him be. We gotta go."

He said her name? That wasn't bright, thought Ian.

"Keep bagging," Zetta said back. In a softer voice she added, "You shouldn't have done this." Ian again looked up. He had to see. There was blood on the marble. Zetta, however, was twisting a tourniquet on the guard's upper arm. The guard was totally immobile, breathing hard, and his eyes stared toward the ceiling. The man looked to be in shock, perhaps even close to death.

A siren broke the silence. No—there were sirens, plural.

"It's past two minutes," said the man with the mustache in a high voice and sweaty face.

"To the car," said the woman, jumping up, and the two men bounded over the counter.

"A hostage," said the burly guy. "Which one?" Ian kept low, thinking to himself, please no, please no.

"I don't know," she said.

"How about one of the tellers?"

"No."

"The woman by your feet?"

"No," said Zetta.

"Who then?"

Not me, not me, not me, thought Ian.

The woman said, "Him!" and Ian's heart leapt, hoping it was someone else, but he was prodded.

"You!" said the ski-masked man who yanked Ian up. "Go!" The man shoved what had to be a gun into Ian's neck. Ian stumbled forward, his mind whirling, wondering if he'd live out the hour.

"Hurry," said the man.

Two people lying on the floor, a young man in blue jeans and a white T-shirt near the front door and a young woman, perhaps his girlfriend, in a yellow short dress, sprang up panicked as if this were their only chance. Stupid! Ian thought, and the gun behind Ian exploded twice more. The young woman fell with just a thud, her head now showing brains, and the young man shouted, his white T-shirt starting to turn red on the side. Shit, shit, they're dead, I'm dead thought Ian.

"Hold your fire, hold your fire!" Ian could hear from out front.

The ski-masked man poked Ian again with his gun and said, "Go on. Walk slowly with your hands up to that white car."

Ian raised his hands and they walked. Is this where it happens? he thought. Is this where I die?

Outside, a half dozen cops behind their flashing black-and-white patrol cars pointed pistols at them. The woman, Zetta, jumped into the back of the waiting car, a white Camry. The ski-masked man shoved Ian in after her and followed. I'm still here, thought Ian. But for how long—ten minutes? The mustached man joined the Asian driver up front. This was a team of four who now ruled Ian, sandwiched in the back. Something smelled terribly bad. Ian's feet mashed what appeared to be a half-eaten Big Mac on the floor. Car doors slammed, and they were off with a screech. They sped down Mission Street, and quickly police cars screamed behind. The police will shoot, thought Ian. I'm dead.

Ian looked at the door handle and considered a quick exit. He knew he couldn't do it, not at this speed.

"Why did you shoot those people!" shouted Zetta.

The bulky man pulled off his ski mask quickly and threw it at her. He was dark-haired and muscular like the man on the front of Brawny paper towels, but unshaven. "Because we'd probably be dead right now if I didn't," he shouted right back.

"Please!" said the Asian driver, a small man in his thirties. "I'm concentrating."

He drove the white Camry fast down Mission Street, past Book'em Mysteries, toward Videotheque, toward Buster's Coffee. Ian realized he should have applied to Buster's instead.

The mustached man up front peeled off his mustache. He pulled off his baseball cap, and long dark hair spilled from it. Ian then noticed long clear-polished fingernails. The robber was a she, but not particularly pretty with her large Roman nose. "Fight later," she said.

Ian wildly glanced at everyone. If they were showing him their real faces, what did that mean for him? Were they going to kill him? Zetta tried to wipe blood off her hands with the ski mask. Nausea rose higher in his throat.

Behind them, a line of police cars blared their sirens. Ian felt even sicker. Bullets or car crash, which would it be?

A half dozen blocks from the bank, they accelerated toward the Gold Line rail station, and the lights at the crossing started blinking red and bells clanged. "Stop!" Ian shouted. The semaphore arms were closing.

They blew through the closing semaphores, and the light rail train, sounding its deep horn and slowing for the station, separated their car from the police pursuit.

"I love light rail!" yelled the Asian man happily.

"We were lucky," said Zetta. She turned to the larger man and said bitterly, "Your killing those people changed everything. No one was supposed to die over this."

"We're not playing games on an Xbox. If you wanted no one killed, you should have done it by computer."

The woman with the Roman nose yelled "Stop talking! We will go over this later in private." Ian understood none of this was meant for him.

The driver took roads Ian never went down and told the others, as he slowed, "A little luck, some good driving, and we're here."

It was then that Ian's stomach's contents purged.

Aleece Medina turned onto her shaded suburban street in West Covina, east of Los Angeles, thinking only of what might be in her freezer. She hadn't shopped in two weeks, so she guessed she might be down to the Ling-Ling dumplings, which probably had freezer burn. Maybe she'd make a toasted PBJ from a frozen bagel. She turned into the driveway of her white ranch house that she shared with only a goldfish—easy maintenance—and parked her government-issued Ford Taurus next to her own Toyota Prius. Her cell phone rang. She loved her job, but she prayed it wasn't the office, which she had just left. She'd already worked twenty-five hours overtime for the week and just wanted to enjoy the October weekend.

"Hello?" she said.

"Aleece, it's Rick." Rick Okinawa was the Supervisory Special Agent, her boss, in the West Covina FBI office.

"I just got home. You still in Virginia?" she said.

"Yep. It's late, but the Landwest branch in South Pas was just hit."

With it officially the weekend, this was a duty agent's problem—unless the incident was extra special. She asked, "Think it was the Busty Bandit?"

"I think so."

Medina's heart surged. Medina was eager now because the leader of this takeover crew had already hit three banks in the San Gabriel Valley. Medina had dubbed her the Busty Bandit because the woman always wore a low-cut blouse. Most witnesses, even the women, didn't remember much about her face because they were looking elsewhere. Also, a good name brought media attention, which helped bring in more people with information. With bank robbery being so run-of-the-mill in Los Angeles, it took something special to get the media's attention.

"They shot a guard, killed two bystanders, and took a hostage," said Rick.

Medina knew instantly the whole office would be on alert. Even the ASAC—the Assistant Special Agent in Charge—from the West L.A. office in Westwood would have to come down, especially with Rick gone.

"All right," she said. "I'll head to South Pas now. Who's the officer in charge down there?"

"Jones."

"Fuck." Jones was the South Pasadena police detective whom she worked with in a bank robbery over a year ago. He'd been going through a divorce at the time so was extremely transparent in wanting to date. Luckily she solved the case in a matter of days. The FBI did not have huge resources in any given city, so working with the local police was often a necessity.

"I thought you liked him," said Rick now.

"God's gift to women? Well, once you cut through that bullshit, he's okay. Give me the details," said Medina.

"I don't know a lot—just heard about it. The same woman and the same two men forced everyone to the floor," Rick said. "They brandished guns again, but there was an extra security guard. He was there early for his shift and had been in the bathroom. When he came upon the robbery, he drew and got shot. The alarm had already been tripped at that point. Your Busty Bandit was trying to stop the guard's bleeding with a tourniquet."

"She has a fucking heart."

"And they were there too long."

Medina nodded. After a silent alarm is tripped, the robber has less than two minutes.

"So the police came rushing over," continued Rick. "The suspects shot a man and a woman, who died, before taking one man hostage."

"And they got away?"

"Yep. Jones has secured the area, and a few specialists from Pasadena will soon be dusting for fingerprints."

"I'm on my way."

"Sorry about your weekend," said Rick.

"My romantic comedy'll wait for another week." She hung up

and stared at the piles of newspapers and bags of aluminum cans against the garage wall in front of her. One of these days, she told herself, she needed to get to the fucking recycler. Hell, one of these days, she needed to vacuum her house and take out the garbage. No time this weekend. She had this robbery to analyze.

When Ian threw up on the car floor, creating a small coffee-colored puddle, the brawny man up front laughed. "At least this isn't our car," he said.

"You don't have a compassionate bone in your body, do you?" said Zetta.

"No, but I have a boner."

She shot him a look of disgust as the car came to a quick stop. "We're getting out here," Zetta said to Ian. He found himself on a verdant side street, one he didn't know, and he spit as he walked, trying to get the taste out of his mouth. The brawny man shoved him from behind toward an old blue van. Ian looked up, hoping for a helicopter, but if there had been one—and there wasn't—the arms of the trees and foliage grew so thickly, a helicopter wouldn't have seen the switch anyway.

"Hold it!" shouted the big guy. The man patted him down.

"I don't have a gun," said Ian.

"Cell phone—where's your cell phone?"

"I don't have one."

"Don't lie to me if you want to live! Where is it?"

"I'm on a student budget. It's just too expensive." He didn't explain he didn't make many calls anyway.

"Hurry," said the short driver, jumping into the driver's seat.

They made Ian lie face down behind the driver's seat. "Why?" Ian said, thinking it was going to make him throw up again.

"Because I said so!" barked the big guy, who then laughed and said to Zetta, "Damn, I sound like my Dad. Maybe I'd make a good father."

"Did he kill, too, Owen?" she said.

His name's Owen, Ian noted. Is that a last name or first name?

"Don't talk to me like that," said Owen. "I helped us all and this is the thanks I get?"

"Stifle it," said the other woman. "Mistakes happened, and we can't make more."

"Keep your face down," Owen said to Ian again. "Or I'll put a bag over your head."

Were they were going to kill him? He realized what he learned about them could and would be used against them. He hoped they didn't think about that. Still, he needed to remember details. So far, he knew the beautiful woman was Zetta, the big guy, Owen. What did they call the driver and the skinny woman? Clearly, this had been a well-planned operation because they had anticipated needing a second get-away vehicle. Perhaps they were smarter than they seemed.

Zetta sat in a seat next to him, and he felt a hand on his shoulder. "You're just a hostage, and we'll let you go in a day or two. It'll all work out," she said.

Ian groaned, but Zetta rubbed his neck and said, "Calm down. It'll all work out. You'll see."

She was bullshitting him. After all, he could ID them.

Shortly after they started moving, he could hear the rush of tires on concrete below them. That had to be the 110 Freeway, the only freeway in the area. They had to be on a bridge going over the freeway, which meant they were driving into Highland Park, across from South Pasadena. Highland Park was a Latino section of town where the houses were little boxes, many of them with grates on the windows, quite different from his small ungrated guesthouse in South Pasadena in what had once been a garage.

After a number of stoplights, they were going up a hill. They kept going up and up. Highland Park was surrounded by hills. The only landmark Ian knew in Highland Park was the largest of the hills: Mt. Washington. They had to be going up Mt. Washington, where the most expensive homes were. It was an island surrounded by the flatland of immigrants and lower-middle class.

When Medina arrived at the South Pasadena bank, a large one-story building with golden bricks, there were many cars and a few news vans in the parking lot along with South Pasadena police cruisers and one Jaguar. She bet the Jag was Jones's. Behind the bank were homes—a lot of Craftsman homes with front porches, pitched shingle roofs, and double-sash windows. The area had always been upper middle-class. These days in the housing market, only couples with large incomes could afford to live in those houses.

In front of the bank, held off by yellow police tape, were a throng of news people, photographers, and undoubtedly curious onlookers. Murders brought the curious.

Medina showed her photo FBI ID to the man at the perimeter, entered the bank, and spotted Jones. He wore a jacket and tie, and his dark hair was neatly combed back. His height and dimpled chin made him look like a well-dressed quarterback. He must have been at dinner— long divorced and happily dating now. He noticed her and whistled.

"Can it," she said, standing in front of him as he gazed at what she wore. Her light green suit with a mauve blouse was conservative and nothing special. She could have been a defense attorney downtown. She'd forgotten how Jones liked women in ponytails—probably his fantasy of something to grab onto. His ex-wife had short hair.

"You're lookin' better all the time, Medina," he said. "Are you thirty yet?"

"Thirty-one," she said, pulling out her notepad and pen from her purse.

"Just my type."

"A Latina FBI agent? Keep dreaming."

"Don't you want babies? You can't wait forever, you know."

"I'm here for a fucking bank robbery—not speed-dating."

"That's the Medina I know! I've missed your zingers."

"Tell me about this scene."

He directed her inside the bank. The tile floor, elegant blond wooden desks, green wallpaper, and framed photographs made the place feel classy. The tellers had no bulletproof glass wall separating them from their customers. The smell of coffee was in the air from Carrie's in the front corner, where two bodies lay under white sheets. The background music still played: mandolins, an accordion, and Dean Martin crooned, "When the moon hits your eye like a big pizza pie, that's amore."

Jones continued, "We've kept a number of witnesses for you here, as well as all the bank employees."

"Get rid of the music," Medina stated.

"Kill the music!" Jones shouted toward the Carrie's Coffee area. In a moment, it clicked off. Medina walked to the first body and lifted the sheet. The young man's eyes were closed, but he didn't look peaceful. Under the other sheet, with blood soaked into the sheet at her head, a young woman stared vacantly. Medina dropped the sheet and said, "This is new for them. Killing."

"The large husky man did all the shooting," said Jones.

Medina looked more thoroughly at the Carrie's area and then across the whole bank. "Where are all of Carrie's employees?" she said.

"Most of them didn't see much, so we took statements and sent them home. The Carrie's manager is here."

They walked into the teller area. "How much did Miss Busty get away with?" she asked.

"Over $200,000."

"Of course it was a Friday, very busy, and I bet they got both drawers from each teller."

"Yep."

"Any dye packs?"

"Nope. They removed the money themselves. They knew what to look for."

She couldn't remember this particular bank ever being hit. Still, greater Los Angeles was the bank robbery capital of the world—sometimes over two thousand robberies a year. That was six a day.

Jones handed her a photo on glossy printer paper. This bank had a digital photo system, so with a good ink jet printer, which the manager obviously had, sharp photos were available in minutes—an advance over the older film cameras that some banks still used.

The photo showed another angle of the same woman who was already posted on Medina's office wall. The woman's long dark hair was probably a wig. The large sunglasses obscured most of her face, but Medina gazed at it as if seeing through the camouflage to the true woman, her adversary. This woman, whom the newspapers loved to write about, could lead to a promotion if Medina could only find her. Medina admired the bandit's brazenness as well as her planning. This was no easy criminal, even if Jones and some of the FBI honchos treated her as stupid because of her good looks. She brandished a .45. Medina herself carried a smaller .38 under her jacket.

"This is her," said Medina.

"She could be a model. Why's she robbing banks?"

"Only ugly women and men should rob?" said Medina.

"This is L.A.," said Jones. "She could be hanging out in the Skybar and attracting celebrities. Hell, hang out at Gus's Barbecue here, and I'll go out with her."

"Support her on your detective's pay, would you?"

"I'm not supportin' anyone anymore." He showed her the photos of the two other suspects. The big guy wore a ski mask as he did in the other robberies.

"He's the one who shot the people," he said. "The skinny guy didn't show a gun."

Medina leaned in closer. The third photo showed a tall thin man in a baseball cap, sunglasses, and an oddly thin mustache. "Look," said Medina and pointed to the man's mustache. "It's cockeyed. Obviously fake."

Jones peered at it more closely.

"You're right. Good catch."

Jones then pointed down a hallway to the left of the teller area. "Your Busty Bandit came from that way, as did the extra guard. The bathrooms are down there. Your big guy came from the right, where we just entered from the parking lot," said Jones. He spun around, pointing to the front door. "Your skinny guy came from the front. The getaway car idled out there at the curb."

"Two entrances, an open teller area," said Medina. "I'm surprised it doesn't get hit more often."

"It's a nice part of town."

Medina looked at the scene, imagined the pandemonium that came in a takeover robbery with everyone on the floor. She knew it'd be confirmed when she looked at the video. Then she thought about the hostage.

"How many customers were here?" she asked.

"A dozen in Carrie's, and another fourteen either doing bank business or in line to do business. Plus there were four tellers, the manager, and an assistant."

"Do we know anything about the hostage?"

"Nothing."

"I want to talk to just two people first, the managers of Carrie's and the bank."

Jones motioned for her to follow. They walked down a hall to the offices.

The door was open to one office, which had the same green wallpaper, the same kind of blond wood desk as out front. Office Max must have made a big sale one day. Jones announced to the people in the room, "I'm back."

The man with the thick gray hair and frown lines had to be the bank manager. He had the appropriate humorless face for the job. He spoke with a young woman who looked upset and worn out. "Special Agent Aleece Medina," said Jones. "This is the manager, Richard Broadmore."

"And this is Tabitha Humphries, one of the tellers," said Broadmore.

Medina looked to see if there was any subtext between the manager and teller. Sometimes robberies had someone on the inside, so she was always suspicious. Broadmore's empathetic eyes and the teller's tears suggested they had been surprised and shaken by the day.

"If you don't mind," Medina said, "I'd like to interview Mr. Broadmore in here, and perhaps you, detective, could get Miss Humphries' statement?"

"Absolutely," said Jones with a wink, suggesting he wouldn't mind being with this young woman. Medina felt like Jones's pimp—except Jones wouldn't risk his job by being too overt.

"And the Carrie's manager?" Medina asked.

"She's waiting for you over in Carrie's Coffee," said Jones.

Once Jones had left, Medina turned to Mr. Broadmore.

"What do you know about the hostage? Why did they take him in particular?"

"He happened to be over by the fireplace—at the wrong place at the wrong time, I'd say."

"Can you show me the takeover on the video?"

"Sure," and he went to his computer. In short order, the scene played out in a wide-angle view from a camera mounted behind the tellers. A time code played in the lower right corner. The Busty Bandit came in from the hallway and looked around. The man sitting in an armchair by the fireplace was sipping on coffee and writing something with a gold pen. He was fairly handsome—a sculptural face with prominent cheekbones, a sharp jaw with a small indent in his chin, and very bushy eyebrows. Perhaps he was part Russian. His dark hair was cropped closely, and he wore a blue blazer.

"What's he writing?" she asked.

"Should I stop this and show you the video from the camera above the ATM?"

"No. Let me see this play out first."

The man by the fireplace looked up to notice Miss Busty walk in. He raised his eyebrows. Miss Busty glanced at him and at a few other men who stared at her. Her looks obviously caused a stir. Miss Busty then turned to see her muscular ski-masked partner enter. He pulled out a gun. She glanced again at her future hostage, withdrew her gun and shouted. There was no sound—just the video. All the customers fell to the ground as if there were a sudden burst of gravity.

The partner with the false mustache entered, carrying two pillowcases. The skinny man handed the masked man one of the pillowcases, and the two men jumped over the tellers' counters like hyenas after an easy kill, and they started opening the tellers' drawers, two at each station. The skinny man started with the commercial window, where the most money would be. The skinny man tested each packet before putting it in the bag. Medina could see that he knew the rule, "If it don't bend, it don't spend." Dye packs would be inside what looked like a banded pack of money, but it wouldn't be money. Rather, inside was a 9-volt battery, an electronic receiver for remote command, and a canister containing liquid dye and tear gas.

At that moment, the extra guard appeared and the ski-masked man shot him. Miss Busty then screamed at the shooter, upset.

Medina nodded—a crook with empathy. All robbers should be women.

From there, Miss Busty helped the injured guard, ripping and turning his sleeve into a tourniquet. Soon she had a teller stay with the guard while the skinny man and the masked man kept clearing out money. In the background, some customers turned their heads toward the front door while still lying on the floor. Outside, flashing lights from police cars could now be seen. Miss Busty pointed to the man by the fireplace, and the two men behind the counter leapt over the counter and joined her. The masked man pulled up their hostage and held his gun to his hostage's neck while the police, who had been approaching outside, backed away. That's when a Carrie's customer stood and got shot.

"All right," said Medina. "I still need to get a good view of the hostage from earlier, where he's sitting."

"Let me try a camera by the ATM," said the manager. He typed on the keyboard and matched up the time codes.

"Can you zoom in at all?"

"Yes, I can enlarge an area."

"Let's see what he's writing."

Broadmore froze a frame and got closer. Only the previous year it took a specialist from the FBI to work and enhance the imagery. Now the video was high definition and the software had become so easy that this manager could do it. Medina leaned closer to the monitor and could make out a Carrie's Coffee logo at the top the page. "Is that an employment application he's writing on?" she said.

"I bet you're right," said Broadmore. "You'll have to ask Maryanne—that's the Carrie's manager."

"Can you print me out a copy of this image?"

"Sure."

"And can you show me two cameras running in a split screen of the same scene? I want to be looking at the hostage mostly. I have to find out who he is." She also realized that there might be the hostage's car in the parking lot. She'd tell someone to look into that.

After he printed the application shot, he restarted the video showing the future hostage.

"Stop," said Medina as the man's face peered toward the camera. He looked to be in his late twenties, and he was eyeing Miss Busty at that moment as if he was at Mardi Gras, ready to throw her a beaded necklace if she flashed her breasts. Men were so simple when it came down to it. Money and sex. Male bank robbers, as she'd learned from most of the criminals when she caught up with them, used lots of money on spending sprees that involved sex. And, of course, criminals never saved for the future. Why should they when there were always more banks to rob and women to have?

"Print his face, please," said Medina. "I'll release it to the media so we can find out who he is."

Just as she was emerging from the back office to give Jones and his team some more instructions, James Wexler, the Assistant Special Agent in Charge out of West L.A., entered with three other special agents. Wexler had the same rubber-nosed face as J. Edgar Hoover, as if cast to type. Wexler was her boss's boss, in charge of everything, and he always showed his power as if he were Captain Bligh on the HMS Bounty, pointing and barking orders, all in his Italian suits. "Medina," he said to her with familiarity. He'd been her boss for a short time years earlier before his promotion. "I want you to fill these fellas in on everything you know about these robbers. Any leads yet on the hostage?"

Medina handed him the photo Broadmore made. "We don't know who he is yet. I'm about to have some of the team looking at the parked cars, hoping one of them is his."

Wexler turned to one of his blue-blazered men, a man she knew as Davis, and said, "Go find Jones and see what he's got." Medina frowned. Wexler hadn't even finished listening to her yet. He was an asshole now as much as he'd been before.

Wexler handed the photo to one of the other men. "I want this on the eleven o'clock news and all the morning newspapers."

"Sir," said Medina, feeling his presence was now stopping the efficiency of her efforts. "I have more. And I thought you'd want me to explain to your team about the Busty Bandit."

"You named her that?"

"Yes, sir."

"A good call. The media already loves the name. That gets us more press."

And that gets *you* more press, she thought.

"Do me a favor," said Wexler, "I need you to fill Davis in on everything here. He'll be taking over the FBI's end." He snapped his fingers at a tall, thin agent with prematurely graying hair. Davis looked more like an accountant than a field guy. This jerk was going to replace her? What the fuck?

"I don't accept this," Medina said as Davis finished speaking with another agent. She realized she phrased it wrong, but really, fuck Wexler.

"What the hell did you say?" said Wexler. Her heart pounded. Her job probably now was on the line. Insubordination would not be acceptable to the man.

"I'm the agent in charge," said Medina firmly, "and you know my record. Why are you bringing in Davis, whom I respect, but bank robbery is not his specialty. It's mine."

"Are you second guessing my reasons?" said Wexler, not backing down as Davis strode over.

"If a man were the case agent," said Medina, "would you even consider that he should drop it?"

"Why do women always have to assume some gender issue?" said Davis.

She could only glare.

"All right, all right," said Wexler, relenting. "I like your balls, Aleece. I'll keep you in charge." He turned to Davis. "Medina is in charge of this. Sorry Jim."

After Davis nodded and left, he said to Medina, "I want that hostage safe and sound, got it? And put these nuts in jail."

"Yes, sir." As she saw one of Wexler's men pass the table where the hostage had been sitting, Medina put her fingers in her mouth and whistled. That stopped everyone including Wexler.

"Excuse me," said Medina, "I'll be brief. This table here is where our hostage was sitting." They could see the table with a coffee cup and gold pen. "The hostage was writing an application for Carrie's Coffee. Everyone please be on the lookout for the application. Also…" She pointed to the man closest to the table, one of Wexler's men that she didn't recognize. "…We need DNA run on the cup as well as dusting for fingerprints on the table and pen." She turned to two others. "I need a team, how about you guys, to canvas the parking lot and run the plates on each car. One of the cars may be the hostage's. That is all."

Medina noticed Jones on the edge, nodding, impressed. Wexler looked the same and said, "And now may I talk with the bank manager?"

"I'm the manager," replied Broadmore.

"Is that okay with you, Medina?" said Wexler.

"Yes. I need to talk with Jones, anyway."

Jones stood politely, waiting, a file folder in his hand. The moment she walked toward him, he nodded. She motioned him toward the front door, away from Wexler's crew. When they stopped, Jones said, "You were dynamic back there, Aleece—taking on Wexler and all."

"Out of thirty agents in West Covina, only two are women. I've learned you have to play hardball with these guys."

"Will you play with me?"

"Stuff it," she said. "Have you found out anything about the hostage yet?"

"Nada. None of the tellers or the people in Carrie's recognized him. Maybe he's not from this area. Is it possible he was working with the crew?"

"I saw the video. I didn't get that sense. He's a real hostage."

"What'd you get from Miss Humphries?"

Jones smirked as if hearing a double meaning. "Miss Humphries was rather freaked out by the guns. She said the burly guy tried to flirt with her, asked her if she liked the movies, said maybe he'd stop by sometime for coffee."

"Was he serious?"

"Probably not. And per your request, I told Maryanne, the Carrie's manager, to wait for you." He pointed to a young woman with shoulder-length hair wiping tables. Medina had to give it to Carrie's Coffee in always finding young people who worked hard.

"Thanks," she said.

Jones opened his file, again looking at the photo of Miss Busty, one that had her in profile showing her assets at a good angle. "This will be a fun case." He stared for what seemed too long.

"They're just mammary glands," said Medina. "What's the big deal?"

"Beauty," said Jones. "It seems beautiful breasts need to be savored."

Even though her coat was buttoned, Medina felt Jones's glance. "Give it up, Jones," she said. "Mine won't make your list."

"You're in fabulous shape."

"If you want to keep working with me, keep it to yourself."

"Sorry."

"We've got to get that hostage back. Everything depends on that."

"You're right. You're always right."

"Stop sucking up to me and get clever." He nodded and moved off. She looked around at the lobby, frantic with the energy of agents and police crisscrossing each other as well as two agents inspecting the teller drawers carefully in case any small clue may have been left. Was it the exhilaration of each new situation that she liked? She realized she preferred the endgame, encircling her prey or running after a criminal and jumping fences, kick-boxing a guy to the ground. Maybe it was the same thrill robbers got in robbing. It was all a balance. Without her and her fellow agents, the city would fall too far the other way.

CHAPTER TWO

The morning after the robbery, in the hideaway house on Mt. Washington, Ian did not move as Owen tied him to a chair at a long oak dining room table. They'd taken off his blazer and tie the night before, so he was in his white shirt and khaki slacks. It was an elegant dining room with wallpaper and two paintings of sheep in a field. Ian's legs and torso were tied tightly, but his arms were free for eating. Of course, with everyone there, he knew the point of the ropes was so he couldn't leap up and run.

Near him, Zetta sat eating cantaloupe, its orange flesh against her red lips. Her white blouse was unbuttoned enough to show off her assets and the horizon of a lacy bra. She had also poured herself a bowl of Fruity Pebbles, apparently not wanting the pancakes and bacon that were cooking. The other woman, the skinny one, wore a printed flowery dress that made her both feminine and dowdy. Reading the morning paper at the head of the table, the skinny woman had long red fingernails that she didn't have the day before, and the nails had roses painted on each one—must be press-on nails. Ian's last girlfriend had them. The getaway driver was busy in the kitchen, cooking. Bacon sizzled.

As Owen finished the final knot, he pointed at Ian, "He knows a lot about us. I still don't get what we're going to do about that?"

"We talked about that last night," said Zetta. "You agreed."

Owen jammed a thumb at the paper. "I didn't expect to see us on the front page today. We're in deep shit."

"Because you *killed* people. This was supposed to be a victimless crime."

"You should have conned people out of money on the internet, then," said Owen.

"We're not after innocent people," the skinny woman said. "Banks are the greedy bastards. Look what they did to everyone in 2007. You were supposed to have blanks in your gun."

"While the guards and police have real bullets? Are you crazy?"

Owen's gun was wedged in his back pocket. Ian thought he should grab it, but by the time he thought of that, Owen was behind him.

"I couldn't sleep last night, either," said Owen. "I changed my mind."

Zetta and the skinny woman glanced at each other. "We have a plan. Let's work the plan," the skinny woman said.

Ian felt nausea rise in his throat again. If Owen shot him in the back of the head, it'd be just blackness forever.

"Oh? So we'll let him squawk to the cops later on?" said Owen.

"We'll be long gone," said Zetta. "We'll let him go when we go."

"You guys are amateurs," said Owen.

"And we've made you rich," said Zetta. "Far better than how we found you."

The skinny woman clapped her hands together. "It's time we split up the cash, don't you think?"

"About time, Navarre," said Owen.

Navarre thought Ian.

The skinny woman, Navarre, pulled a duffel bag up from the floor, unzipped it, and dumped out bundled stacks of cash. "Four equal parts. That should make everyone happy. Let's make it into even stacks, and then we'll divide."

The driver emerged from the kitchen and watched as Zetta placed the cash in banded bundles, side by side, until there stood four big equal squares of cash.

"Choose which one you want, Owen," said Zetta. Owen slid over the share closest to Zetta.

These people were getting away with it, thought Ian, each rewarded with more money than he would earn over years.

"Fuck casting agents," said Owen. "I've got money now." He strode into the kitchen and returned with a roll of gray duct tape. "If I may borrow a section of your paper," he said to Navarre, and Navarre pushed the sports section toward him before pulling it back. "One sec," she said. "Look." Navarre held up the page of the newspaper. It showed a man in a yellow T-shirt on a sailboat, shouting something, raising his arms in victory. "A U.S. boat won a regatta that leads up to the America's Cup," said Navarre.

"What the fuck's a regatta?" said Owen.

"Sailing. These twelve-meter yachts are the most precise and beautiful things in the world."

Owen scoffed.

"You've never sailed, Owen?" said Navarre.

"I'll go sailing with you two. The marina has sailboats for rent. Of course, our happy witness here is taking all this in."

"I'm not listening," said Ian.

"That's the way to be," said Owen. "Or you're dead meat."

Getting the newspaper back, Owen placed a few stacks on a single sheet, wrapped his cash like a Christmas present, then with the duct tape, sealed it shut. He lifted his first taped bundle in triumph, echoing the color picture of America's Cup winner on the stack.

Owen knelt down to Ian's level. "Hey, last night's news flashed your picture, asking people to call a certain number to identify you. Hey, if you live, you'll easily get a job."

Zetta touched Ian's shoulder. "Of course you'll live."

"Right," Owen said to Zetta.

Zetta and the skinny woman looked at each other again, which only seemed to amuse Owen.

Ian considered his own picture on the newscasts. Who might call to identify him? Surely someone he knew watched the news. His whole family, though, lived in Canada. Maybe his landlady would ring up. Or someone from his classes would call. Wouldn't it be ironic if it were someone on his orals committee?

Owen stood and touched Zetta's bare arm. "Now that I have money, I should take you to Morton's Steakhouse sometime. Beverly Hills. Now there's fine food."

"Sorry. We won't be around that long."

"Movie stars like to go there. We might see some. There are other places I could take you, too. Have you been to the Farmer's Market— the big one by Television City?"

"No time."

"Oh. But otherwise you'd go?"

She didn't answer.

Ian realized Owen must live in L.A. and Zetta did not. Owen came around to the other side of the table and flexed his arms in tandem like a body builder. Then he looked right at Zetta. "The most exciting thing to happen to laundry since… Heck, it's the *only* exciting thing. Tide Kick."

Tide Kick? thought Ian.

Zetta said, "You're excellent and you know that. That's why I asked you to be with us."

With the bit about casting agents earlier, Owen must be an actor, Ian thought.

"There're lots of things I can show you," said Owen.

"That's not my need," said Zetta.

She ate another dab of cantaloupe, not looking at him at all. She shoved the melon aside and poured milk into her cereal.

"Why don't you like pancakes?" said Owen.

"This," said Zetta, "I like the memory of it."

"It's a kids' cereal."

"Exactly," she said.

Owen appeared flummoxed and said, "Pancakes. The asshole has to be finished by now," and Owen stepped into the kitchen.

The skinny woman leaned toward Zetta and said softly, "We need a plan B for Orono."

"It's Owen, remember?"

"And he's mean. A meany. We got to get out of here soon."

"Don't worry."

Owen/Orono? thought Ian. They all had false names, he realized.

"My point is," said the skinny woman, nervously twisting the diamond wedding ring on her ring finger. "Owen doesn't get us. He's a loose cannon."

"We'll be out of here soon."

Ian prayed this was so. They hadn't killed him yet. If he kept quiet and cooperative, maybe it'd work out. He'd just watch—maybe help the police later—something he remembered from a play about hostages. None of them had many details to offer the police later. He noticed then that Zetta wore no rings. What was Zetta's and Navarre's relationship? Navarre had a husband—where? Best as Ian could figure out, the robbers were renting the place, a Craftsman home from the looks of the inside—an old place.

From the kitchen, there was loud murmuring, and then, "Fuck you, man," from the getaway driver. "I want the food out all at the same time."

"Like you're the boss of me?" said Owen.

Playwright David Mamet's book on acting, *True and False,* sprang to mind, where Mamet said that, "As actors, we spend most of our time nauseated, confused, guilty." How true that was for him this very moment.

"Might you let me go soon?" said Ian. "I've got a puppy to feed." He didn't have a puppy, but everyone liked puppies.

"Aww," said Zetta. "What kind of puppy?"

"A cute little dachshund."

"What brand of food do you give it?" asked Navarre.

Brand? Ian searched his memory of pet food ads. He'd never had a pet let alone a puppy. What brand? "Pet Corp," said Ian. "I buy Pet Corp's best food." Wasn't that the name of the pet store on Arroyo?

"Pet Corp?" said Navarre.

"Pet something," said Ian.

"Pet Island?" said Zetta.

"Sure," said Ian.

"There is no Pet Island," said Zetta. "And no puppy. Good try."

Navarre smiled while shaking her head.

I'm shit as an actor, Ian thought. A plan, he needed a better plan.

Owen returned, and Navarre's smile evaporated. Owen seemed to notice because he pointed at Navarre." You don't think I'm as good as this guy?" indicating Ian.

"I've said nothing," said Navarre.

From his pocket, Owen yanked out a piece of paper, unfolded it, and started reading. "It says here, Ian, you can work seven days a week, and you're able to work overtime." Owen held Ian's Carrie's Coffee application.

Ian glared at him.

"You went to high school in Winnipeg. Where the fuck's Winnipeg? College at McGill with a major in English, drama and theatre option—like that's a needed degree for Carrie's." Owen came closer and leaned into Ian's face. "And a master's in theatre at USC. What do you need a degree in this shit for? This town is full of good acting coaches."

"Leave him be," said Zetta.

Owen ignored her and paced behind Ian. "Aren't you a little overqualified, buddy, to hand me a cup of coffee?"

Ian strained his legs against his bonds with a surge of energy, ready to do battle. For a second, Ian thought the flash of adrenaline would bust him free, but to no avail. Calm, calm, he told himself. This has to be about wits. "No," said Ian. "Everyone has a degree these days. Overqualified would be to write on the application that I attended UC Irvine, the doctoral program in theatre, which I used to do."

"We have a smart one," said Navarre.

Owen gleefully continued scanning the application. "Under the question, 'Have you ever visited a Carrie's Coffee location? Where? Describe your experience,' Ian wrote, 'I am not a particularly avid coffee drinker, but your location three miles north of here, with its interior post-modern look of exposed ductwork and the vertiginous aroma of your dark Zambian beans excites me.'"

Zetta, Navarre, and Owen burst out in laughter.

Ian only looked down as he realized how completely idiotic he could be.

Navarre held up one finger to make a point. "Did you want the job?"

"Of course. What am I supposed to write on an application?" Ian said.

"You like getting rejected, is that it?" said Owen.

"Vertiginous?" said Zetta, still laughing.

"And look," Owen added. "He says he's good at computers and knows 'the interface for the Now Casting website thoroughly.' You want the Carrie's Hollywood location, is that it?" Everyone laughed again.

"I just wanted to show I know computers, and I'm a fast learner."

"Important for adding that extra shot of espresso into a paper cup."

The driver walked into the room from the kitchen. "What's so funny?"

"I lost my position in teaching recently," said Ian, "and that's a grand laugh."

"He's a loser," said Owen, laughing.

"And you're a winner?" said Ian reflexively.

"Ouuu. This guy's got balls."

Ian stared into the guy's face. It was the face of Professor Cromley, too, the disarrayed white-haired jerk who had forced him out of school. Dismissive Cromley.

"You don't think theatre has its uses?" said Ian mostly to Navarre, who he considered the smartest. "As a director, I'm concerned with many details about people including accents. From yours, Navarre, I hear a Canadian twang like mine—or maybe it's Minnesotan as in the movie *Fargo*. And yours," he turned to Zetta, "I hear a little Southern." He turned again. "I'm guessing you, sir," he said to the driver, "were were born and raised here." Last, he glared into Owen's face. "You're definitely from around here. Southern Californian all the way."

Owen nodded and turned to Zetta. "You Southern as he says?"

"The less we know about each other, the better," said Zetta.

"I heard the South is a nice place," said Owen.

"Whatever," she said.

Ian realized that while Zetta and Navarre seemed to know each other, Owen and the driver were new to the group.

Owen shot a thumb at Ian. "Look at how much he knows. And we're just going to let him go?"

Ian's heart pounded as he realized how stupid he had been.

"The simplest thing," said Owen, "is no witnesses."

That night, tied and gagged and wedged against a Maytag washer—no more bed for him—Ian was still alive. He thought of something musician Bruce Springsteen said in an interview when talking about his song "Racing in the Streets." He said there was a lot of pain in life, but that one had to persevere and be resilient. That's what Ian realized his job was at the moment. Persevere.

Shortly thereafter, the room's walls were becoming wavy and his ears began to ring. He realized horribly that the water Owen had recently given him must have had a drug in it. Before he became completely overwhelmed, he wished he could be Harry Houdini. He'd get out of his tight bonds and smack Owen left and right—right and left—and then run out and shout for help and get an antidote.

Since breakfast, Owen had only given him liquids, allowed him to pee, and otherwise tied him up in the laundry room where he had to sleep. No bed. When Zetta wasn't around, Owen would kick him in the ribs, slap his face, and belittle Ian with, "How's it feel, Mr. College Man? You're smarter than me?" When Zetta would later come in, she would tell Ian things like, "Don't worry. We're nearly ready. You're only tied up for your own safety." Her voice was gentle, but he hated her, too. And now this.

This is just a drug, just a drug, Ian chanted in his head. But his bonds felt too tight. Did he have enough blood going to his hands and feet? Would they have to be amputated? Would he die before any amputation?

He could feel that he was thinking strangely, and knew he was in deep danger. What was the drug? It was a hallucinogen. LSD? Was it something that he could control?

The door was open a crack, and he could hear Owen come out of the bathroom. "Hey, Navarre," shouted Owen. "You plugged up the toilet again. Can't you wipe your ass right, or is it one of your tampons?"

He heard Navarre's heels click down the hall and she then said, "You can be very rude. You should be respectful of me, you know."

"Excuse me, your highness. Might you fix it, please? Or am I supposed to fucking unplug your shit?"

"I'll see if there's a plunger around," said Navarre.

Ian considered what he heard. It was just so odd. Would it have been odd if he were not drugged? He hadn't imagined the conversation, had he?

The crack in the door seemed to spill in vanilla light. Ian then saw shoes, black high-top shoes, Owen's shoes.

Ian glanced up and saw a blob for a face. "So, Mr. Know-It-All, Mr. I-Have-a-Ph.D-in-Theatre. How do you feel? Feel a little different?" Owen laughed. "Sure hope the spiders don't get you!" Owen flicked off the lights and slammed the door shut.

Spiders? There were spiders here? Concentrate, Ian told himself. Spiders can't hurt you. Yes, they could. They could crawl all over a person's body and bite little bits of flesh until he was a man without skin. The police would find a skinless man with spider eggs all over him.

But maybe he could become Spiderman. Then he could tie Owen up in super bonds of webbing. Wouldn't muscle-man Owen be shocked, then? Yeah, he would.

Ian found himself breathing hard, and the rational part of him told him to simply ride it out. Ian could hear Navarre say, "What're you doing to that poor man?"

"Nothing, don't worry."

The door opened again. Ian could see high heels as ruby red as Dorothy's from *The Wizard of Oz*. Ian wished the shoes were Dorothy's to click together and take him home. There's no place like home.

"Why's he sweating like that?" said Navarre.

"Wouldn't you?"

"Why's he moving his head around like that?"

"I gave him a little somethin' to help him sleep."

"What?"

Owen said, "Let's say he'll be dreamin' real well."

"Why would you do that?" said Navarre.

"Hey, you heard him earlier, commenting on our accents. He'll give the police too much—this'll confuse him."

"We had a plan," said Navarre, "Why do you do this shit? When you deviate from a plan, you hurt us all."

A thump resounded like that of a skinny woman being slammed against the wall. Ian imagined Owen leaning into Navarre. "Listen, Bitch," said Owen. "I've had it with you and your critical mouth. I'm only here because of Zetta, and I'm even getting sick of her. Enough said?"

"That sounds like bad movie dialogue," said Navarre.

Exactly, exactly, thought Ian.

"You'd better think again if you think women, beneath their veneer, are helpless," said Navarre. "I'd think twice if I were you."

"A bag of bones like you?"

"I assure you, you don't want to fuck with this woman."

Kill him, thought Ian.

"I don't believe it," said Owen. "But, hey, I'm not mad anymore."

"I'll take that as an apology," said Navarre.

"Navarre, you are so bizarre," and Owen's laugh spilled into an echo.

Ian swore he was falling—falling like Alice, falling like Major Tom. Take your protein pills and put your helmet on.

A strange ringing skated around in Ian's ears. He must not have a vacuum seal.

Owen spoke again. "When Zetta gets back, I say let's shoot the guy and get outta here."

Ian gasped. He started choking.

Ian realized he needed to concentrate. For the next two hours, Ian concentrated on his breathing. He knew if he breathed, he was alive. Yet, against the washer, Ian hyperventilated as if the air was as thin as on Venus. The darkness reminded him, too, of outer space. He could die in outer space.

In the faintest of light, waking up on the floor, he could see a washer and dryer. Now he remembered: he was in the laundry room and he was tied up. He'd been sleeping, dreaming about Oz, and he'd been in the Technicolor land as himself, not as Dorothy. He'd poured water on the wicked witch and she'd melted. What would the monkeys do now for a job? At least in Oz, he was free.

He could smell bleach, the same smell swimming pools had of chlorine. Had someone been doing laundry while he was out? There were shadows and light on the ceiling. The light, he realized, came from outside of the window above the washer. Was the window something he could use if he could get his hands free? It looked too small and too high.

His shoulder was sore. The floor was hard. He was also still hearing voices, and at first he assumed he was still hallucinating. No, they were real voices, voices outside of the window. That's why the light was on out there. One female voice said something about "good years in jail." He recognized the voice. Not the leader but the other woman. Why couldn't he remember their names?

Ian's heart beat faster. Were they going to kill him? The next clear words were the leader's: "I would rob more banks for him. He's the world for me," she said passionately.

"Even if he doesn't know you?" said the friend.

"He knows me. You can't say that," replied the leader.

Ian considered: the leader loved him?

The friend shushed the leader, and their voices stopped.

What? What was going on?

"It's love that even defies description," the leader said strongly. "It's every heartbeat, every cell that grows and dies." Again, Ian had to wonder if he was still hallucinating. She loved him? This did not make sense. What he could remember, she'd been nice to him. She'd selected him from all the others to be the hostage at the bank. There was a bank robbery—now he recalled. And the leader had allowed him to be beat-up, drugged, and humiliated by that big guy—what was his name? Why couldn't he remember the man's name either? What happened last night?

Ian took stock of what he knew. He was in a house. He had been kidnapped. He'd been drinking coffee, he remembered that, and it was at Carrie's Coffee, which was at the bank.

A screen door slammed—the one on the side by the kitchen. "What're you two plotting?" said a deep voice, the big guy. "Getting rid of me?"

"No, nothing like that," said the leader's friend.

"We've got to leave here at first light," said the leader. "We've been cleaning the house while you've been sleeping."

"Why the rush? I thought you wanted to stay low."

"We need to get out of here. We have to use might-oh procedures," said the friend.

"Might-oh? What the hell're you talking about?" said big guy.

"We're sitting ducks. We need to split up—not a second to waste."

"Then let's get rid of him and go."

Ian gasped, and he pulled at the bonds on his wrists. He found they were loose. They'd been so tight before—how was that possible? Had the leader come in and loosened them while he'd been sleeping? He had to assume so as he yanked his arms free. Maybe she did love him. Mamet's words about the human condition sprang to mind: "All of us. All of us. We're doomed." Weird that he could remember Mamet but not other things. He sat up, took out his gag, and untied his feet and stood, feeling extremely light-headed. The light at the edge of the window had a strange glow—probably from the aftereffects of a hallucinogen. Ian had to lean against the washer. He didn't want to be doomed.

The screen door slammed again, and he guessed the big guy had reentered the house and was coming for him. The light came on in the hallway, and footsteps approached. Ian knew the other door in the laundry room led to the garage, and he ran for it. The garage was deeply dark, but he could smell oil. Switch, there had to be a light switch. He found it. A bare bulb went on mid-ceiling, showing a roomful of metal shelving loaded with cardboard boxes—and boxes on the floor, boxes everywhere. There was no room for a car, but to the right was a side door, and he leapt for it just as he heard the big guy yell, "Hey! He's gone! What the fuck?"

"What?" the leader yelled. "Impossible!"

Ian was out the side door, and when it slammed, the big guy yelled, "He just went through the garage! Fan out!"

Ian raced out into the cool night air and looked around running, running, and the trees felt like hands trying to grab him. That made him spin to get his bearings. A half moon among the branches zipped by. He paused. He stood in an unfenced back yard and the hill ran down steeply from the corner to the right. Not there, he said to himself, and he ran to his left. He spotted a street and sped for it. Rushing onto pavement, he noticed a light on a front porch, a friendly front porch of a Craftsman home, yes, yes. He ran faster than all his races in elementary school and leapt onto the porch and started hammering on the door.

"Help!" he shouted and pounded more.

He heard footsteps on the street as well as in the house. "Help," he shouted again.

"Off my porch or I'll shoot!" came a deep male voice from inside.

"Don't shoot. Call the police!"

The big guy in the street yelled, "Over at that house. I got him!" Ian turned and saw the big guy's bulky figure. Ian had no time to explain his situation to the homeowner, nor did he want to test the man's paranoia.

Ian vaulted over the white balustrade railing of the front porch into the side yard and dashed into the back, which was very dark with all the trees that edged the yard. The hillside had to be there, he surmised—his last refuge. Just run, he told himself. Run fucking hard. Ian's legs were stiff, but he ran hard onto a wooded path that quickly became steep—the hillside. He realized his white shirt reflected the moonlight and made him stand out in the night. Get behind something, he thought. No, just run.

Over the next rise, Ian stumbled and then tumbled down an embankment. As he spun, he could see the path he'd been on skirted a narrow canyon, and Ian fell into the canyon, slowed by the thick soft grass on the hill. He righted himself so that he slid on his behind, and he shot quickly down at an angle. He heard his pants rip and saw he was headed right for a tree. Ian leaned hard and missed it. He could see even thicker tall grass ahead, and he plunged right into it and stopped. He was in one piece, scratched and dirty but okay. Lying on his stomach, he breathed hard and listened.

"Where is he?" shouted the big guy way above him, passing where Ian had fallen.

Close behind, the leader's friend said, "Did he go this way?"

"You skinny bitch, you helped him somehow—I know it since you didn't want him killed," said the big guy.

"No one helped him," said the leader. "Our lives are at stake here. Keep looking for him. We need to find him fast."

"I'm going to kill him no matter what," said the big guy. "I don't care about anything else."

Ian trembled. He lay low in the grass as they turned on their cell phones in the flashlight mode. Four flashlights scanned around on either side of the path. If the fourth guy, the driver, had been sleeping, he was now up. "Down here?" the driver said. A light flashed his way, but they didn't see him. Clearly the lights weren't strong enough or the gang didn't read natural signs well. Otherwise, they might have noticed certain grass on the hillside was flatter. He wished he had a gun and could pick them off like ducks in a shooting gallery. His fear evaporated, and pure hatred ran through him now. He realized he could indeed kill them. One thing he knew: he wouldn't rest until these four got their due.

When the four had all gone farther away from him, and with dawn approaching, he followed the canyon up until he found a well-worn path that ascended above the house where he'd been held hostage. When he got to the top, there was a park bench that gave a stunning view toward downtown Los Angeles, its skyscrapers well-defined against the now light gray sky. Ian hid behind a tree as the big guy yelled, "I know you're out there, shithead!"

Sounds carried well because he distinctly heard the thin woman say, "Now you've done it. If no one's called the police yet, they will now. We gotta go."

Below him, the line of four cell phone lights clicked off, and the four figures, the hour-glass shaped one in the lead, moved into the shadow of the backyard. He couldn't see the house itself—blocked by the hillside and trees, but the getaway van was visible in the parking area above the house. Ian watched. Within two minutes, the four had rushed up the stairs to the van with suitcases and garbage bags of things. They hurried back down, and about four minutes later, they had more stuff that they threw in. They hopped in and took off.

Was this a trick to get him out of his hiding spot? No, they couldn't have known he could see them. They had to assume that he got away and called the cops—from someone's cell phone or maybe from a neighbor's house.

Still, just to be sure they wouldn't return, he didn't move. As he waited a while, no police came. *No one called?* That was shitty. And what would he tell the police if they did come? He couldn't remember things. Was it because he'd been panicked? Was it because of the hallucinogen? He tried to remember something, anything. One thing: the leader's skinny friend had said they needed to use "might-oh procedures." He'd heard the term somewhere previously, and then he just knew it was "MITO procedures," meaning "minimal interval take off," used by Air Force pilots for a rapid deployment of planes. Ian then remembered *All My Sons,* a play that involved pilots in World War II by Arthur Miller. Ian had directed it once and had consulted with a military commander and historian, who explained the term "MITO procedures." Ian wondered why he could retrieve that memory but not much about what happened recently. How long had he been a hostage? Hours, days, weeks? It was as if he'd been given an Alzheimer's pill.

Convinced they were gone for good, and with a part of the sky now pink where the sun would rise, he moved toward the house. Every fiber of his being said stay away from the house, but he needed something to give the police. Because he didn't know where he was, if he called 911 from the house, the police would have the house address automatically—very clever, he thought. Plus he'd get the police right away—better than knocking on another neighbor's door and getting shot at as an intruder. If he could find a morning jogger and borrow his cell phone that would be better, but no one was around.

In the parking area above the house, standing where the van had been, Ian stared at the house, which didn't look like much of a house at all. Two tall trees like giant's legs stood at the back, their branches and leafy canopies touching the flat roof of the single story. The house, tucked against the hill, was a poorly kept up Craftsman. Some of the siding now was cheap fir, the kind that came in sheets and their seams covered with a narrow board. In the backyard, old wooden ladders lay on their sides, partly overgrown with vines, and a rusty red wheelbarrow slept upside down. It was a backyard with long forgotten intentions. No lights were on. The thought of going into the house spooked him. The sooner he put space between this house and him, the better he'd feel. Still, Ian needed to get the police.

The front door was locked. So was the side door and even the garage door. As he walked around, he looked in each window just to make sure no one was there. No one was. Near the side door stood a neat stack of wood for the fireplace. He grabbed a small log and rammed it into a window in one of the bedrooms. He carefully removed the remaining glass from its hold into the windowsill. Once it was clear of glass, he climbed in.

Clicking on the light, he saw the bedroom was amazingly clean. There was no bedding on the queen-size bed, no trash, no dirty socks even on the bare oak floor. It even smelled clean, sharp with chlorine. There was also no phone. Ian moved out into the hallway and then turned into an open doorway. It was the laundry room where he had been. The rope he'd been tied with was gone. No single sign of the trauma he'd endured was evident. He bet that they took anything in the house that they couldn't wash—the sheets, the rope, his blue blazer and all other possible clues. He noticed the dryer door was open and the light inside was on. There was something in there and he moved closer to see a cloth inside. He pulled the pink cloth out to see that it was a sexy thong with a very narrow band. Surely these were the leader's. What was her name? He read the tag. Victoria's Secret. He threw them back in. Leave them for the police. He needed a phone.

In the living room, he switched on the lights. He'd never seen the living room, which was elegant—a fireplace with a mantel, a Persian carpet, and etchings on the wall. All was very orderly. Clearly they erased as much evidence as possible including fingerprints. That's why they were up most of last night. No sign of a phone there, either. Next came the kitchen.

In the kitchen, tiled white, a white phone with a long curly cord was mounted on the wall. He picked it up. There was no dial tone, so he couldn't dial out.

It was then, with the dead phone at his ear, that he noticed a package on the floor by the tall pantry closet. What drew his attention was the color picture of a yachtsman shouting, arms raised in victory. The picture looked familiar, but he didn't know why. He ran over, picked it up, and tore back the picture. Underneath was money. It was real money. In their rush to get out of there, they must have all been panicked. This package must have fallen out. Surely they hadn't meant to leave a clue—or money. Maybe they'd figure it out soon. Maybe they'd be back. Ian realized he'd better get out of there.

Yet was he going to leave this money for them? God no.

That meant he should he give it to the cops, right? What if that made the cops suspect him? Surely they'd have to see he was truly innocent—a true hostage. Then again, in Mamet's play *Oleanna*, the professor was innocent of sexual harassment, and look at all the trouble he got into. Ian shook his fists into the air. God, he wished he could think more clearly right now. All he suddenly knew was that the only evidence in the house was this money and his fingerprints in a few places. What if he erased all evidence that he had returned to the house? It would be clearer that way. He could ditch the money in the woods to keep anyone from getting it.

Also, another notion struck him. Once the case was long closed, he could come back for the money. He deserved it after all he'd been through. Maybe he could even get into another graduate program and the money would pay for it. He found a large zip-lock plastic bag in a drawer and put the money in it.

Ian quickly returned to the bedroom and tossed the packet of money outside. Starting at the window, he considered the places he'd touched. In this room, he'd touched the windowsill and the light switch. He ran into the attached bathroom and grabbed a purple washcloth that was hanging. With it, he wiped the windowsill and around the light switch. He went into each room he'd been in and was methodical, wiping such things as the closet doors, the light switches, and the phone. He really hadn't touched a lot.

He pictured what would happen when he finally got to a phone and contacted the police. He'd be questioned, maybe brought here, then brought home where at last he could sleep. God he was tired. He returned outside and wiped his fingerprints from all the glass pieces on the ground and from all the doors on the outside. He buried the packet of money under leaves in a depression on the hillside, a place that was remote yet he could find easily again.

He had only one option now. Get to a phone and call the police. Get this whole thing started. He'd walk down the hill to a big street, and he'd find someone with a cell phone. He was turned off by the thought of a paranoid neighbor shooting first and asking questions later.

Tucking his shirt into his pants, he walked up to the hillside steps to the parking space and the road. He noticed a street sign he had not seen before: Pisa Terrace. He started walking down the hill. Houses were built only on one side of the road, and a line of cars—Mercedes, Toyotas and various SUVs—were parked on the same side, leaving a single car width for traffic. As he walked the narrow asphalt, the Munchkins' song popped in his head: Follow the yellow brick road.

Twenty minutes later he approached a car wash not yet open, and he spotted a pay phone near a Coke machine. There were still pay phones? He ran over. The instructions said that dialing 911 was free. He dialed the numbers.

For two days, Medina and her team had tried to find out who the hostage was. They released the hostage's photo to the local news stations and newspapers, giving people a number to call. They were inundated with leads, which took a lot of manpower. She slept little and worked hard. Now on the third day, in her office with hundreds of calls to make, Medina received a call from Jones in South Pasadena.

"Aleece," he said rather friendly. "The hostage just called from a payphone. He broke free from his captors."

"What's his name?"

"Ian Nash."

"You're sure it's the hostage, not a crank?"

"He sounded scared enough. A cruiser's picking him up now."

She immediately went to work finding out as much as she could about Nash's background. He'd never had any dealings with the law, she found, and he'd been a doctoral student in theatre until recently. He had not earned his Ph.D. He wasn't deeply in debt from the financial records she'd obtained, but he clearly needed money if he wasn't working.

Less than an hour after Jones's call, Medina walked toward the open interrogation room in South Pasadena. The room was plain—acoustic tiles on one wall and the ceiling, the rest of the room beige. In a ripped and dirty white shirt, looking much like a beaten and homeless man who'd been found huddling in a bathroom, Nash sat with Jones at the dark table, looking down, lost in thought. A crushed aluminum wrapper of a 7-11 hot dog and a Big Gulp stood before him. He had the same face, the same jaw with the same indentation revealed on the videotape. Yet he looked as defeated as his hot dog wrapper.

Jones stood when she entered. "Thanks, Detective," she said, and turned her attention to the man sitting. "Mr. Nash?"

"I'm sorry, yeah." He looked up, then back down. He remained seated and smelled like a gym bag. He'd been held hostage for two days so it had to be expected. Beneath his stubble and exhaustion, she could see he was a handsome guy, short blond hair and blue eyes, but a few things were off, such as his ears stuck out and his sideburns were a little long for this century. He was also rather lanky, an ostrich, the kind of guy who'd get sand kicked in his face, which is why perhaps he'd been selected as hostage.

"Ian, this is FBI Special Agent Medina," said Jones. "She's been in charge of this case and really put a lot of manpower trying to find who and where you were. She's the *best*."

Medina glanced at Jones to show him he was laying it on too thickly, then she looked at Ian and said, "This one is important to me. We're here to help you."

He didn't return eye contact and said, "Yes. My dissertation committee said something like that."

"From your tone," she said, "your dissertation committee didn't go well."

"No."

He wasn't going to trust her, but then again, she wasn't ready to trust him. He was in theatre, after all. Maybe he was acting.

"All right," she said. "You've been through a lot, and we just want to know what happened from when you were taken away."

"There's a lot."

"I'm listening."

"They did something to me. Drugged me. I'm only getting pieces, and it's very frustrating."

"You were taken from a bank in South Pasadena," she said. "Do you remember that?"

He squinted as if doing so would help him see into his past. He slowly nodded. "It gets kind of surreal. I remember being tied up and my eyes being covered. Ah, shit. I know I know this stuff."

"Do you remember being in the graduate program in Irvine?"

He glared at her, now not withdrawn. "Perfectly. It's only the last few days. I feel so damn scattered."

"What kind of drug?" she said.

He looked at her as if she just spoke Erdu.

"Did it make you sleep? Where you sleeping a lot?"

"We have a phlebotomist we can use just down the street," Jones told Medina as if to impress her. Ian looked confused.

"With your permission," Medina told Ian, "we'd like a sample of your blood. If we can get evidence of drugs still in your system, we can use it in court later against these perps." It would also tell her if the drugs were real. If not, then maybe he worked with the bank robbers. She couldn't rule that out.

Ian nodded weakly. He looked extremely tired. "It made me hallucinate. I don't know if it was LSD or what. Are you going to catch these people?"

"Bank robbery is my specialty," said Medina. "And I have a strong record."

"Good," said Ian.

"In many ways, bank robbery is a dumb crime," she told Ian. "Robbers put themselves at risk in a high security situation for only a moderate amount of money generally—and it's an automatic federal crime. Imagine planning a crime where your picture will be taken, you're likely to have many witnesses, someone will set off an alarm, and the money you get can become instantly useless thanks to an exploding dye pack. I'm on their heels."

"It seems like they got a lot," he said. "I saw them divide it into four."

"Did you get any names of your captors?" When he looked confused again, she said, "When they talked with each other, did they use any first or last names?"

Ian frowned. "I think so. I should know that. I'm just tired."

"You're tired, and you may be suffering from post-traumatic stress syndrome too, which plays with the memory—perfectly normal. You'll be all right, okay?"

Ian nodded, but he still looked worried. She knew she was wringing him out, but she needed to use him more immediately and paused before offering him what was only the right thing under the circumstances: "Would you like to sleep before we talk? I'm just trying to find out who did this to you."

"Me, too. I can't sleep. I want to get them."

"One thing I'd love to know then," said Medina, "is where you were held."

"It was a house on a hill somewhere near where you found me, but I don't know the area."

"Would you like to show us? If we drove you back, explore the area, would that help?" She didn't offer him another opportunity to sleep.

"Drive me over there."

He had no hesitation. He'd seemed so fragile—now he wasn't scared? She'd expected to have to talk him into it. She nodded. "I'll arrange for a SWAT team to follow, too, in case we find the house, and then we can act on it right away. Sound good?"

"Do you need a SWAT team? I think my captors are gone."

"How do you know that?"

He looked puzzled. "I don't know," he said. "I was thinking they'd probably hurry out of there if I escaped. You're right. Bring the SWAT team."

"Okay." However, her instincts said there wasn't something right about his reactions.

"I also learned no one recognized me from my picture on TV," he said. "Kind of sad."

"We had many calls," said Medina. "Surely there're a few in there that were correct. Have you had a chance to call home—friends or family?"

"He didn't want to," said Jones, giving her a look that showed he'd asked.

"I'll make calls later," said Ian. "We have to get after these people first."

"Yes," said Medina. "If you want to write names and phone numbers down, Detective Jones can probably have an assistant make calls for you to say you're safe and you'll call later."

"Not needed," said Ian. "I only have my parents."

Medina nodded and smiled to make it seem normal, but again, something odd: did this man have no friends?

"You went through a lot," said Medina. "We've got a counselor you can talk with later. She's really good in helping with post-trauma."

"I don't need anyone."

"Okay. Before we go to the house, I just need to learn a few more things. How did you escape?" she asked.

"I remember being tied up and left on the laundry room floor. I awoke to voices this morning. It was the women talking outside, near my window, and one of them seemed upset by something."

"Someone was angry?" said Jones.

"Just let him talk," said Medina.

"I couldn't hear all their words but I learned they were getting ready to leave the house. I listened closely. I wanted to know what was going to happen to me. Then the big guy's voice came in, and he was clear. He was saying to kill me, leave no evidence. I struggled with the ropes on my hands and found they were loose, which was odd because they'd been very tight. I wasn't Houdini."

"Who loosened them?" said Medina.

"Probably one of the women. I must have been hearing wrong, but it sounded like the leader told the other she loved me."

"She did?" said Jones.

"It's weird and I don't get it but she was always nice. Anyway, the rope around my hands came off easily. I quickly untied the rope around my ankles and I ran out of the house. I could hear the big guy yell in the house that I'd escaped. I ran to the nearest house. Pounding on the door and yelling for help, I must have sounded like a mad man because the guy inside said he'd shoot me if I didn't get off his porch, and then the big guy was getting closer to me, so I ran into the woods. I tripped and fell down a hillside, which I guess was good because soon all four were looking for me and never found me. I just stayed hidden. After the four gave up and it got lighter, I walked down the hill where I spotted the pay phone. I didn't want to try another house in case there was another guy with a gun."

"I'm glad you made it," she said. "One last thing. You mentioned your dissertation committee hadn't gone well."

"I lost my stipend and teaching position," he said. "But that's another story—fucking academia."

"You were filling out an application at Carrie's Coffee," she said.

"Seems so long ago." He nodded, remembering. "I needed something to tide me over."

"So you're low on cash?"

"Rent's coming up and—" His expression hardened. "Are you implying I had something to do with the robbery? Fuck this shit, I can't believe this!"

"You've been through a lot. You misunderstand."

"That's bullshit. I was tied, beaten, and drugged, and you're not fucking on my side here."

"I am. I'm also doing my job."

"I want those criminals captured and flayed."

Jones piped in, "We'll get them. We're with you. You can be sure we're doing everything we can."

"Are you doing the good cop, bad cop thing? You think I helped in the robbery?"

"Truthfully, we don't know," said Medina. "The facts will show us the way. Let us arrange a few things, and let's get going to the house."

Ian nodded but didn't seem as eager as before. "How many cases are on your plate right now?" asked Ian.

"Thirty."

"Thirty cases?" he said with disbelief.

"Be assured this case is a priority."

"So you're forgetting about the other twenty-nine?"

"I do my job well," said Medina. "You don't have to worry."

"Thirty," Ian said, looking at Jones.

"You don't really have much option, do you, Mr. Nash," said Medina. "I'm in charge of this case, and for months, I've been following this woman, whom we call the Busty Bandit."

Ian flashed on seeing the woman first at the bank, noticing her breasts. Maybe he shouldn't have smiled at her then.

"We'll get the crew," said Medina. "Can you take us to where you were held?"

"Absolutely," said Ian.

Medina looked at Ian, wondering about him. There just was something odd about this guy.

CHAPTER THREE

It took thirty minutes before they left because Special Agent Medina had to finalize the SWAT team, which had been on alert. Ian also had a blood sample taken by a young Asian woman who hurried in, then out.

Medina allowed Jones to come as a courtesy for his help. Jones sat in the back of Medina's car while Ian sat up front. As they drove, Ian thought of how he'd driven to Carrie's some days earlier—had it been three?

"My car," Ian said.

"Pardon?" said Medina, starting the car.

"I left my car on the street near the bank. Can we stop for it later? Do you think it's been towed?"

"I'd been wondering about that. We'd checked every car in the bank's lot."

Jones leaned forward from the back seat. "What kind of car is it?" he asked.

Ian had to think. "An old blue Toyota Corolla."

"Give me your keys, and after this, I'll assign someone to find your car for you."

"This is a side of the police I haven't seen," he said.

"We're a full-service company," Jones said, leaning in further as if to see Medina's reaction. She swatted him back. It sure seemed like they were partners.

Ian, too, could see Detective Jones's interest in her. Her trim body, long blond hair in a ponytail, and natural good looks had made Ian gaze more closely when she first walked in. She had two small diamond studs in her earlobes that he found attractive. Her Spanish surname at first threw him, but when he'd looked again, she could be Latina in a young Jennifer Lopez way. Married? He didn't notice a ring. Her attraction faded, however, after she had spoken a while. She was the anal type—good for an agent, bad for dating. After what happened with his last relationship, Pierra, he didn't need more "bad."

"What if my car's been towed because it's been there a few days?" Ian asked, now that he thought about it.

"No matter," said the detective. Ian handed him the keys.

As they drove and Ian let himself relax, he felt the lack of sleep push down on him as if there were too much air pressure. He sat up straighter to keep alert. If he had to stay up another day without sleep, he'd do so.

Yet that very lack of sleep brought another notion, which had been in the background all day. He remembered the leader saying, "It's love that even defies description. It's every heartbeat, every cell that grows and dies." Had she really loved him—or still loved him? It had to be someone else—or else the talk he'd heard had been staged for him to get him to escape without making it obvious to the big guy. He had to admit he was alive thanks to the leader. She had helped him just like the guard in the bank. Was it right to do everything to capture her? Yes. The law's the law, and she had put him through a lot of misery, and he did not love her. However, he would say good things about her at the trial.

As he looked out the window, the stores they passed on Figueroa Boulevard did not look familiar at all. One had in its window a mannequin that wore a wedding dress. "Vestidos de Boda," said the store's sign. The life-sized doll beamed as if she were ready to throw her garter to the next dummy. What if that doll were the leader? Then it occurred to him—his memory was partly back.

"Hey," he said to Medina. "I just remembered something."

Medina turned in her seat to look at him. "What's that?" she said.

"The Busty Bandit, as you call her. Everyone called her Zetta. And the big guy who shot the guard. They called him Owen."

"Excellent," she said. "They may be real last names, but likely code names for each other. How about the others? What were their names?"

Ian pictured their faces but no names sprang to mind. He still felt so fuzzy and tired. God knows if he could find the house.

Ian cranked his head around to peer through the rear window to see an unmarked white panel van in which, he imagined, sat a number of bulletproof vested SWAT team members with rifles. Or would they have automatic machine guns?

"So what else can you tell me about your captors?" said Medina. "No detail is too small."

Ian remembered sitting at a table, but was he tied up? Was that part of his hallucination? Everything was so fuzzy. And he was so damned tired. "I'm sorry," he said.

"How about the other person?" said Medina. "Jones, do you have the file with you? Show him the other fellow."

Jones showed Ian the photo of the man with the pencil thin mustache. Ian looked. "First of all, he was a she. The muchache was fake."

"I assumed that," said Medina. "But she's a she... Have a name?"

He knew he knew it, but it didn't come. "She had red press-on fingernails, if that helps—with roses on them."

"Her name may come to you later," said Jones.

"Okay," she said.

"What kind of prison sentence will they get?" asked Ian.

"Two counts of murder, two counts of attempted murder as I look at it," said Medina. "Life sentences or the death penalty. Of course, the prosecutor will have to decide."

Medina picked up a manila folder wedged next to her seat and pulled out a photo. Ian moved to see. It was of Zetta during the bank robbery. "Life in prison," said Jones, "will turn those good looks into a wrinkly grandma."

"Maybe she had a good reason to rob," said Ian.

"I learned long ago," said Medina. "There are only two sides, the good and the bad. Yes, good people sometimes do bad things, but they need to be held responsible."

"I agree," said Jones. "They should ban psychologists testifying about childhoods. Yes, people have lousy childhoods, but does that give them carte blanche to commit crime?"

"Exactly," Medina said.

Jones looked pleased, as if he'd finally said something to impress her.

Medina pulled into the car wash just off of Figueroa. "Is this where you were picked up this morning?"

"Yes." Ian pointed straight ahead. "I came down this road. Keep going straight up the hill."

"Good. Let me talk with the team behind us, and we'll go up."

Medina hurried to the van now parked behind them and spoke with the driver. When she returned, she said, "They'll wait here for our go ahead."

As they drove up the hill, Medina said, "Where did you pop out onto the road? You said you took a path to a road. We follow that path and that should take us to the house, right?"

Ian realized he'd actually never gone down the path to the road. He had only used the road from the house. His little fib now put him in an awkward position. Still, as the victim, he shouldn't feel guilty. Because he'd called from the gas station, it was best just to stick with the simple story: he'd hidden in the canyon, and at daybreak, he walked down the path to the road to the gas station. "Now that I think of it, I may not recognize where I came out," said Ian. "I was too panicked. But all roads lead to the houses, don't they?"

"I know this area," said Jones, "and a lot of the houses can't be seen from the road."

Medina turned to Ian, seriously. "You've got to look closely for where you came out. We've got a whole SWAT team waiting on us here. You told me you could take us there."

"I will," he said. "I'm sure if we drive around, I'll recognize something. I'm sure of it."

Medina frowned, and looked as if she was about to say something, but stifled it. She drove ahead. They kept going up the hill, and Ian recognized different houses. They were on the right route—he just couldn't tell her. When they came to a fork in the road, Medina said, "Left or right?"

"Right. Definitely right. I remember that swing set over there." He hoped that would make Medina feel better. Yet as she drove, Ian did not recognize anything else. It all looked new. Did they miss another fork? They made it to the top of the hill and nothing looked familiar.

"Was the house all the way to the top?" said Jones.

"No."

"Where do we go?" she said.

"Let me think," Ian replied.

"You'd been drugged, remember," said Medina. "Had you ever taken a hallucinogen before?"

Ian sensed the anger in her voice. "What the fuck does that have to do with anything?" he said before he caught himself, realizing he was doing what he'd done with Pierra, meeting anger with anger. "And no, I've never taken LSD or whatever. I'm sorry. Maybe we could go back a ways." He could see her jaw clench. Maybe humor was needed. "I studied Edward Albee's weirder plays and survived," said Ian.

"Right," she said, opened her door, got out, and slammed the door.

"I'm a bit tired," Ian said to defend himself to Jones.

"She hasn't been sleeping much herself," Jones said.

Ian watched her pace back and forth.

Jones looked concerned and reached for his door handle when his cell phone rang. He answered it with a simple, "Jones." The woman's voice on the other end was loud enough for Ian to know whoever was there was not happy.

"I'm not the Bank of America," said Jones. "I told you that if you want me to go halfsies with you on anything, you have to tell me in advance. I have a cash flow problem. The dogs are your responsibility anyway. You wanted them. Listen, we've got to talk later. I'm on a case."

He hung up and looked at Ian. "Sorry. My ex-wife isn't exactly good with her money."

The door opening startled Ian. Medina got back in. "You're right," she said to Ian. "Let's go back down to the last thing you know you saw."

"That would be the swing set by the fork in the road."

"Maybe we took the wrong fork," she said.

"Let's try the other fork," said Ian.

They did and soon Ian noticed a sign, "Pisa Terrace." His heart jumped. "This street name I remember. We're getting close." Medina, like a dog with a sensitive nose, looked eager and drove ahead. After a few more turns, Ian said, "Stop."

"Is this it?" said Medina.

Ian opened his door and walked toward the gravel area. Yes, this was it. There was the house below and the stairs. Medina stared at him through the windshield. He stared back—then nodded and signaled for them to come forward. Medina and Jones exited. Their feet scrunched in the gravel on the way over.

"So this is the place, you're sure?" she said.

"Absolutely. I remember these stairs, those windows, everything."

Jones scanned the horizon as if trying to understand something, then he said, "I thought you were blindfolded when you came here."

"I wasn't when I left. I hung out in the canyon and got a good look at the place in the light."

"But that would have been from the other side," Medina said.

"It looks the same on the other side."

She nodded, then gazed at the ground where they stood. She frowned, then walked over to a dark area in the gravel and kneeled down. She touched one of the rocks with her index finger, then rubbed that with her thumb. She stood, looking closely at the gravel.

"You see something?" said Ian.

"There's oil here in the gravel. Maybe the van you mentioned leaked oil. I can see a footprint in it, which means someone got oil on their shoe. Maybe there's a better imprint somewhere else—could be evidence."

Ian nodded. She was good. He also realized it could be his foot-print from when he returned, so he hoped there were no other impressions. Maybe he'd made a mistake in not telling her he'd been here. Too late now. "Are we going down?" he asked.

She shook her head, then pressed a button on her cell phone. She spoke into it. "Bring the full team up." She gave the address. "I also need forensics on a possible footprint."

Ian sat with Jones and Medina in the car farther down the block while eight members of the SWAT team surrounded the house. Ten minutes later came the all-clear signal. No one was in the house. "Don't move anything, but start dusting for prints and searching for DNA evidence," said Medina into her phone. "We'll be right there." Medina turned to Ian. "I need you to give us a tour of the rooms and what you remember. Maybe seeing the place will remind you of things. Any details can help us."

Ian nodded, thinking of how efficient she was. She'd make a great stage manager if she were in theatre. Even with a dozen actors, she'd be great. No surprise would stun her.

Jones said, "I need to return a call. I'll be in in a little." He pushed buttons on his cell phone.

Ian walked behind Medina down the street and down the stairs toward the house. As they stepped into the house, she paused and sniffed. "Chlorine bleach. They're good. We're better."

They walked down the hallway and came to the hallway bath-room. Medina stopped at the doorway, and she and Ian looked in. A young man was crouched in the dry tub, eager and focused, and he poked down the drain with what looked like a stick. He withdrew a giant swab and examined it closely. "I've got some hair and what I bet is some hair dye," said the young man.

"Good," said Medina.

"DNA, right?" asked Ian.

"Yes. We always need to think about the court case. The more evi-dence to tie them here, the better. If you live in a place for a while, you can't avoid leaving stuff."

"Ah."

"The toilet's plugged, too," said the young man. "I bet we'll have fecal matter."

"Probably Navarre's," said Ian. "Ah, that's her name: Navarre! I remember Owen getting mad at her for clogging it."

"Good," said Medina. "And where is the laundry room?"

He pointed ahead. "Down the hall."

As they walked by the bedroom, a man wearing latex gloves was dusting the floor beneath the window that Ian had broken. When the man saw Medina, he smiled. "There's a very clear footprint here and maybe another," said the man. "Looks like he had oil on his shoe that carried dirt. Maybe this is how they got into the house the first time."

"With all the cleaning they did," said Medina, "Why wouldn't they clean in here?"

"They were in a hurry to leave after I escaped, I imagine," said Ian.

"Or maybe someone else broke in," said the detective with the latex gloves.

"Can you tell anything from the footprint already?" said Medina.

"I'd say it's a size eleven athletic shoe. Converse All Star."

"Are you kidding me?" said Medina. "You know that many shoes?"

The man held up a piece of paper that he'd used for transferring the print. In the middle of the page of the shoe shape were the fuzzy words: "Converse All Star."

Ian caught his breath. He was wearing those very shoes now. He noticed Medina looking at his shoes.

Medina peered straight into his eyes, and he knew she knew. She took his arm just under his armpit, like a teacher might do with a small student, and dragged him back outside. Once they were away from everyone, she said, "Let me see the bottom of your shoe." He reluctantly lifted his foot, and she saw.

"Why did you come back here?" she said.

"For the phone, actually. You'll see what I found—there's no phone service. The phone is dead."

"Why didn't you tell us this earlier?"

"Because I entered without permission. I broke the window."

"Now hold it," she said. "You were frightened of these people, yet you came back?"

"I saw them go. I figured 911 would bring the police to this address."

"But you called from a payphone."

"As I said, the house phone didn't work. I'm so sorry. I feel badly."

She considered it and slowly nodded. "I don't like that you lied to me."

"It was wrong. As David Mamet says, 'Always tell the truth—it's the easiest thing to remember'."

"Who's Mamet?"

"A playwright and director. I told you about him. My dissertation."

"Did you touch anything else in here? Are we going to find your fingerprints around and no one else's?"

Ian flashed on the rooms he'd been in: the bedroom, laundry room, and kitchen. He'd touched very little and had wiped his fingerprints, so he wasn't worried about that. He thought, though, about the money in the hillside depression not far from the wheelbarrow. He should probably mention that.

"I didn't touch much," Ian began, "and I just want to help. I wanted to call as fast as I could."

"Your lack of complete honesty has me question things."

"Am I in trouble?"

"I'd say yes. This has really thrown a wrench into things. I don't know what to believe."

"I'm tired, okay? I haven't slept, and all I've eaten is a hot dog. Those nitrates do weird things to me. I think I have to reevaluate how you've been treating me, frankly. I'm trying to cooperate, and I *still* need sleep."

A few minutes later, upon Jones' return, Medina took them into the kitchen. "I've always found there's a lot that goes on in the kitchen," she said. "Does this place jog your memory at all?"

It was where he found the money. Should he mention it? Would he get him in more trouble? He was so damn tired. Shit, he wish he could think better. Be conservative. He could tell them later. "The driver, an Asian man, did all the cooking," Ian said. "I only had two meals until they stopped feeding me, but even his pancakes had flair—fresh blueberries on top with whipped cream and real maple syrup, not the fake kind. This guy only served the best."

"Interesting," she said.

"Some guys like to cook," said Jones. "I make a great morning omelet, for instance." Medina ignored the remark.

"What else?" said Medina to Ian.

"Owen was an actor. I've seen enough of them. And..." He remembered that breakfast more. "He quoted from a Tide commercial, so I'm thinking he made some money at one time in commercials."

Medina nodded again, seemingly impressed. "Navarre?" she asked.

"I couldn't really place Navarre. Her accent sounded a bit Canadian, you ask me, but she seemed so out of place with the others."

"You know accents?" said Medina.

"I'm in the theatre. Accents are a stock in trade. Anyway, Navarre was the intellectual type. If I had to guess, I'd say Navarre was good at finalizing the details, but everyone revolved around Zetta."

"Why's that?"

Ian held out his hands as if it were obvious. "She has charisma. She's likeable, frankly."

"Good cop, bad cop," said Medina.

"Pardon me?"

"Owen treated you brutally, and Zetta treated you well, yes?" said Medina.

"Yes, but—"

"If Zetta were truly in charge, as I suspect, too, then she'd have Owen do those things to you because you'd want to help her after what he did to you."

"No, she didn't seem the type."

"You said yourself he was an actor. She hired an actor to be a brutal guy. He'd do what she'd ask, right?"

"Yes, but he *was* a brutal guy. You don't fake that. I know."

"Because you're in theatre."

He felt cornered and said nothing.

She added, "And you weren't fed for two days because…?"

"Because Owen wouldn't allow it."

"I thought Zetta was in charge."

Why was Medina being hard on him suddenly? Ian looked for help from Jones, driving. Jones smiled. He was the good cop.

"I don't know," said Ian. "I think she was just keeping the peace is all. She wanted money but no death." He realized then that if Zetta were not caught, he wouldn't be upset.

"I have a question," said Jones. "What was the relationship between Zetta and Navarre? Do you think it was sexual?"

"You'd like that, wouldn't you?" said Medina.

"Lesbian lovers always adds a nice twist," said Jones.

"I noticed," said Ian, "that Navarre had a wedding ring and Zetta had no rings."

"Interesting," said Medina. "Maybe down the line, marriage records will help us."

"What about the press conference?" said Ian.

"You don't need to be there."

"But I want to."

"Why don't I have Detective Jones drive you home, you get some sleep, and we'll see how you are this afternoon."

"From my point of view," said Ian, "you've got thirty cases you have to deal with, and this is my one and only priority. I don't want to be cut out of the loop."

"Mr. Nash. There is no loop for you. Let me just do my job. If you have ideas, you can certainly call me or leave me a voice message." She reached into her waist pack that she wore and pulled out a business card. Ian looked at it. An FBI gold seal was the biggest element. Her name, Aleece Medina, stood over the italicized words "Special Agent." There was no address, just her telephone number, fax number, and a 24-hour message line number.

"After I get some sleep, I'll be good as new," he said. "Maybe I could just ride along. I'm an instant resource."

"That's not the way the FBI works."

"You're cutting me out!"

"I know you want to help, but the speediest thing is let me do my job. Are we done, or is there something else we should know?"

Ian looked at her face. So dismissive. He'd considered pleading his case, but he knew her type—so in control, taking help from no one or at least him. Fuck her. He'd be nobody's doormat anymore. If the FBI couldn't find these people, he'd have do something himself, work under the radar. He had no idea what, and he knew he wasn't at his best in terms of thinking, but he had to trust his instinct. No more being treated poorly. It's what Mamet would do. It was time to stop analyzing and just *do*. All there is is action.

As for the money near the wheelbarrow, he wouldn't mention it ever. Let her find it, and if she doesn't, well, it's not going to matter to the case one iota. In fact, it might have to be used for other purposes, such as to fund his own investigator. "Yes," said Ian. "I guess we're done."

Five minutes later, Jones was driving him down the hill in Medina's car, taking him home.

"Something happen with you two in the house when I was gone?" Jones asked.

"No," said Ian, though he knew Jones would find out later. Ian didn't want to talk about anything now. Jones didn't look like he wanted to talk much, either, so after Ian gave him his address, they said nothing for most of the way.

Ian's insides rumbled. He realized as complicated as the situation was, this tenuousness was reflective of his whole life. After he'd been kicked out of the doctoral program, he had found himself angry—as angry as he was at this very moment.

"Sleep will do you well," said Jones.

"I don't know," said Ian. "Everything has been figured out, except how to live."

"You lost me."

"Sartre said that—an existentialist. He wrote the play *No Exit*, about three people trapped in a room, each longing for a person who doesn't return the interest. Hell is other people."

"Sounds like my last marriage."

"He also said that all human actions are doomed to failure."

"Don't think I'll invite that guy to a party."

Ian wasn't going to tell him the guy's dead but said, "I'd rather have playwright David Mamet to a party. He said that the phrase 'nothing matters' debases the human spirit. From where I'm sitting, everything fucking matters."

"I know Mamet. My wife dragged me to one of his plays, about Hollywood; can't remember the name of it."

"*Speed-the-Plow*," said Ian.

"Yeah. It was kind of funny, a lot of F words, but so what?"

"The point is the magic happens in front of you. There are no retakes. It's actors alone on a stage for ninety minutes, and they can capture your soul. Theatre is about what we as people do—how we're so fucked up and different."

"I don't need a play to tell me that. Every day of my job is that," said Jones. "I have to say, though, what people do when you corner them is interesting. Some try to run, some break down and cry. Some stand there and say nothing. People are different, and that keeps me on my toes."

Ian nodded, thinking about what he had done when cornered by Medina about his shoes. At first he was thrown, but he told her the truth and she saw he was okay. He had to keep up the momentum.

"You going to be all right, buddy?" said Jones. "You should call a therapist of some sort."

"Like I have a health plan anymore."

"The city has some sort of victim assistance program. You can't do this alone."

"All I know is there are people out there who did me wrong, and they must pay."

"Yeah, we'll find them. In the meantime, you should talk to a shrink."

◆

Ian's mailbox at the edge of the driveway was stuffed to overflowing with circulars. Hadn't that been a clue for his landlady that maybe he hadn't been around for more than two days? Hadn't she seen his image on the TV or newspaper? Why hadn't she called the police?

He yanked out all his mail. Much of it, he could see, was flyers for grocery stores, for real estate, for pizza specials and more. Even with so much of it junk, he always felt he needed to go through his mail carefully, so he always stacked his letters on his desk to be examined more thoroughly later. This batch would join the stacks already there.

The door to the main house opened, and Mrs. Brown came out to water the numerous hanging plants on the front porch, green plastic watering can in hand. She had an old Craftsman home. A tall woman in her early seventies, she'd lost her husband a few months before Ian had moved in to the converted stand-alone garage in the back. Ian was her first tenant ever. She needed the extra income.

"There you are, Ian. I was wondering where you'd been."

"Mexico," he said, not wanting to get into a discussion. Perhaps, too, it'd explain why his clothes were ripped and dirty. She was a good woman, but he didn't want to talk now.

"I thought it was something like that. Where's your car?"

"Getting fixed," he said to cut off inquiry.

"Anytime you go on a trip, I'm happy to take your mail, water your plants."

"I don't have any plants."

"Would you like some?"

"No thanks. I don't have a green thumb. I'm sorry, I'm a bit tired, but I'll talk with you later."

"Very good," she said. "Welcome back."

He walked down his driveway to the back where his small guesthouse was. He unlocked the door, made a slow beeline for the bathroom, and undressed once he was in there. The powerful steady stream of hot water felt good on his body. He shaved in the shower, washed, and walked naked into his cluttered dark bedroom. The familiarity of it was comforting. Rather than turn on the light, he pulled on fresh underwear from a drawer and crawled into bed. He could eat later. He was far more tired than hungry.

In the moments before he lost consciousness, he pictured Zetta. After Owen, he'd like to kill her, too.

CHAPTER FOUR

Returning from the South Pasadena police department, Medina called into her West Covina office to find out that her boss, Rick Okinawa, had returned that morning. He would be at work by the time she arrived. It was already after lunch and she hadn't eaten, but she'd grab a Del Taco burrito on the way.

As she ate it in her car, she returned to the question that Jones brought up: why was a beautiful woman robbing banks? Also, how did Zetta choose Owen and the driver? Who was Navarre?

She knocked on Rick's third-floor office suite. Rick was a short man with black hair. He always wore a gray suit, a white shirt, and a plain tie, even though the FBI had okayed color and style post-Hoover. He looked more intense than usual, as if something was bothering him. "Now that Nash is safe, where are we?" said Rick without his usual pleasantries.

"A lot's happening," she said. He pointed to his café-style chairs and round table by the windows. She sat and glanced at Interstate 10 and the flat San Gabriel Valley beyond. The hills just to the east could be seen where the freeway rose, only later to dip down into Pomona.

"The Busty Bandit—Zetta," she said, "and her three friends fled around dawn this morning. Airports, the ports, police stations, even train stations were alerted to look for these people when Nash was first taken, and they've been given updates." Rick nodded as she spoke. "However," she said, "I imagine the suspects took cars. From what Nash said, they probably went their separate ways. I don't imagine we'll find them easily."

"And tonight you're having a press conference?"

"Yes, at the Federal Building in Westwood. The public has loved the drama of this case, so I can hope people will come through with leads."

Rick held a photo of the house where Ian had been held hostage. "Whose house was this? Where are the owners?" It was as if he was double-checking her work—very unlike him.

"Jones and a number of police have canvassed neighbors and local retail shops. The house was owned by an elderly couple who died over a month ago in a car accident—on a 110 Freeway entrance ramp."

"And still we don't know the real names of these hoodlums?"

"It'll happen. Don't worry. The neighbors say the daughter lives in New Zealand and just couldn't deal with selling the house, so she found house sitters. From the descriptions, they sound like Zetta and Navarre. They were living there a month before the South Pasadena robbery."

"Any evidence in the house?"

He had to know she'd be getting to this. "Are you okay?"

"What the hell did you say to Wexler?" he said.

Ah. Wexler had called. "He was about to replace me," said Medina, "with Davis after all the work I'd done on this."

"Now he's worried. He wanted to know if there were any infractions against you, asking how reliable you were."

"I hope you said good things."

"I did, and he basically said my ass was on the line. If you mess up, then he's going to swap *me* out for Davis."

"Typical for Wexler. Replace brilliance with mediocrity."

"Both Davis and Wexler are better at internal politics than I am."

"You know you can rely on me." She looked right at him so he'd know. "Anyway, we have some DNA evidence—some fecal matter, some hair—but I don't expect any of this will lead anywhere. They don't seem like career criminals."

"But it's been well-planned."

"This is a smarter-than-usual bunch. They used chlorine bleach, for instance, to wipe down the house. They did their best to remove any evidence."

"And did Nash offer any helpful details?"

Thinking about the guy, she nodded. "Some small stuff. He'll be most helpful at a trial."

"From what you said earlier, he was abused at their hands."

"Yes, but he's been less than truthful. Evidence shows he broke into the house to use the phone after the suspects fled. Why didn't he admit to that at first?"

"So you think he's hiding other things?"

"The odd thing is he basically wants to be my partner, and I told him no. He wants to find these people badly, but he's only had a background in theatre."

He nodded. "How much sleep have you been getting?" Rick asked her.

"Not a lot while Nash was a hostage."

"Go home now. Get some."

"I'm okay," she said.

"No, I want you to get a few hours sleep before the press conference. You need to be rested."

"But I just got here."

"Please," he said.

She nodded, looking at her watch. Maybe she could sleep.

A half hour later, as Medina pulled into her garage once more, her cell phone rang. The readout said it was Jones. "Yes, Detective?"

"Hey, you're always so formal. Call me Jones, like everyone else."

"What's up?" she said.

"I keep having press people call me asking why save anything for a press conference?"

"That way we control the imagery. I want the impact of Nash to wash over them. I want to see him pointing at the pictures of the suspects and demanding people find them. It's more personal."

"So you want to use Nash after all."

"Yes, if he'll be cooperative. Tell him so."

"And the press conference is at six—live for the evening news?"

"Exactly. See if you can turn up anything else by then."

"I've still got officers in the field asking around, and the Highland Park police joined in, too. I left a message for the daughter in New Zealand. I may have more answers when I see you."

"Excellent," said Medina. "I'm off-duty for a few hours."

"Need any help doing what you're doing?"

"Get a girlfriend already," she said.

"I'm trying."

After a quick hard nap, she glanced at her watch. Two hours fifteen minutes until the press conference. She had to admit she felt better. Now she had just over an hour to get ready, cook, and eat.

Minutes before she had to leave, the doorbell rang. Irritated, expecting the usual suburban kids either selling candy "for a valuable program so we can stay off drugs," or a wayward Mormon trying to convert people at the dinner hour, she yanked the door open to find Jones standing there, smiling, his dimple prominent. Why did men think boyish charm was anything?

"Detective," she said.

"I thought we might drive to the press conference together."

"I never gave you my address."

"I wouldn't be a good detective if I couldn't find it."

"This is inappropriate."

"You don't want to hear what I found? Fine. Drive yourself." He started to walk off.

"I'm sorry," she said. "What'd you find?"

"Appropriate now?" he asked. "I tried calling your cell, but when it wasn't on, I came here."

She grabbed her cell phone from her belt. It wasn't on, and it wouldn't go on. Shit. She hadn't charged it in a few days. That was a rare mistake.

"I'm sorry," she said. "I don't mean to be unfriendly."

"I've been putting in hours, too, and this was an extra that I thought you'd appreciate."

"You're right. Sorry. We'll caravan. I don't want you to have to drive all the way back here."

"It's no problem for me."

"It is for me," she said.

"But I've got lots of news," he said. "I need to update you."

"Tell me now."

He nodded. "I finally got a hold of the daughter in New Zealand. It was five p.m. here and noon tomorrow there—isn't that weird? They already know what's happening tomorrow because they're living it."

"Yeah, weird," said Medina, "like those jars you can buy with peanut butter and jelly already together." He frowned at her, and she realized he still didn't get her sense of humor.

"Anyway," he said, "she had put up signs in a few stores on Colorado Boulevard in Eagle Rock looking for a house sitter. She interviewed a few people, but she liked having two women, Meredith Brown and Eleanor Green, who we know as Zetta and Navarre."

"Brown and Green? And did they have references?"

"Yes, which the daughter never checked out. We did. All false."

"Did she say anything about them that we could use?"

"That they liked movies. They knew a lot about the director Peter Jackson, who's from New Zealand and a huge cultural hero there. He did the *Lord of the Rings* movies."

"I know."

"So you like movies. Maybe we should go to one sometime."

"When hell freezes over." She shook her head in awe. The guy was an Energizer bunny for rejection. "Are you hitting on me, Jones? I've made it clear—"

"You're my type."

"Forget it."

He laughed.

"Enough already, okay? We're keeping this professional," she said. She pointed out the door to indicate they were leaving. She locked her front door.

"I figured you'd say this, Medina, but listen. Cops and FBI are the same kind of people. Look how well we work together. And you can't tell me that when you date so-called normal people, they understand you one whit." They walked toward their cars, his an unmarked Crown Victoria, not his Jag. "I bet they even feel hurt when you can't call them back right away—that sometimes it's days before you can return a call. Plus you work nights often. That's when the criminals come out to play. Do other guys understand this?"

The fact was, they didn't. The few guys she dated in the last year were impressed she had a house and two cars. They wondered why no pets, and they couldn't stand the fact they always got her voice mail and couldn't talk to her right away. Jones was right—sometimes it was days. She had explained to her dates that it wasn't them, it was her job. They didn't get it. Even so, Jones was a player—he knew it and she knew it. He wasn't looking for a relationship.

"No, most guys don't understand that," she said.

"I know: you think I'm a cop, and you're FBI, so I'm a peon and you're not."

"That's not it. I wouldn't think such a thing."

"I get roast beefed all the time by the FBI," he said. They stood by her Ford Taurus.

"We're in the same field but have different responsibilities," said Medina.

"I get your drift, Medina. We'll keep it professional, don't worry. But you have to realize I have eyes. You're gorgeous."

He winked at her—again he actually winked. "I've got your number," said Jones, and then he looked ahead with that smile of his. She knew this wouldn't be the last on the subject.

Ian's car showed up late that afternoon when a South Pasadena police officer knocked on his door, and Ian's mouth was full of a peanut butter sandwich. "Jones can't pick you up," the man said, "but here's your car." The officer handed him the keys to his Toyota. "Make it to the Westwood Federal Building, seventeenth floor by 5:30, okay?"

"Okay," said Ian, clearing his mouth, who'd heard from Jones earlier in the hour. They wanted him after all, which made him feel better. The sleep had helped, too. "Where's the Federal Building?"

"Eleven thousand Wilshire at Veteran Avenue. Try Mapquest."

"Thanks."

Ian changed for the press conference, putting on best clothes—a black Italian suit that his former girlfriend Pierra had selected for him at a used clothing store, a white shirt, and a red tie. He considered how he could use the TV coverage to best advantage. Ever since Jones had driven him home, he'd been thinking of ways to help find this gang—and now he had a plan if the timing was right at the press conference.

Ian arrived early to the Federal Building. Out front, three news vans set up their satellite dishes. Before he got to the receptionist on the seventeenth floor, a woman in a suit and red nails approached him. "Are you Ian Nash?" she asked, her make-up a bit too bright.

"Yes," he said.

"You look like your picture."

"Is that good?"

"Of course. You're handsome. Nice suit."

"Thanks," he said. Ian liked this woman, whoever she was. Thin and confident, she was like an infomercial spokeswoman, someone selling a new set of knives. He would buy. "And you are?" he asked.

"I'm Rebecca Goode—with an E on the end. I'm a spokesperson for the FBI. I'll be introducing you. You're only saying just a little, that's it. The idea is people can see you as a real person and want to call in tips to help." They shook hands, and she led Ian into a small waiting room where there were doughnuts and coffee, which made him smile as did the short woman in a tight orange T-shirt who stood when he took a doughnut.

"This is your makeup artist, Vicki," said Rebecca. "Because you'll be on TV, you'll need a non-glare base."

"Oh," said Ian, who bit into his doughnut, supplementing his earlier peanut butter feast. "Nice to meet you, Vicki."

"Nice to meet you. I'm glad you're safe."

"Thanks."

Soon, Jones and Medina arrived, nodding to Ian when they entered.

"People are gathering now," said Medina, "and, Ian, you'll see about thirty reporters. You're just saying basically a little bit about—"

"I told him that already," said Rebecca.

"Yes, but I want to be clear. Rebecca will introduce us. I'll make a statement, then you and Jones can add onto it, then I'll be more thorough. I'll take a few questions. Don't be nervous," she said.

"Are you okay?" Jones asked Ian.

"If I can't talk about the case, what am I supposed to say?" Ian asked.

Rebecca spoke up. "Don't get into specifics because we need to keep the details for the trial. Just be general—that you were treated roughly, they were going to kill you, and you escaped. The key is to be brief. People want to see you're all right."

"That's nice to think," Ian said.

"Anything you say'll be interesting," said Jones. "It's sort of like looking at a car accident."

Ms. Goode in the suit seemed to take offense. "He's not a car accident—just the opposite. He's fine. But we need information."

"Red leather, yellow leather, red leather, yellow leather," Ian said, "Zanzibar Zanzibar," he added, stretching his mouth this way and that. People stared at him. "These are just voice and mouth exercises for actors," he said. "Don't you do them before you're in front of people or the camera?"

Vicki looked at him as if he were plankton from Pluto.

"These are standard things in theatre," he said.

Vicki applied powder to all their faces. Ian watched as she spent extra time with Medina, lining her eyebrows and giving her a light shade of lipstick.

"Please don't make me look like Bozo," said Medina.

"You say that every time, and I never do," replied Vicki. "You have a gorgeous face—beautiful—and this brings out your best. I love your hazel eyes and their flecks of green."

"Thanks," said Medina.

Ian nodded, too. When Medina wasn't talking, she was a looker.

At two minutes of six, they strode down the hall and into a room with bright lights, a raised platform with a podium, and a roomful of people who, unlike in the movies, didn't shout questions when they walked in. A few reporters quietly spoke into microphones before their cameras. Ian heard one reporter say, "Rebecca Goode, spokesperson for the FBI, will begin."

The wall behind the stage had a giant seal of the FBI, and on either side, seals of the Los Angeles and South Pasadena police departments. There were also three poster-sized boards on stands. One board held an enlarged photo that showed the Landwest Bank/Carrie's Coffee surrounded by police cars, and Ian, hands raised, was walking out with Owen and his gun, followed by Zetta and Navarre. Another offered an aerial photograph of the house on Mt. Washington. The last were photographs of the four robbers taken in the course of the robbery. Next to Navarre's photo was an artist's rendering of her as a woman.

"Good evening," said Rebecca. "As you know, three days ago, the Landwest Bank in South Pasadena was robbed in daylight by the Busty Bandit and her gang, and two people were killed, Northrop Ogden, a student at the Art Center College of Design, and his girl-friend, Jaq'lynn Nader-Russo, an intern at radio station KPCC. Ian Nash, to my right, was taken hostage. We're happy to say Mr. Nash fled to safety early this morning. The perpetrators are still at large, and there is presently an intensive search now that clues have been found in the house where Mr. Nash had been held captive. Special agent Aleece Medina, who is in charge of the investigation, can add details."

Ian could see they were not wasting time on pleasantries. With their being live on some stations, they couldn't dawdle.

Medina stepped to the podium and said, "Actually, I can't add a lot of details at this point for investigative reasons, but we do have some leads after searching the house where Mr. Nash was held hostage for three days on Mt. Washington." She gave a lot of the basics of the initial robbery, the getaway, and the house on Mt. Washington, a photo of which she pointed to next to photos of the perpetrators. She gave a phone number that people could call and said, "There's a ten-thousand-dollar reward for any information leading to any of their arrests." She turned to Ian. "Mr. Nash, would you like to tell us briefly what happened to you?"

All eyes were on Ian. Those closest to him just below the podium held out microphones as if to suck in all the sound he could muster. He cleared his throat. This was far different than any acting he'd done. This was about his life.

"It wasn't fun, let me say that. For most of the three days, I was tied up and gagged and left in a dark room. I was beaten." He could feel his eyes water as if his body was humiliating him in front of everyone. This wasn't fair. He coughed so he could quickly dab an eye. "I was drugged. And I escaped. If you have any information, please call the FBI."

Some of the reporters clapped, which Ian didn't expect. He mouthed "thank you" to them. While Medina pointed for him to exit, and Rebecca held out her hand to take him off camera, Ian felt he should add more. It'd help.

He ambled to the board, and he pointed to Owen. "We believe he's been an actor pursuing commercial work." He stepped to a photo of the driver, whose name he still couldn't remember, taken through the side window of the white Camry, the original get-away car. "Apparently he's good at carjacking and driving." He pointed to Navarre. "He's a she and very smart."

Last, he pointed to Zetta, and he was seized with a feeling that he might faint. The room felt as if he were on a moving boat. His mouth also seemed very dry, too, and he moved his tongue under his top lip to help him. He hoped he could finish without making a fool of himself. "Zetta," he said, "was the leader, and—"

"Thank you, Mr. Nash. I'd now like to introduce Detective Lanford Jones of the South Pasadena Police Department."

Turning her eyes from the cameras to him, Ian could read plenty in her glare. He'd just stepped over the line and he could kiss good-bye any thought he'd "be in the loop" again. Rebecca indicated he should get off-stage, but he stood next to Jones.

Jones moved to the podium as if he owned the place. "I'm very proud of my men and all the work they've put into this case, and proud to see that Mr. Nash has made it through a very traumatic time." He clapped and looked at Ian. Ian nodded in return. Many of the reporters clapped again, too. He was glad he stayed there.

"And now I'll take questions," said Medina.

In an instant, reporters blurted out questions all at once, many of them raising their hands. Medina pointed at the woman closest to her. The woman said, "Special Agent Medina, can you give us any background information on the leads you have?"

"We have suggestions from where they may be headed as well as DNA evidence. Leads are like anything else. You go with what you have."

The reporters barked out questions again, and this time Medina pointed to a person, an older man with a full beard. The reporter asked, "Isn't it correct that even with the full weight of the FBI, you weren't able to find this house after three days, and it's only thanks to Mr. Nash's escape that—"

"We had thousands of leads," Medina injected. "Our staff was working overtime. We would have found the house."

"May I finish?" said the man. "At this point, the suspects have more than half a day on you. They could be anywhere in the country at this point and unfindable, isn't that right?"

"You won't solve cases with a negative attitude," Medina said. "Every case has the possibility of failure, and no agent solves every case. The point is, you have to believe. I put puzzles together. I'm good at that. It's one piece after another, and we have some pieces now."

"Listen," said Jones, getting in his own interjection. "I've worked with a number of agents with the FBI, and Aleece Medina is one of the finest. It's just the way her mind works. Let's give her a hand," and he clapped hard. Others joined in. Was she blushing?

"Oh, one more thing," said Ian, realizing he had to act on his plan.

"Yes?" said Medina, her eyes saying "no!"

"To all of you who have suffered setbacks in your life, just know that sometimes things can turn a corner. I don't expect to be sleeping well for a while, but yet right at this moment, I feel like a sailboat captain winning a major race and cheering. I did it!" He held his arms overhead in victory exactly the way the photo in the paper showed, the one used to bundle Owen's stack of cash. With the reference to sailing and with his arms high, Owen should get the hint: I have your money. Come and get it, sucker.

Applause erupted. Medina looked frustrated but smiled as if she meant it, but her tilt of the head said, "Get off stage now, fucker."

Right after the press conference, Medina approached him with her glare again, so before she said anything, he said, "I'm sorry if I said more than you wanted. I was just trying to make people see I was real, as you said."

"You've done everything you can," said Medina, "Thank you for your help, and now you can go on with your life. If you want to speak with our trauma counselor, I urge you to do so. Just leave a message at the number I gave you."

"That's it?" asked Ian.

"Not much more to do, buddy boy," said Jones. "Sit back and see what happens. Special Agent Medina will follow through. Don't worry."

"Are you placing a watch on the house?"

"We've been through the house meticulously," said Medina. "Is there something else you didn't tell us?"

"No, not at all."

"You expect them to come back?"

"Don't you?"

"Why would they?"

"Scene of the crime? I thought that's the way it was on TV," said Ian.

"I'll be talking with you in the next few days," said Medina. "Probably even tomorrow. Periodically if you want an update on the case, call the number on my card, and the receptionist can fill you in."

Ian stared at her. "Receptionist?"

"An 'assistant,' I should say. Like everywhere else, people do double duty."

"I see," he said, knowing now he'd have to go onto part two of his plan. That was okay. In his heart, he expected this. He didn't have time to argue. He had to prepare.

After thanking everyone, Ian hurried to his car, a man on a mission. First stop, Big Five Sporting Goods for a gun. He knew that since he gave Owen a challenge, he, Ian, had to defend himself. Owen would surely try to grab him in the wee hours while Ian slept at home, demanding the money. Ian would surprise him, get needed information, and solve this case. He drove to the store in Pasadena.

Forty minutes later, having pulled off the 210 freeway, he stepped into the bright white two-story store. The gun section was easy to spot, and he walked to it. He'd always been opposed to the easy acquisition of guns in America, and had even been a member of Handgun Control, Inc. But that was before. Now he had to be ready for Owen. The one thing he knew about California gun laws was that if someone broke into your house and you feared imminent harm, you could shoot and kill him. Owen would certainly come without knocking, and Ian would be ready.

"May I help you?" said the salesman behind the counter.

"Yes," said Ian. "I need a handgun—for protection."

"We're required to tell you that handguns cannot be carried around without a permit. May I ask you why a handgun?"

"They're easy to shoot, right?"

"Is this for protection in your home?"

"Yes. Exactly."

"Have you ever used guns before?"

"Never."

"Then let me recommend a shotgun. You don't have to be as accurate in aim, and they will take down any intruder. May I show you?"

"Okay." Ian liked a knowledgeable salesperson.

"We happen to have on sale a Mossberg 500, a wonderfully light-weight gun with synthetic stock and forearm. It's a twelve-gauge, which means it's powerful, and it has a short twenty-inch barrel, meaning you don't have to be a good shot. A wider spread to kill them dead."

Ian nodded.

"And it has pump action—eight cartridges, one after the other."

Ian was convinced this was what he needed. "I'll take it and a box of cartridges—to go," he said.

"I need you to fill out a few forms for your background check."

"Background check?"

"Yes, we have that in this state."

"I'm perfectly legal to own one," said Ian. "I've never been to any court."

"I'm sure you'll have no problems. These aren't my rules, but the government's."

"Except I need one tonight," said Ian, panicked. This made the clerk look at him differently.

"There's a ten-day waiting period in Los Angeles County," said the clerk. "And there's a twenty-five dollar fee for the background check—not my fee, it's a county fee. And you need a gunlock, too. The Mossbergs, come to think of it, come with gunlocks, so you're okay there."

"Oh, man," said Ian, wondering what to do.

"I'm not happy about it either," said the clerk, "but those are the rules. Ten days goes really fast. It's twenty-one days on handguns."

Ian realized he hadn't thought out the plan with Owen well, but he had acted quickly because he was never going to have an opportunity to be on television again. Yet now Ian could see that in a day or two, he could be dead thanks to no gun and no contingency plan. He needed to think quickly to adapt. "Do you have flare guns?" he said. "I saw a movie where a kid saved himself with a flare gun right into the guy's stomach."

"Are you in trouble?" said the clerk.

"I'd been kidnapped, so I just don't want that to happen again."

"I know you." The clerk smiled—then pointed eagerly at Ian. "You were in the paper, weren't you? For something, right? I saw your picture."

"Yes, I was taken hostage. Now I don't feel safe. That's why I want a gun."

"All right, I see where you're at. You can go to a mall to get a taser or stun gun—those things with electricity."

"Ah—those zapper things. The police zap people all the time."

"We don't sell those, though. You'll have to go elsewhere."

"What can you sell me to protect myself today?"

"A knife? A crossbow?"

Ian looked around the store helplessly. He'd read of people buying guns illegally in parking lots from trunks of cars, and at gun shows, but he had no idea where either was. He needed something now. "I've got to think about my options. Maybe I'll be back." He gave a half wave and left. A better idea surely would come to him later.

From Big Five, Ian moved into the next part of his plan for the way he'd know Owen was near. He drove to the Radio Shack in South Pasadena—ironically just up a couple blocks from the Landwest Bank. When he stepped in, the store was completely empty except for a young man with a pencil-thin mustache wearing a red shirt and tie.

"May I help you?" said the man.

"Yes," said Ian. "I'm super paranoid about burglars. I need an alarm system with cameras and everything. What do you have?"

"First, do you want outdoor cameras or indoor ones?"

"Both. And I need motion detectors indoors and out, too. I need the best. Money is no object—but I need it simple enough to install myself tonight." While money normally was an object, for this Ian could not let anything stand in his way. He needed to stay alive and to succeed in his mission. He'd worry about paying down his credit card later. The young man smiled grandly, the kind of sale that happens rarely in a lifetime. He started with the Plug 'N Power Wireless Security System, which would allow Ian to set up sensors and motion detectors wirelessly—no wires or drilling needed. It was expandable to thirty-two protection zones, which would be more than enough.

"If there's an intrusion," said Ian, "I don't want a loud noise to scare anyone away, actually. I need like a mild buzz or something just to tell me someone is there."

"No problem," said the clerk. "You can adjust the volume or, if you want, any light you connect to a module will flash on and off."

"Perfect," said Ian.

The video cameras were another matter. While the "best" was a color quad observation system with a pan-and-tilt dome camera, it took cabling and time to get it set up. The most practical was clearly the wireless black-and-white security system that was quick to install, and infrared technology on the cameras allowed the camera to see in complete darkness. There were also microphones on the cameras, so sounds could alert him, too. Ian took that and four cameras.

When they moved to the cash register, the man happily tabulated away. It came to over a thousand dollars, and Ian gave him his credit card and his driver's license for proof of identity. Moments later, the register beeped, and the man frowned.

"I'm sorry. It says 'declined.' Do you have another card?"

"I don't understand."

"Did you hit your limit?"

"I guess I did."

"Do you have another card?"

"No." He'd been charging too much for a while. Teaching assistants didn't make a lot—but he needed this system tonight. Owen could intrude, and Ian could die. There was the cash under the wheelbarrow. He'd grab some of it, get the security system first, then he'd have to hurry to the mall and buy a taser. This was the best of his options.

"I can hold this for up to ten days," said the clerk.

"Hold it for today," said Ian. "I'll be back."

"We close at eight," said the clerk, pointing to his watch.

"I'll give you another two hundred—in cash—if you stay open a little longer. I need it tonight. You've seen my ID, so I'm not hiding anything. Just wait, and I'll give you the cash."

"Hey, you were on the TV tonight." The young man pointed over to the bank of televisions, which were all playing the same thing, a reality show of some sort with a barely clad young woman kissing a handsome man in shorts. "You were on the news."

"Yeah, I'm the guy. Can you stay open just a little longer? I have cash at home, so I'll be right back." Ian figured the sale would look good for the young man and probably boost him into a new sales level for the month. Salespeople always worried about their monthly totals. And the two hundred dollars cash extra wouldn't hurt.

"Yeah, I'll stay open, and if you can't make it, call me. Here's my card." The young man handed Ian a card.

"I'll be quick," said Ian, and he ran to his car. He quickly calculated the shortest route to Mt. Washington and the cash. On the way, he remembered how dark it could get outside the house and he'd need a flashlight if he were to find his way to the money. At the next stoplight, he looked at the sky through all windows to see if, perchance, there might be a full moon. He didn't see any moon. It'd probably be coal black atop Mt. Washington. Luckily he thought of it, and his home was on the way, where he stopped and ran in for a flashlight. He was in and out in less than a minute.

Driving down Figueroa, he recognized a few stores, including the wedding dress shop. As he turned off Figueroa and turned up Mt. Washington, he felt a chill.

As Medina drove home, she ran over in her mind the events of the night and probable outcomes. By moving Ian more into the spotlight, her hope was that the suspects, feeling the pressure, would make a dumb move, and someone would notice and make a call. If she were lucky, too, she'd get another piece of real evidence.

The odd part of the evening was Nash himself. What was that whole sailboat captain thing, cheering as if he'd won a race? And why for the second time did he suggest that someone watch the Mt. Washington house? That bothered her. As much as she hated to do it, she grabbed her cell phone and pressed the speed-dial number for Jones.

"Hello, Aleece," he answered. "What's up?"

"What did you make, if anything, of Nash asking that someone watch the Mt. Washington house?"

"I don't blame him," he said. "He wants to work with you."

"What do you mean?"

"Aleece, he's lonely right now—and traumatized. Of course he wouldn't mind being around a beautiful woman so sure of herself."

"Don't give me that crap. I want to know if he's hiding something. Should we have someone there at the house?"

"If you're worried about it, I'll go up there myself right now."

"I don't want to waste your time. I'm asking if there's anything we overlooked?"

"Can't think of anything. Tell you what: I have no family waiting for me, so I'll zip to the house for a little bit and if I think it's important, I'll call one of the night shift people to watch."

"No, it's not that important," she said, but she could hear the call had dropped. She was in a dead zone.

Ian drove to the house he hated. He didn't realize he was moving particularly slowly up the hill until a car behind him hit the accelerator and screeched past him where there were no parked cars. The monstrous black SUV roared ahead of him and careened around the next corner. Ian briefly considered what would happen if he didn't get the security system tonight? He would need to stay elsewhere, but he might also miss entrapping Owen.

At the house, the parking area above the stairs that led down to the house was empty as he had expected. He had to hand it to Zetta for finding such a place because the house was truly hidden. Thanks to the forest-like setting and the shape of the hill, none of the nearby neighbors could see the house. Right now, the night was so dark, he could hardly see his hand. There was only one street light behind him on the corner and something was wrong with it, nearly out. It glowed like a dying cigarette.

The air was nippy. The end-of-the-summer nights were starting to get cold. Wanting to be done with it and out of there as fast as he could, he quietly jogged down the steps using the flashlight. He looked at the front door then headed to the right, around back. A loud snap near the edge of the property—a stick breaking?—had him freeze on the spot. He turned off the flashlight to listen better. All he heard was the wave-like sound of the crickets. He listened carefully beyond the insects. He crept forward in the dark and pressed himself against the back wall of the house. He felt his heart pound in his ears. This is the stupidest thing I've ever done, he thought. No, he was fine. His imagination was simply on full. He hated the dark.

He could smell smoke. Was something burning nearby? It wasn't this house. It was likely someone on the hill barbecuing or using a fireplace.

He stood there and listened for a long time and finally he heard a snap again directly ahead of him. He clicked his flashlight on and aimed it in the general direction of the sound. At the base of a large, fat tree, a giant dog-sized rat was strolling right toward him. He screamed and dropped the flashlight, knocking the light out. Was the giant rat now racing toward him, ready to leap at his throat and rip out his jugular? He felt for his heavy flashlight on the ground and grabbed it, hoping he could fix it.

Switch, switch—where's the damn switch? His fingers fumbled, and he finally felt it. He clicked the switch, and the light came back on. The giant rat was receding, and then he knew what it was: an opossum, damn ugly and big. He had no idea they could get that large. Then again, things seemed larger in the dark.

Ian aimed the light over toward the back door. There was the wheelbarrow, still upside down. He shined the light further down the hill and found the depression. He hurried over, swept aside the leaves, and found the package, still there. Ian ripped the paper off of one end. How much money to take? The whole thing? What if he got caught with all of it? It'd be hard to explain away. He pulled out one banded pack, and the flashlight showed they were fifties. This whole pack, if it held one hundred bills, meant he had five thousand dollars. That was a lot.

Never wanting to come back here again, he decided to take the five grand. That should cover expenses for a while. He placed the bigger bundle into the hole again, covered it with leaves, and lifted the wheelbarrow back over it. As he silently moved back toward the edge of the house, a very loud sound like two firecrackers went off. Where? The front of the house? He clicked off his flashlight. Someone had to be out front.

A bright beam of light lanced the air from the other side of the house—and it was moving toward the rear, closer to him, and in that instant, he knew the sound he'd heard had not been firecrackers. But who shot what?

Ian glanced for a place to hide. There was nowhere. He looked past the wheelbarrow to the side of the house and ran there as fast and as quietly as he could. He jerked around the corner just as the light slashed across the backyard. He could tell the person— Owen?—was looking for him. He considered briefly whether to press himself against the corner of the house and use the flashlight as a blunt weapon, which was still in his hand. It would be flashlight against gun. That wasn't going to work, so he turned the light off. He ran toward the front of the house using one hand against the siding to guide him.

As he turned the corner to the front, he clicked on his flashlight directly on the ground for a moment to see where he was. The light landed on a face. Jones's lifeless eyes stared at him. Ian gasped. Blood pooled around the body, and the front of Jones's shirt was drenched in blood. He wasn't breathing.

Ian aimed his light at the stairs up to his car and ran as fast as he could. His unlocked car stood at the top, right next to a police car, Jones's. Ian darted to the front door of his own car and yanked it open, leaping inside and quickly locking the door. He fumbled for the keys in his right pocket, but he was so frightened, he couldn't get his hand out of his pocket. He noticed no light had yet followed him up the stairs. Did the person take the side street at the rear of the house?

Ian started his car—thank God. Then he heard another car start.

He yanked the gearshift into reverse and backed out quickly. As he jerked the gearshift into drive to move forward, the passenger door's window suddenly exploded, and the whole door smashed in. He had been rammed.

Still with enough sense, Ian hit his accelerator, but nothing happened. His car had died.

The car window on his side now exploded, and the butt of a gun broke through. A hand reached in for the door lock, unlatched it, and yanked open the door.

"Guess who!" said Owen in the dim light from Ian's dashboard. "Remember me?"

Before Ian could say anything, Owen grabbed him by the shirt-front and hauled him out of the car like a rag doll. Glass shards glittered on Ian's pants. Throwing Ian on the ground, Owen kicked Ian in the side over and over. Ian screamed in pain, and shouted "Help! Help!" Ian helplessly tried to stop the kicks with his hands, but they were getting bloodied and perhaps broken, too, like his ribs.

Owen stopped and bent down, reaching into Ian's pants and finding the money. "I didn't get to the backyard fast enough to see where you got this," said Owen, "because the cop showed up."

Now that he wasn't being hit, Ian sensed his whole body throbbing, pain spiking like thousands of needles around his body. Ian managed to say, "You killed him?"

"I just need the money, and I'm out of here."

"I'm not telling." He coughed. "You'll kill me afterwards."

Owen grabbed his gun from his waistband, aimed it at Ian's leg, and fired. The gun's sound, a red-hot-poker sensation in his thigh, and Ian's own scream merged in the same instant.

"You can die slowly or quickly," said Owen. "You take me to the money, and I'll be merciful."

"But you're just an actor," Ian said, between gasps. Nothing mattered now.

Owen laughed. "Clearly I had the wrong calling. I'm better at this. I even took Klemma's share when mine came up missing. The asshole was easy to find—how many Mannys and Moes are there around here, right? Anyway, he'll be in the hospital a few weeks most likely, getting to remember me."

Ian groaned as he moved his leg, which burned anew.

"I saw you on the TV tonight," said Owen. "You looked good. I also got the reference to the sailor photo on my share. You wanted me, you got me."

"You're too quick."

"Yeah, I'm good," said Owen, who kneeled down and scooted one arm behind Ian's back and lifted Ian to a standing position. With the other arm, he held his flashlight. "Lean on me but walk with your good leg," said Owen. They headed down the front walk slowly.

"You don't have to kill me," said Ian. "Killing me won't help anything."

"No?" said Owen. "Think of it as grabbing the gusto."

"Like beer? I can help you find Zetta. You want to find her, right? You're attracted to her."

"Doesn't matter," he said. "She's got a kid, I don't need that. I'm going where the best women are."

"Beverly Hills?"

"Aspen, dude."

"You ski?"

"Snowboard, guy. Only old people ski."

At that moment, a set of headlights shot over their heads. A car door slammed.

"Shit," said Owen and he launched forward, dragging Ian with him, and Ian screamed out in pain. Owen dropped him. "Stay here!" Owen whispered loudly to Ian. "Maybe it's nobody," but a strong beam of light hit first Ian on the ground, then Owen.

"FBI! Put your hands up!" came Medina's voice. Ian put his hands up but Owen ran. Medina fired. Owen disappeared behind the house. Medina's fast footsteps approached and passed him by as her flashlight cut into the darkness. On his back, he watched her beam scan in a wide spread. Minutes later, her running steps returned. Breathing hard, she was already on her cell phone.

"That's right," she said. "Put a roadblock at the bottom along Figueroa and send as many patrol units as you can get up here immediately." She kneeled next to Ian, still speaking. "I tracked him down a trail but lost him. Helicopter surveillance would help, too. One sec."

She lay down her phone on the lawn while she lifted up his knees, telling him, "I don't want you to go into shock. Keep your legs this way." She examined his wound with her flashlight. "It's not bleeding profusely, so no major vein or artery was hit. You okay?"

He felt nauseated. "I've been better," he said.

She picked up her phone and spoke, "We need an ambulance, pronto. Ian Nash has a gunshot wound to the leg." She again spoke to Ian. "Have you seen Jones?"

Ian pointed down toward the house, and her flashlight picked up on his body. She yelled into her phone, "Officer down, officer down!" She hurried down to Jones. Ian watched her flashlight alight on Jones's face. "Oh, man," she gasped. She again spoke into her phone, but Ian couldn't hear what she said.

She and her light returned, the phone no longer in her hand. "Shit," she said.

"I'm so sorry."

She wiped her eye. They said nothing.

She aimed her flashlight on his leg. "It's still bleeding a bit, but it doesn't look like it hit bone." She clicked her flashlight off. "I don't want the light to attract him in case he returns," she said. "We'll wait for backup and your ambulance. Okay?"

"Yeah," he said.

"Why were you up here? Meeting Jones?" she said more softly.

"No. When you said you weren't going to be watching the house, I thought I would."

"Why?" said Medina. "Why would you come here?"

"I thought criminals always returned to the scene of the crime."

"Only if there's a reason to."

Ian groaned, still deeply in pain. "Can we talk about this later?" he said.

"Sure."

For now, this was the reprieve he needed because he didn't know how much he should say. He didn't want to go to jail for taking money, although the money he had had was in Owen's pocket now. Owen still didn't have the bulk, though. Ian considered: did he want to turn control of that over to Medina? In telling her about it, would he be taken to court for obstructing justice? He probably should talk to a lawyer first before getting in deeper.

Medina gently took his hand and said, "Can you hear it?"

"Hear what?"

"A siren. That's your ambulance. You'll be okay." She squeezed his hand. This was a side to her he would have never expected.

"Thanks," said Ian before passing out.

The first thing Ian focused on was acoustic white tile of a ceiling. Turning his head, he perceived a man in blue scrubs and a white doctor's coat tossing bloody gauze into the garbage. Ian realized he was in an ER. Medina sat in a nearby chair.

"Hey," said Medina, leaning closer. "You're stabilized."

"Your vitals look good," said the young doctor who didn't look like he'd shaved in a day. "The bullet was small caliber and didn't hit bone, major nerves, or artery, but you lost a lot of blood, which is why you were out. A vascular surgeon on call patched you up. How do you feel?"

He looked down at his leg. It was wrapped in gauze. While he still had on his suit coat and pants, the right pant leg had been ripped off to get at his wound. His coat, too, had a spattering of blood. There goes that suit, he thought, and in that second, his side and leg throbbed so hard, he thought he might pass out again. He couldn't talk right away.

"My side really hurts," he managed. "So does my leg."

"I'll get you something," he said. "I have a little more work to do on you, but we'll get you to a room soon."

"How much is this going to cost?" said Ian, grimacing again.

"I found your health card in your wallet," said Medina.

"I hope it's still good," said Ian.

"The hospital and county will work it out if nothing else," said the doctor. "You were a victim of crime."

I'm a victim of stupidity, Ian thought. What had he expected from Owen?

The doctor excused himself but said he'd be back with pain relief. Ian looked at Medina and blinked, feeling as if he were hallucinating. She covered one hand compassionately. One of his wrists thumped in pain now in unison with the pounding he felt in his side and leg.

"What are you doing here?" he said.

"You're welcome very much."

"Yes, thanks. Didn't you have to stay on the scene—to deal with Jones and things?"

"I did. Then I came here, and I'll go back."

He nodded. "Thanks again. I'm sorry Jones died. It's all my fault."

"I'm the one who sent Jones there—into a situation I didn't foresee," she said.

"But it's my fault," said Ian. "I made Owen come after me so I could trap him."

"How so?"

He shrugged. He'd felt too guilty to explain. "Which hospital am I in?"

"Huntington Memorial." She leaned in. "I'm not clear. How did you make Owen come after you and why?"

She looked at him hard—not a lot of compassion there. What should he say? He hadn't had time to consult an attorney. Still, between his guilt and his physical pain, he had to tell her. "I found a lot of money in the house the time I'd returned to make a call. I saw the bundle on the floor in the kitchen, and I recognized it as Owen's from the way he had wrapped newspaper around it."

"You stole it?"

"I hid it knowing Owen would likely come back for it. At the press conference, I gave Owen a hint that I had it."

"So you purposely withheld information from me."

"I didn't know what to do. You weren't eager to include me, so I needed to act on my own."

"Oh, man," she said, shaking her head.

"I wanted Owen to find me, where I'd be ready for him." He told her about his aborted efforts to buy a gun, taser, and security system. "I thought he'd come to my place, and I didn't think he'd come until much later in the night."

"You thought you'd stop him alone and with a taser?"

"Yep."

She stared at him. "So where's the money now?"

"It's buried under leaves and dirt under the wheelbarrow in the back yard."

"Does Owen know that?"

"No—but he knew I had it within easy access somewhere in the backyard. Maybe he found it by now."

She immediately pulled out her cell phone, and, searching in her pockets, found a business card. She called the number on the card. "Banayan, it's me, Medina," she said into the small device. "Are you still on the scene or is anyone?" She grimaced and said, "Someone needs to go back. I just found out there's money in the backyard. The suspect may be looking for it as we speak."

As she talked, the doctor came in and held up a syringe. "Morphine," he said. "This should help you." Ian expected to feel the sting of the needle, but he noticed the doctor injected it into his IV. Ian followed the IV into the big vein on the top of his hand. The veins in the crook of his arm had never been good—too deep and hidden, so they'd used his hand.

Medina said into her phone, "Yes, use the siren, and get back to me whatever you find. Thanks." She flipped her phone shut. "We'll see."

"I'm sorry," Ian said, knowing he should feel bad about the

whole thing, but he was just so exhausted. "I'm just shutting my eyes for a second," he said. "But I'm still listening."

"Sure you are," she said. And that was the last thing he heard.

CHAPTER FIVE

He opened his eyes. His side under his left arm throbbed in pain, which is what must have woken him.

He was no longer in the morgue as he'd been dreaming. Ian found himself in a gown in a bed in a private room with a huge door open to a nursing station. His arms felt odd as if someone were squeezing them. He lifted them with some effort. He had a cast around his right wrist and forearm and gauze bandages on the other arm. An IV was in one hand, and that wrist in particular hurt. His chest felt tight and sore, too. If someone could invent a formula for feeling the worst physically, he had it.

He slid his better hand under his gown, but he didn't feel any bandages or wrapping around his chest. Then he flashed on Jones's face as Jones last looked, dead. Ian decided he didn't hurt enough. He was a piece of shit. He wished he really was in the morgue.

A black man in a green hospital uniform swept in carrying a tray. "Ah, you're awake. Good mornin'," he said.

"Hardly," said Ian.

"At least you're alive."

"Maybe I shouldn't be."

"You got yourself a breakfast here. Some jello, some weak tea if you like it, apple juice, and Seven-Up." His accent was unmistakably Caribbean. "My name is Cuervo," and he pointed to a white board on the wall where, scrawled in red marker was: "Nurse: Cuervo."

"I've never had a male nurse before."

"Are you implyin' I'm gay?"

"No."

"Well I'm gay, but it makes no difference." He pronounced the last word "DEEFer-aunts" and put a straw in the Seven-Up. "Drink up."

"For what?"

"Feeling bad, are we?"

"Yes, we are. And I'm not hungry."

"There's nothing to eat. It's just drink. The doctor has to see you before he approves solid food."

Cuervo pulled over a tray table already set for the proper height. Ian sat up in bed, feeling fresh pain in his side. He stared at the cast on his right arm that left his thumb and fingers free.

"You have a fracture of the radius," said Cuervo. "You have a cracked rib, too, but there's no cast for that. Plus you have stitches in your leg."

"I'm not worth repairing."

"I doan believe in that cry-me-a-river stuff. You're alive, and thank the Lord for it. The guard outside your door certainly thinks you're worth saving."

"I don't believe in the Lord, either."

"You're one of those high-maintenance guys?" Cuervo looked at an already-prepared hypodermic on a nearby counter, checked the syringe's label, and then injected its content into a tributary in Ian's IV. "This is morphine for the pain. You should be feeling better in a minute."

"Maybe I'll bleed internally and be a low maintenance guy down in the morgue."

"Step up to the plate, man. This is your life. Now do something with it."

The magic potion must have hit his bloodstream. Soon Ian felt not only less throbbing in his side and limbs, but also he felt as if he could breathe more easily. Stepping up to the plate, he thought. He didn't do that enough in his life.

Cuervo threw the used needle into a receptacle in the wall. Ian tried to guess the man's age—perhaps mid- to late-thirties. Cuervo looked at him. "Drink your breakfast and you can always reach me by pushing the red button on dat controller by your head."

Ian cranked his head to look at the controller when he heard, "You're feeling better?" Medina had just walked in. She looked as she did yesterday, unruffled, but there was something different, more angelic. Maybe it was the morphine, but he saw the love in her. She was an angel.

"You're…" Now don't say anything stupid, he realized. He cleared his throat. "You're here."

"A Pasadena cop guarded you, but at the end of his shift, another wasn't available for a few hours, so I came."

"You look so… rested." He wished he could say he loved her.

"No. Your little incident kept me busy all night."

He looked down, considering again that his quest had brought Jones's death.

She leaned toward him. "I guess I didn't make myself clear enough that I was in charge of this investigation and you weren't to interfere—such as going to the house."

"You made it clear you weren't able to do a lot."

"According to what? Your instinct?"

"He wasn't supposed to be there," Ian said. "I'm sorry."

The way she glared at him skimmed away his good feelings.

"This is a real mess," she said. "In a matter of hours, I'll be off this case. Wexler in Westwood will take over. He's the big boss. Under him, you'll be on the news for a few days and a few of his guys will be assigned, but if nothing comes up, your case will join the hundreds of others on his back burner and disappear."

"With a guard shot and a cop dead, this has to be high priority."

"Wexler doesn't have the attention span of a flea. Those of us in the field would stay on it, but he won't. You fucked it up."

Ian stared at her. Despite his guilt and his entire body feeling like road-kill again, she wasn't letting him off. He asked, "How can I keep you on it?"

"You can't. You go your way, I go mine."

"What's my way?"

"Back to school? Back to Canada?"

"Owen is still out there. Am I going to get more protection?"

"Up to Wexler. The Bureau is strapped for cash. Best to go home to Canada, ask me."

"With a cop killer out there, the police won't have a huge manhunt?"

"They will, a massive one. Doesn't mean they'll protect you, either."

"You don't have the least idea what it's like for me, do you?" said Ian. "I'm almost killed twice now. I've been physically and mentally pounded, can't remember everything, have little money, then I find out the FBI is basically going to abandon me. The agency's more concerned about Arabs in America or Mexicans swimming across the Rio Grande—terrorism, right? So issues such as bank robbery, shootings, and kidnapping get fewer resources. Okay, I fucked up. It's the best I could do. But you or that big cheese Wexler don't care if Owen kills me?"

Ian was breathing hard and in doing so, his sides felt as if he were being jabbed with knitting needles. That's where anger got him. Medina simply stared at him as if watching a caterpillar crawl.

"I'm telling you to go to Canada."

"No one cares about me in Canada."

"Your parents?"

Ian shook his head. It was one of the things that ate at him, too. "As you know, I have no money."

"Friends?"

"No one that I can endanger."

"Thanks to you," said Medina, "I'll have no authority on this case within twenty-four hours."

"Can you keep me alive for a day?"

"To what end?"

"Fuck you."

She stared at him without blinking. "Maybe we'll see my boss, Rick. See if he has an idea."

"And wouldn't you love to show up Wexler? Wouldn't you really love to stick it to him?"

"How would I do that?"

"Use me—help me with my memory. I must know things."

"How is that a plan?"

"You have something better?"

"Yes. I move on."

"I shouldn't have gone to the house," he said, "and I shouldn't have been mad just now. If I know one thing, though, it's that you want to stay on this thing."

She again stared. As she turned to leave, he reached out to stop her, but he was too slow. "Last night," he said quickly. She glanced back but kept moving. He blurted, "He said once he got the money he was going to Aspen."

"What?" She stopped.

"Owen said he's going to Aspen—for the women." He realized something, and it felt as if another shot of morphine had surged into him. "Hey, I remember the driver's name now. Klemma."

Medina moved closer. "So we have Zetta, Owen, Navarre, and Klemma."

"Yes, and we have Aspen and the women."

"That's not really anything," said Medina. "Most bank robbers are men, and they spend it immediately on sex, drink, and cars. I can't believe Aspen because criminals lie. Getting laid, yes, Aspen, no."

"And evil, yes."

She shook her head. "Good, evil. We're all gray."

"So you're thinking he had a bad childhood or something?"

"Doesn't matter."

"Your big boss Wexler. He's gray, too? What's his agenda?"

She paused, tellingly. "He's on my side."

"Not if he's taking you off the case."

She shook her head and said, "What else do you remember about last night?"

"I had a dream," said Ian, "where Klemma was in this hospital with me in the morgue."

"Bizarre."

"No," said Ian. "Owen told me he had to beat Klemma up to steal his share. Owen wasn't happy when his share was missing."

"Is this true? The driver was beat up?"

"He'll be in the hospital for weeks, Owen had said."

She looked off as if considering what to do.

"You're helping me remember things," said Ian. "Maybe you shouldn't just dismiss me, but work with me. You can show up Wexler."

As if she hadn't heard, she said, "Owen told you this last night—or earlier?"

"Last night."

Medina pulled out her cell phone and hit a speed-dial button. "Hello, Rick, it's me, Aleece. I'm still at the hospital with Nash."

She was talking with her boss, Ian realized, and she called him by his first name. As she explained his memory was coming back and what she learned, it struck Ian that Owen last night mentioned that Zetta had a kid, and that kid was probably who Zetta meant in her declaration of love. Her words made sense now. After all, she would have a love for her son that would defy description, every heartbeat, every cell. Her son had to be her motivation. Maybe she was like so many people, out of work, underwater on her house, behind in her mortgage—but rob banks? He was sorry, but at least three people were dead and his own life was forever changed because she loved her son and she needed money? While he could empathize, her actions were wrong.

"Yes," Medina continued, "And Owen supposedly beat Klemma severely enough to send him to a hospital—maybe this one or another nearby ER… Yeah, okay… Okay, that's great… Yeah, I surely will. More later." She tucked away her cell phone and as she was about to speak, a police officer entered in a black uniform. A patch on his shoulder said "Padadena Police."

"Excuse me, are you Agent Medina?"

"Yes."

"I'm Sergeant Bradford. I'm supposed to be guarding this gentle-man, I understand."

She thanked him, introduced Ian, and explained more of the sit-uation. Ian thought the beefy man with graying hair looked more like an accountant than an active cop but was glad someone was there. The man went out front, and Medina turned back to Ian. "Rick is sending me someone to help find Klemma. I'm first going to see if Klemma is in this hospital. Of course, I don't have his real name, but at least I know what he looks like."

"Where's this put us?"

"You can be useful. Wexler's boys may call at some point. I don't want you to lie about anything—but also don't offer any information if they don't ask. Maybe we can crack this yet."

"We?"

She left. No good-bye. She was just gone.

CHAPTER SIX

Medina zipped to the hospital's registration desk and was directed to the person in charge of registration, Mrs. Stefano, a thin young waif in a brown suit who called to mind a cigarillo. Showing her ID, Medina introduced herself and said, "I need to find a possible patient in this hospital—an Asian male who may be here from a beating."

"An Asian male with an externally induced trauma," said Mrs. Stefano, restating it as she typed in her search words.

"Yes," said Medina.

The young woman's fingers still clicked on her keyboard. "With Alhambra and Monterey Park not far from here, I'll have more than a few Asian males."

"I just need a name or list of names," said Medina. "Anything violent—gunshots, too."

Mrs. Stefano nodded at it as if she were used to reading such things. "It's just so sad, our society."

"I suppose," said Medina, feeling impatient.

"Yoko Ono said it so well: all you need is love."

"She broke up the Beatles," said Medina, flatly.

"I mean it's sad there're so many victims of violence."

Medina wanted to throttle this person for the inane small talk—but then that would add another victim to violence. Medina only said, "What's your screen saying?"

"I'm almost done," said the young woman. She tapped some more on her computer. In another minute, she had a printout for Medina. There were five men on the list, five different rooms.

Medina glanced at it and said, "Thank you."

In the first room that Medina went to, a large man, at least 350 pounds, lay asleep with casts around both arms while a tiny woman in her early twenties—his wife or girlfriend, no doubt—watched him carefully with glistening eyes. Medina considered the couple on better days. How did two such different-sized people fall for each other?

The next man was in ICU with a number of machines and monitors overseeing him. This was a gunshot to the stomach, which would be mighty painful later if he made it through this part. He wasn't Klemma—a far different face. In fact, over the next thirty minutes Medina saw everyone on the list, and none of the men matched the pictures of Klemma. This was the closest hospital to Mt. Washington if he was still in the area and went to a hospital, but more footwork at other hospitals was needed.

As she walked to Ian's room, she imagined her boss's boss, James Wexler, had the news now of Jones and was trying to replace her. Rick would fight for her, maybe even stall for a day, but Wexler had bigger ambitions. With the FBI's mandatory retirement age of fifty-seven, he needed all the recognition he could get to get a promotion. If you were near the top and pulling in the big bucks, you had a great retirement package. This case was likely to bring him the attention he needed, and she'd be in the way. If she could have a breakthrough this morning, it'd take the wind out of Wexler's sails. She sensed it wouldn't happen and that Wexler would effectively cripple her career in the FBI for his needs. Her fists clenched, and she wanted to smash something.

Cuervo came in with more pain medication, this time a shot of Dilaudid. "It's stronger than the morphine, and it should help," he told Ian, who was sitting up in bed.

"Is it addictive?"

"Like shootin' up in an alley addictive? You're far from that."

"I like alleys," said Ian.

"Pain interferes in the healing process," said Cuervo. "You want to cut the edge off of *tings* and let your body do its work. The doctor will order something non-narcotic in pill form when you leave the hospital."

"When will I leave?"

"Up to the doctors, but the way they race people through here, I'd say tomorrow. We still need to observe you, make sure you're stabilized."

The shot made the searing needle points in his side fall away again. He could breathe more easily. He didn't have anything to read, but he didn't think he could read anyway. It wasn't as if he could concentrate. He lowered the upper angle of his bed to be flat, and he soon fell asleep. When he opened his eyes, he could sense someone was in the room. A doctor, with his back to Ian, pulled a needle from a plastic Wonder Bread bag. A Wonder Bread bag?

"Doctor?" said Ian.

"Pain," said the doctor. "It'll soon go away."

"I'm not so bad," Ian said. What time was it? How long had he slept? He looked for a clock. Why wasn't there a clock in his room?

"I mean," said Ian, "Cuervo gave me a shot not long ago. I'd rather not feel so out of it."

At that point, Ian noticed Sergeant Bradford crumpled on the floor, off to one side. "What's wrong with the officer?" said Ian. It was very strange.

The doctor turned around, and Ian took in the broad shoulders and scraggly face of Owen. "He's dead," said Owen. "And you're next."

Owen held his syringe and moved quickly toward Ian. Gasping, Ian grabbed Owen's hand.

With only a thin blanket on him, Ian shoved his feet at Owen and jabbed the man's chest, forcing the man back. "Hey!" Ian shouted. "Help!"

"It'll only take a sec," Owen said, charging at Ian again. Ian flung himself off the table, bellowing out and managing to soften his landing with his pillow.

"What's going on?" said Cuervo, from a distance, probably the far side of the nurse's station.

"I'll look," said a stocky older nurse, entering, her photo ID clipped to her smock's lower pocket.

"He's NOT a doctor! The officer's dead. Stop him!" Ian shouted from the floor.

As if without thinking, the nurse leapt at Owen, circling her arms around the man's chest.

Owen struggled for another step, then whirled around and jabbed the needle into the nurse's neck. The nurse screamed in pain and fell to the floor, writhing.

"No!" shouted Ian.

"Look what you made me do," said Owen.

Staff including Cuervo gathered around the close end of the nursing station to peer in.

"Until we meet again," said Owen. He dashed out and ran around the nurse's station before anyone seemed to understand what had just happened.

"The nurse has been injected with something!" said Ian as he staggered out of bed, feeling his head quickly clear. The woman's body was already still. Ian couldn't see her face. "The needle's on the floor," he said as Cuervo hurried in. "Help her."

"Inna crosses," Cuervo seemed to say and immediately knelt and felt for a pulse in her neck.

Ian noticed the gun in the dead officer's holster and fumbled for it. Surging with adrenaline, gun in hand, Ian speed-limped out of his room into the hallway. When he got to the corridor, Owen was turning the corner at the far end, where there were a half-dozen people.

"Stop him!" Ian yelled while running as best he could with a bum leg, but the people screamed, clearly reading the situation wrong, a gowned patient with a gun running after a doctor. "I'm FBI," said Ian desperately. "Stop that man. He's not a doctor."

When Ian rounded the corner, the hallway stood completely empty. Owen had to have gone through one of the near doors. One was marked as an exit, a stairwell, and he pushed through, breathing hard. A door closed a flight down. Ian hurried downward in his bare feet.

On the first level, people walked normally as if nothing unusual had just occurred. That meant Owen had to be walking, looking normal. In one direction, three people in the white coats of doctors calmly strode, and in the other direction there were two more. He yelled holding his gun aloft, "FBI. Stop that doctor," hoping someone would bolt. And someone at the far end of the hall to his right did.

People screamed seeing his gun, opening up the hallway for him. Ian ran after Owen. However, a tall man in a tweed suit, trying to get out of Ian's way, kept moving one direction then another until they collided. They both fell down.

"Sorry," Ian shouted and got back up, his side now hurting again. He could no longer see Owen, who must have turned down the next hall. As Ian ran into the hallway, his side now really pounding in pain, absolutely no one was there. He tried run-limping again, but each step was a white lightning bolt of pain. Walking, barely seeing anything now, he did not find Owen. At the end of the hallway, a doorway led outside. As he limped toward it, a blue flash, that of a body hurtling toward him, streaked from his left, and he tumbled toward the ground. As he slammed down hard, he screamed out in ultra pain. The gun scuttled away to his side.

He could only make out a blur, but the voice he recognized. "Nash?" said Medina. "What're you doing here—with a gun?"

He mustered the energy to speak as she got off him. "Owen," he could only say. He took a few more breaths before he added, "He tried… to kill me."

"How'd you get a gun?"

"From the cop… Owen killed him."

Medina straightened her shirt. "I heard shouts that a patient had a gun. I didn't think it'd be you. You're hurting—sorry about that."

His eyes could focus finally, and only now did he see she had her own weapon drawn, a snub-nosed revolver. "If you didn't know it was me, why didn't you shoot me?"

"I don't kill if I don't have to."

Ian moved his arm up and pointed to the door at the end of the hall. "Maybe he went that way."

"I'm impressed with what you did. Wait here," she said.

"As if I can move," he said as she raced away, shoving through the door. A few minutes later, the door opened again. By then, he was sitting against the wall and no one had come by. This must be a minor hallway, he thought. Medina approached with a nurse. "This is Mr. Nash," she said to the nurse. "He was up in Room 212 on the second floor. Can you get him back there?"

"Sure," said the young woman.

"I'll be up soon," she told Ian. "I just want to be more thorough down here."

◊

Medina checked every waiting room on the bottom floor before finding a few witnesses who saw Owen slam through a particular door, and then found another witness who saw Owen run to a car and tear out of there. That was that. She called a Pasadena police detective she knew to tell him about what happened and about his now-dead colleague. Then and there, the man alerted his chief. They'd be enlarging their efforts in hunting Owen.

On the way back into the building, before calling Rick to update him, she saw a man and woman standing and holding each other closely in the waiting room for Imaging and Radiology. In a hospital gown and frail, the salt-and-pepper-haired man in his fifties looked like a federal judge she knew, and he stroked the woman's hair as if he were leaving for a long trip at an airport. The woman, a few years younger than he, blond hair in a bun, wore pearls against a yellow dress as if to evoke cheer, but her stoic smile quivered as if to say she knew. Knew what? That he was dying? A tear fell on her cheek. He brushed it away with a finger and pulled a loose strand of her hair around her ear.

This small innocent moment, this silent love, was such a contrast to Medina's last day that for a flash, she pictured herself holding Ian the same way, stroking his hair. Ian had been brave and stupid chasing Owen—and incredible. Even going to the house had been daring. Why, oh why was she attracted to this guy?

The man in the gown spotted Medina standing there, smiled as the woman turned to look, too, and Medina nodded and said, "Good luck."

As she walked away, she wondered what she'd say to Ian. She knew that while she could be attracted to him, she couldn't let it show. She'd made that mistake once. As an FBI Special Agent, she could not mix in romance. Still, the guy had something there.

Ian was given a new room, along with two hospital security people who had police-like uniforms and stood outside his door. As he settled in, Medina entered, and even if he knew she'd shield herself with her all-work demeanor momentarily, he sensed her concern. She was his personal angel.

"I'm glad they got you a new room," she said. "But Owen's gone. A witness saw him tear off in a brown beat-up car of some sort."

"It could have been me dead back in my other room," Ian said, back on an IV drip with pain medication. "You think your boss Wexler will now see you're onto something?"

She touched his shoulder, and he understood she was on his side. "No. He'll blame me," said Medina. "I expect a call later."

"You have to keep going. You can't let him take you off."

"It doesn't work that way."

"Freelance with me then."

She laughed. "Really? You think that could be a reality?"

Was she mocking him? He couldn't tell because she'd turned so he couldn't see her face. "You're not going to find Owen otherwise," he said. "You don't want Wexler to fuck it up, right?"

She turned back. "Why is Owen after you? Why's he risking so much?"

"Pure evil? Except you don't believe in that."

"People don't work that way. What'd you do to him?"

"I don't know. Piss him off? If Mamet were writing him as a character, he'd probably say Owen felt a threat of emasculation."

"Fuck that."

"Perfect Mamet. Still, the way Owen showed off for Zetta, he was pushing the masculine thing. There's also the greed thing with Mamet. Human beings are greedy."

Her phone rang. She nodded and kept saying "Okay" to her

caller, and then she explained everything that had just happened with Owen and Ian. Her poker face revealed nothing. Ian wondered if it was Wexler. She hung up and stared at her phone, lost in thought.

"So that's it? Wexler told you that you're off?"

She looked up. "No, it was Rick saying that a check of other hospitals didn't find Klemma, and he'll call Wexler about Owen. That means I'll be taken off it soon."

"That's not right," said Ian.

"Rick said the police manhunt for Owen is massive, and expect news helicopters over this hospital soon."

"Maybe Owen will be caught soon."

"Did Owen know Klemma well?"

"I don't know." Then Ian recalled the pancake breakfast. "I think they didn't know each other at all."

"So how did Owen find Klemma?"

"Owen had said Klemma was easy to find. He said there were not a lot of Mannys and Moes. I don't know a single Manny or Moe."

"Manny, Moe, and Jack?" she asked.

"What?"

"They're the Pep Boys—the auto parts chain of stores."

"Is there one around here?" he said.

She pulled out her cell phone and punched it expertly with her thumbs.

"Yes," she said. "A Pep Boys is at 55th and Figueroa. We must've passed it going to Mt. Washington."

"Let's go there now," he said.

"Let's? I can't bring you along."

"Why not? I'll check out of here. They can't keep me. You only have a short time before you get a call from Wexler. Use me. Time's a wasting—and thanks to you, I'm remembering things."

He sensed he may have gotten to her because she looked out his sixth floor window, apparently considering her options. She spoke. "I'm not being fired. I'll just have to work on other cases, not this one."

"You want this one. You're better than Wexler and probably most of your colleagues. Besides, you know I'm in danger, and as you said, Wexler may not care. He won't use me. What's my only option? I'll just have to disappear. And Jones died for nothing. The bad guys win."

"Listen," she said, pointing a finger at him the way a parent might when pissed off. "I know the rules and the boundaries. The only rule I'm going to bend is I'll protect you for a day or two."

"How?"

"I don't know. I have no answers. I promise to protect you, but I don't know how yet."

"I can't stay here."

"Fine."

"Fine? What about clothes? The ones I had are ruined."

"I have some fresh sweats in my car. They're big for me, so they should be good on you. Hospitals don't work quickly. It'll take an hour or two for you to get released. In the meantime, I'm going to zip over to this Pep Boys and see if I can find Klemma."

"But I want to come." And, he thought, I need you.

"You never know when to stop, do you?" And with that, she took off.

"You're coming back for me, right?"

With her lack of response, he assumed so.

CHAPTER SEVEN

The Pep Boys' automatic door swished open as Medina stepped near it. Inside, she came to a line of cashiers with blue counters. Only one line was open, with a male Mexican-looking cashier. "May I speak to the manager?" she asked the man, whose nametag read, "Javier Perez, Jr."

"I'm the manager. Can I help you?"

Medina showed him her laminated FBI ID and explained she was looking for a particular man and maybe he could help.

"Why would I know anything?" said the manager.

"He may have worked here." She presented Klemma's photo in a shot taken when he was in the car outside the bank.

"He kind of looks like an employee, but only vaguely. This photo is probably someone else."

"Which of your employees does this look like?"

"Freddie Liu, a guy who works at the parts counter in the back."

"Is he here today?"

"No. He's sick."

"Have you heard of the Busty Bandit?" asked Medina.

The man looked puzzled.

"Freddie Liu may have been the driver in a series of bank robberies," said Medina.

"Not Freddie," said Perez. "He likes his cars, and he likes auto racing, too, but he's an honest person, a great employee. It's not him."

"The last robbery was five days ago in the morning. Was Mr. Liu here?"

He thought. "No, Freddie was on vacation last week, but he'd never do such a thing. Truly."

"When did you see him last?" asked Medina.

"He called me Monday night saying he was feeling really bad—and he sounded it, too. I told him I didn't want to catch the flu or nothin', so call me when he was feeling better. He hasn't called yet. I'm sure his girlfriend is helping him."

"Who's his girlfriend?"

"This week? I don't know. He's kind of a player—but a real nice guy."

"Might his girlfriend be the woman I'm looking for?" Medina showed him the photo of the Busty Bandit taken at the most recent robbery."

"I never see his girlfriends. She's a beauty, eh?"

"And here's a shot of her driver taken from a citizen's cell phone." She laid it in front of him. The photo did not have the best lighting and it was highly pixilated from being blown up so much. The driver was mostly a series of dots in silhouette—but a form could be seen.

"It's hard to say. Sort of yes, sort of no," he said. "Could he be the guy?"

"I won't know until I talk with him."

"I hope it's not him because he's so good—even my wife loves the guy. He's very friendly."

"May I have his address and phone?"

"Okay." He yelled out "Sonia! Cashier stand!"

A young voice replied, "Coming."

A young woman strode down an aisle to take over, and Medina followed the manager to an office in the back, past all the tall shelves that held parts.

The office was cluttered. On a wall, a Rigid Tools calendar featured a pinup girl in a bikini, which gave the sense that no one got hurt in this world. Perez read from a file folder and wrote on a small piece of paper. He handed Medina the paper.

"Here," he said. As they left, the manager asked, "Is there a reward in this if it's him? You know, for my helping and all?"

"The reward was for people who called in."

The man looked disappointed.

"You can still get the reward if you hear from him and call me." She handed him her card.

"Thank you," he said. "Very good."

"Thank you, Mr. Perez," said Medina, and she moved quickly out of the store. In looking at the address, she saw Klemma's home wasn't far away. She could arrange for a SWAT team to surround the place to take him, but more likely, Perez was calling him. She had to get there right away.

Five minutes later, she was on his Highland Park street, looking at Liu's one-story beige house with peeling paint—as sad looking as a crumpled cigarette pack in the mud. Bars on the windows and a chain-link fence around the property didn't stand out because all the houses on the street had barred windows and some kind of fence. She parked two blocks away. If by chance Liu had not been alerted, she needed the element of surprise.

From her trunk, she pulled on a Kevlar vest. The body armor had helped her once before, months earlier, when a fleeing suspect shot at her. Over her vest, she strapped on her shoulder holster and revolver.

She knew that, alone, she could be walking into a dangerous situation. Nothing said Liu was not by himself nor that he would be as friendly as he was with his Pep Boys boss. This was not the kind of situation the FBI encouraged. In fact, the safer way was to call for support while keeping an eye on the house. She guessed, though, that Rick would tell her to get out of there—it wasn't her case anymore.

Rather than cover her vest and gun with her light blue windbreaker with the letters FBI emblazoned on the back, which would give her away, she donned one of two pink sweatshirts from her gym. It had the word "Pink Iron" on the front. Her plan was just to stroll up and knock on the door as if she were selling something. A Hispanic woman in a Hispanic neighborhood wouldn't look out of place.

She sauntered to his house as casually as she could, but her heart beat rapidly, and she was hyperaware of the sights and sounds around her. Her eyes took in the asphalt street whose patchwork of filled potholes, variations in grays and blacks, gave a sense of a quilted blanket. Yet the tall skinny Italian cypresses in a number of yards, as well as the still-green jacaranda and giant leafy eucalyptus trees created a landscape worthy of painting.

She pushed the doorbell, but did not hear any ring inside. She knocked on the door, her hand on her chest, ready to grab her pistol. "Mr. Liu?"

Still there was no answer.

She walked into the side yard, doing her best not to make a sound because she spotted a window open, a screen beneath. When she passed the window, she smelled something as bad as rotting fried chicken and very bad cheese.

The back door wasn't locked. It's something she'd noticed over the years. People would have two or three locks on the front door, but the back door was often flimsy and many times unlocked. Burglars much preferred the back.

She opened the door, and the smell was now stronger. "Mr. Liu?" she said, not expecting any response. She stepped into what must have been a screened back porch at one time, now walled and windowed in. A set of French doors led into the house proper. She drew her gun, just in case she was wrong about what she'd find. She noticed a few flies on a window. The bedroom was probably where the open window was. She passed the French doors and now stood in the dining room, which had a card table and four folding chairs, and a lot of mail on top of the table. She could peer into the kitchen and see a stack of dirty plates in the sink. That had to add to the aroma of the place, too.

As she approached the bedroom, she pulled her sweatshirt over her nose.

Freddy Liu, a.k.a. Klemma, lay flat on his queen-size bed atop a messy bedspread. His head was on a pillow, his mouth gaping, and his eyes seemed to be moving until she realized the illusion came from the many moving maggots atop the closed lids. A few flies buzzed above the body. The skin of Liu's face was gray, very dark in spots as if bruised, and the way his lips were stretched, he looked like a snapshot for pain.

Medina stepped closer and looked closely. He seemed to have been beaten severely. The autopsy would likely say he died of internal bleeding. She supposed after he called into work, he stayed in bed rather than go to a hospital. He might have lived if he had.

Owen, she thought, is just mounting up bodies. For not being a career criminal—their face recognition software hadn't pulled him up—this guy was brutal.

Now it was time to call in the specialists, the team that would comb over this room, and other people who would take Liu and perform an autopsy. With one phone call, it would all start. She wasn't reaching for her phone, though. Rather, she returned to her car, took off her hot sweatshirt and vest and grabbed a pair of latex gloves and a small digital Canon camera. She went back to Liu's bedroom.

With the camera, not much larger than a credit card, she photographed the scene and took a few shots of Freddie up close.

As she shot him, she thought about the first time she'd studied someone dead—at the Academy. A domestic terrorist had been found and killed in a Washington D.C. shootout, and her class got to see him on the autopsy table. "You have to remember, this isn't a person," her instructor had said, pointing to the body. "This is just his remains. Think of it like a mannequin or even a memorial to the man he was once known as. I'm sure he had his good points. Some people surely liked him. Don't view him as good or evil. We're too complicated for such divisions. Our job is to find the clues and follow them where they take us. We are an important element in keeping freedom and democracy alive."

She shook her head at the memory. Freddie here wasn't an idealist and probably never thought of freedom or democracy. He just wanted to make some money, seduce a few women, get fucked up occasionally, and maybe pull ahead of a few others. Unfortunately shortcuts, such as Freddie tried, sometimes led to dead ends.

"I don't like to think this will be me someday," she remembered saying to a cohort about the dead terrorist. She still didn't like to dwell on how all life ended, hers included. Still, she was good at what she did, and while she was alive, the Wexlers of the world wouldn't stop her.

On the nightstand next to the bed was a copy of *Road and Track* magazine. On the floor were copies of *Sports Illustrated*, *Beckett Racing Collector* and *Penthouse*. She again looked around at the mostly messy bedroom. The walls had two framed posters. One showed the huge words "Monaco XVIII Grand Prix" and in smaller letters under a stylized graphic of a race car were "29 Mai 1960." The other poster showed a pit team swarming like locusts around a formula one car. This was the room of a grown boy.

Medina turned her attention back to the nightstand. In the open drawer was a small well-thumbed little black book. She picked it up with her gloved hand. It was his address book. She'd have to leave this for the team to find, but she laid the address book on the bed and photographed each set of pages, which she could go over later. She realized then that no matter what other cases she'd next be working, this case would be her off-hours focus.

She methodically went over the whole room, looking for anything else that might be as valuable as the address book and found nothing. She made sure everything was as she'd found it exactly. Then she strode outside to make the call she'd been delaying. The fresh air didn't ease her tension any, especially since the smog on the horizon felt more like bats on a ceiling.

"Rick, it's me, Aleece," said Medina when he answered. "Things have happened rather quickly—so fast, I hadn't had time to call until now." She explained how she'd learned of Freddie Liu, the real name of the driver, and she was at Liu's house now where she'd found him, dead. She answered his questions on the order of events.

"I spoke to Wexler personally," said Rick, "and it's official. You're off. You're not to be involved in it any more at this point."

She stared at the ground, unable to stop the feeling of a system against her. "I'm still expecting a few calls on this from people I've questioned."

"You refer them to Wexler's office. He made it very clear that Westwood is taking this over. It's a priority for them."

"Yeah, for how long? A week?"

"We can't do anything."

"Then maybe this is an appropriate time I took my vacation."

"We have too much to do right now."

"I feel the flu coming on. Must have overworked myself."

"Don't do this to me."

"Rick, I need some time off."

"All right. We can cover you for a week."

"Thanks."

Ian glided down the hospital hallway toward the exit and felt incredibly light as if balloons helped carry him. After all, Medina was back, and she seemed different, getting the doctors to sign off she could take him—to her house, she said.

"Isn't that against FBI rules?" he'd asked.

"It's my problem."

Medina now held his bag of prescriptions as well as a plain black cane that the hospital had given him. He was wearing all pink—Medina's sweats that had the word "Pink Iron" on them. A young man from the transportation department pushed him.

Outside, they parked by a bench. "I'll get the car," said Medina.

When Medina drove up, Ian stood up from the wheel chair. She hurried around her car and opened up the back door. "Scoot in the back," she said, "You can stretch out for your leg."

"We're off to your house?" He was happy.

"Yep—and don't get any funny ideas. I know how guys think. This isn't any romance."

"I'm not thinking that," he said, thinking it.

"I'm keeping you out of Owen's way," she said. "What is he, the Terminator? Why the hell's he after you?"

"I have no idea. I thought you were the expert."

"This is the strangest case."

He nodded. He'd be happy just to work with her and get Owen

and the others for once and for all. Once settled and she was back in the driver's seat, he said, "You didn't tell me what happened at Pep Boys."

She checked her rearview mirror, then drove forward. When she approached the end of the driveway, she spoke. "I got a good lead. Thank you. It worked out."

"What worked out? Did you find Klemma?"

She looked preoccupied.

"You did find Klemma, didn't you?"

"I did, but I'm not on the case anymore. Wexler made it official. I can't talk about it."

"Sure you can. Is Klemma in custody or what?"

Again she looked at him in the rearview mirror. "I have to be careful what I tell you and what I do."

"You can't let that piss-ant win."

"And you're not in charge of me, either."

"I'm sorry. I'm just trying to help. You'll see I'm a good team member."

"Team member? What?"

"You came for me. I'm in your back seat, aren't I?"

Her eyes in the mirror looked at him with confusion. "I said I'd protect you. This is what I'm saying about guys—you misunderstand things."

"I'm not misunderstanding that you're off the case but don't want to be. Together we can figure it out."

"Doubtful. Things like this don't get solved quickly or by chatting. I'm not going to tell you anything more right now. I'm going to take you to my home, then pop in to talk with my boss."

"With Rick."

"Yes. Rick. Rick Okinawa. As far as he knows, you've left on your own."

"How about if you used me as bait? Maybe there's a way Owen can find me again and this time you're there. I'm not crazy about the idea but it's all I got."

"Bait?" Her look said, Yeah, right. "No way."

Ian at that moment wished they'd smash into a brick wall. Everything was fucked. He stared out the window a while, first letting everything be a blur. Then he paid attention. They were on Interstate 10 passing houses on a green hillside. Life must be great in the hills. Every day was a view from the top.

He noticed on the back seat a camera. Maybe she shot something with it, perhaps Klemma. It was a Canon. He had an Olympus, but he'd used plenty of digital cameras. Most were easy to use. He clicked it on, pressed an arrow to get photos, and it opened on the last shot she took, a book of some sort. He zoomed the photo for a closer view and could see it was an address book. He flicked past the pages, recognizing a name here and there and wondered if this was Klemma's. He couldn't ask.

Then he came to a shot of a man's head, grotesque, brown, worms or something on his eyes, and his disgust came out in a gasp. He even said, "Yuck." He wasn't thinking. Medina's eyes flicked back in the mirror.

"Hey!" she yelled. "I didn't give you permission. What the fuck do you think you're doing?"

"I was just curious, I'm sorry." He clicked it off and put it back on the seat. "I thought it might be your vacation or something. Or close-ups of flowers. No harm."

She quickly pulled off at the next exit and grabbed her camera from the back. "Here you think we'll be partners, and then you do something like this."

"Ease up, officer. I'm sorry. Really. I mean, isn't curiosity the element that you use every day in your job? Who was that face, anyway? Klemma's?"

She put the car back in gear, crossed the street and pulled onto the on ramp. She merged back onto the road. "Yes, Klemma," she said. "He's dead. He didn't survive the beating."

"And those pages were his address book?"

"That's confidential."

"Here's a truth," said Ian. "If you don't allow me into all this, we're not going to get anywhere. You just want to control everything, right?"

"I'm the expert."

"And I can help. For instance, I recognized a name in that address book."

"You did? Who?"

"See how you need me?"

"Okay, okay."

"Marilee Sato. He must know her," he said.

"Who's that?"

"If it's the same Marilee Sato, she's a wonderful actress. I saw her perform with East/West Players."

"East/West Players?"

"It's an Asian group downtown doing major plays with non-traditional casting. Marilee played Jill Mason in *Equus* a few years ago—and was quite lovely."

"The nude role?"

He looked at her, surprised. "You know the play?"

"I had a theatre class in college."

"Well, she wore the part well."

Medina handed back the camera and then reached in her pocket, retrieving her cell phone, which she also gave to Ian. "Try Klemma's number for Ms. Sato. If she answers, just hang up. I only want to see if it's a working number."

Ian did as he was told. "Her number's not in service," he told Medina when he heard.

"Shit," she said.

"I could call East/West Players. Or better yet, her headshot might be on NowCasting.com. I belong to the service."

Medina seemed to consider, then nodded. "Go ahead, try."

He connected to the web and used his Now Casting account from months earlier. Once inside, he entered the search feature. He found Marilee's photo as well as her home and agent phone numbers. "I can call her if you like," he said. "If I pretend to be casting a film, she might be more chatty. All L.A. stage actors hope to hit it big in films. I can tell her Freddie Liu recommended her."

"Call her."

He pressed the numbers for Marilee's phone number, and she answered in the same memorable sexy voice he had heard on stage.

"Hello, Marilee?" he said.

"Yes."

"My name's Ian Brown," he said, using the false last name, "and I'm casting a small film. I happened to find you on Now Casting dot com."

"How small a film is it?"

He tried to make it as real in his mind as he could. That's the way the best improv worked. "It's a graduate film at UC Irvine, and—"

"I don't do student films."

Damn. He should have said it was a film at Paramount. "I'm making it to qualify for the short film category in the Academy Awards."

There was a long pause. "What's it about?"

He had to think quickly. The protagonist needed to be a woman in a meaty role to interest her. A farm girl might be a good role. He thought of *The Wizard of Oz*. "It's about a young woman on a farm in the Central Valley." Make it historical, he thought and he added, "Just before World War Two. She and her family are on their own small cotton farm, and war breaks out. She does everything to keep the farm." He realized at that moment that he was starting to make it *Gone with the Wind*.

"Why's her farm in danger?"

That was a good question. For Scarlett O'Hara, it was back taxes. Then the answer was right in front of him as he looked at Marilee's picture. "She's Japanese, and everyone of Japanese descent is being rounded up for the camps."

"Interesting," she said.

"I saw you in *Equus* at East/West, and you were fabulous."

"Thank you."

Medina whispered "Freddie."

"Besides, Freddie Liu recommended you, too."

"You know Freddie?"

"I live in South Pas and I got to know him at Pep Boys in Highland Park."

"I haven't seen Freddie in a while, maybe two years. I'd rather forget about him."

"Why?"

"It's personal."

Medina whispered to Ian, "I need to meet her."

"Can we meet for casting?" he said into the phone.

"We?" said Marilee.

"We?" whispered Medina.

"My producer, a woman at the college. I'm the director."

"When?" Marilee said.

"How's today?—a location of your choice. Whatever's convenient."

Marilee agreed and gave him her address in the Hancock Park area. He said he could be there in a half hour. When he hung up, he shouted, "Got it!"

"A half hour?" said Medina.

"She's expecting us. We're a team. You've got to get used to that."

"What's the address?"

He gave it to her, and as if she had Mapquest in her head, she entered the on ramp for the freeway. As she raced to freeway speed, she said, "I'm not sure I can get used to a partner."

🌢

A lot of the old apartments in Hancock Park were now expensive condos, Ian knew. He'd been to a building once on Rossmore where Mae West had lived—and where she died in an armchair.

They arrived to the area within the hour. Marilee's condo bordered Koreatown. The place had a doorman, just as in New York.

"I'm here to see Ms. Sato," said Ian, hobbling in using his cane. His leg was hurting more now, even with another Vicodin. He was doing too much walking, but he wouldn't tell Medina that. The doorman looked at him warily, glanced at Medina who clearly looked better, then back at Ian.

"What happened to you?" said the doorman.

"The ravages of smoking," said Ian.

The doorman looked at Medina for some kind of confirmation. She only said, "Unfiltered Pall Malls."

"Ms. Sato is waiting for us," said Ian. "The name's Brown," he said giving his fake name.

The doorman found his name on a list, and he let them in. They ascended in the elevator.

A small woman in her late twenties with short dark hair answered the door. She wore shorts and a silk blouse, and she turned her head from Ian in his pink sweats to Medina in her business attire.

"Hi, Marilee, I'm Ian," he said. "Sorry I didn't have time to change. And this is Aleece Medina."

"Hello," Marilee said and extended her hand slowly, seemingly confused by a man with such odd clothes, a cast, and cane. "You're directing?"

Ian shook her hand and nodded assuredly. "John Huston directed his last film from a wheel chair while needing oxygen."

Marilee extended her hand to Medina. "And are you the producer?"

Medina pulled out her FBI identification. "Actually, I'm with the FBI. I'm not here about a movie but about a bank robbery. Ian was a victim in it."

"I don't understand. Bank robbery?" said Marilee, her eyes moving from person to person, as if seeing her words to the press at the Academy Awards quickly fading away. "Aren't you doing a film?"

"I'm sorry that we used a ruse," said Medina, "but this is important. I'm here to ask you about Freddie Liu. He was found dead today and may have been involved in Ian's kidnapping."

"I know very little about Freddie, I'm sorry." Marilee tried slamming shut the door, but Ian inserted his cane between the door and the jam. "You were involved with Freddie," he reminded her. "You don't care he's dead?"

She sighed and opened the door again. "Freddie was nice. I'm sorry he's gone."

"May we come in?"

She hesitated. "I sent my husband to Starbucks for this interview, so we have to be quick. I don't want him to hear about Freddie again."

"Why's that?"

"Because I had an affair with Freddie, and my husband found out."

Marilee showed them into an elegant living room with antique furniture and a view of the Hollywood Hills and the Hollywood sign. Ian was impressed. This was far more than a struggling actor working in 99-seat theatres could afford. "What's your husband do?" Ian asked.

"He imports restaurantware from Japan. He has his own company. He's been doing it for twenty years." Ah. The husband was older than she. Medina gave Ian nodding approval and pulled out her notebook.

"How did you and Freddie meet?" Medina asked.

"At the Long Beach Grand Prix, actually. He loves racing, and so do I. It's an awesome event on the streets of Long Beach, but my husband doesn't like it."

"So you went by yourself?" said Medina.

"With a girlfriend actually. We met Freddie in the stands. He bought us beers and was very sweet. I'd been married a year and was too young, really. Freddie was just a good escape."

"Freddie knew you were married?"

"Oh, yeah. I learned later he liked only married women. That's fine. I didn't need another relationship, just someone who cared for me for an evening every now and then."

Ian couldn't believe someone like Marilee was ever lonely. Then again, from among the many actors he'd known, he'd come to realize an actor's need to be seen and appreciated was perhaps higher than most people's. Still, having an affair was crossing the line. Everyone should have ethics.

"How often did you see him?" Ian said. Medina's glance indicated to let her do the asking.

"If I was in a play, I wouldn't see him for six weeks or more, depending on the length of the run. *Equus* went two months. Freddie and I might have chatted once in a while. He could make me laugh. He must have had others, but we always used protection. As I say, he was a nice guy." She looked saddened. "How did he die?"

"By a beating, likely from one of the men in the bank robbery. Did you know Freddie was involved in crime?"

"He alluded to it, but I never took him seriously. One time he couldn't meet me because he said he had a freelance job, driving. When I asked driving who, he said I didn't need to know. That kind of made Freddie more exciting, frankly."

Ian nodded. He sensed sometimes from the actors and actresses he directed that they liked acting for its very sense of danger. To be in front of people for two hours without a script, to be without a director reminding them where to walk, to be in front of many sets of eyes scanning from the audience, took a special kind of person. That person needed things normal people didn't.

"And you said your husband found out?" Medina asked.

"Yeah. He followed me to a restaurant one night when I said I had an audition. He found me and Freddie sharing a steak. He said he'd pound Freddie to a pulp if he saw me again. I didn't know my husband cared so much, and it's been fine with us ever since."

"And where was your husband three nights ago?"

"We were entertaining here. I thought you said someone else was your suspect."

"I need to look at everything. You brought it up."

"He was with me and two other people. I can give you their names. Are we done?" She was looking anxious.

"Yes," said Medina. "Except one more thing. Do you know anyone else Freddie might have been seeing more recently?"

She hesitated. Her look revealed she did know someone. "Yeah, I ran into Freddie at the Long Beach Grand Prix again last year, and he was with a woman, a little older than me but lookin' good in her pink short shorts. Irma's her name. I remember it because it seemed like a grandmother's name."

Medina wrote the name down. Once they were back in the car, she looked for the name in Freddie's entire address book in her camera. "No Irma in here."

"How about we go back to the Pep Boys? Didn't you say the manager was helpful? Maybe he heard Freddie talk about an Irma," Ian asked.

"And there's another possibility," said Medina. "The manager said he and his wife liked Freddie." She looked at Ian deeply as if considering the possibilities. "Freddie liked married women. What if his wife's name is Irma?"

Medina called the Pep Boys store and spoke again with Javier Perez, the manager. Medina broke the news that Freddie wouldn't be coming in anymore. He was dead.

"Oh, man," said Javier. Medina's phone was loud enough that Ian could hear what Javier said. "That's a bad flu. Was it that bird virus from Vietnam?"

"It was murder."

"Oh, my God… It wasn't one of those random gang killings, was it?" Javier asked.

"No," she said. "Do you know of any reason someone might beat him to death?"

"Freddie, are you kidding? He was a nice, honest guy."

"I'm interviewing everyone who knew Freddie, even a little bit. Might I interview your wife?"

"Irma?"

Medina nodded and pointed at Ian.

"Irma won't know anything," said Javier. "She just knew him from the store and a few dinners at our place."

"Every bit helps," said Medina.

"Okay," he said. She was home, and he'd set it up. He gave Medina the address, and she hung up.

"You're good," said Ian.

"I know," she replied, and they were on their way.

CHAPTER EIGHT

The Perezes, Medina noted, happened to live on Mt. Washington, much farther down the hill from where Ian had been held hostage. The pale blue house had a view of the park just across Figueroa. It'd be a pretty area, she thought, if most of the homes didn't have bars on their windows or if cars weren't parked on the lawn across the street. In one driveway, two young men worked under a car on cement blocks. This wasn't a rich neighborhood like those farther up the hill, but then again, it was higher than the flats. Status was often about how far up a hill you were.

Ian appeared to have difficulty with his cane as he walked uphill. "You okay?" she asked.

"My right wrist is starting to hurt," he said, walking unaided but slowly.

"Why don't you sit this one out in the car, then we'll go to my place. I don't want you back in the hospital."

He stopped. "I just have to catch my breath a moment. It's like I'm an old man. Jeez."

"This is silly. We can come back later."

"We can't," said Ian.

"Of course we can—or I can."

"I have to pee," said Ian. "I couldn't earlier because there's a knot in the strings now."

"It's supposed to be tied like a shoe."

"I thought I did, but there's no bow anymore. Can you unknot it?"

Medina tried to understand what he was asking of her. "I have to pee badly," he said. "It's embarrassing."

"Is it just the knot or… more? Like something needs holding?"

"No, no. If you can help me with the knot, then if someone's home, I can do the rest. It just seems stuck, and I can't bend well to look."

Medina peered over to the next driveway to see that the young men who were working under the car were not in the line of sight. She bent down to work the knot. When it wouldn't come easily, she knelt down and tried more. She felt stupid peering right at his crotch, but this had to be done. Using her teeth as well as her fingers, she started to get it loose when she heard the front door open.

A young woman, late twenties, wearing a blue shirt, strode out, and from the top of the concrete stairs that ran up from the street said, "What are you two doing! This is a good neighborhood."

With a surge, Medina stood, getting the last of the knot out. "No, sorry. He had a knot."

The woman looked skeptical and said, "Yuh huh."

"Are you Irma?" said Medina, hurrying up the stairs, and the woman looked surprised. "I'm Special Agent Medina with the FBI. Over there is Ian Nash." The woman was now frowning, gazing toward Ian, who approached, hobbling and holding up his pink sweatpants.

Medina extended her hand to the woman. "Thank you for meeting us." Pinned on the woman's sky blue knit shirt was a CVS Pharmacy clerk's badge that read "Irma." With puffy eyes, she looked as if she'd been crying. A fresh tear fell against her large nose, not her best feature. But she was a thin woman with a figure, and Medina could see why she might attract men.

Ian slowly followed up the steps, holding the handrail with his one semi-good hand, but he was wincing.

"You okay? I can help," said Medina.

"Stop it. I'm fine," he said.

Irma frowned. "My husband called and said you'd be coming. Freddie's dead? Is this true?"

"Yes. Before we get into that, may he use your bathroom?"

"Of course. Down the hall to your left." She pointed the way in.

Ian approached the front door, breathing hard once again. Irma did not comment on Ian's clothes.

"Are you okay?" Medina asked Irma.

"It's just sad when someone you know dies. Come in."

They stepped into the front entry, a small space in Mexican pavers. Ian moved down the hall to the bathroom.

"My husband had Freddie over for dinner a few times," said Irma, showing Medina into the living room, which had madras throws over the two couches, and trinkets were spread like snow on side tables. A bookshelf contained DVDs and framed photos. The place had a cluttered feel, like grandmothers had run amok in a tourist shop.

Before sitting, Medina stepped over to look at the framed photos. One showed Irma and Javier standing before a fountain of spitting fish, and in another, they held each other with a mountain view behind them. They were a matched pair in their smiles. How could she betray him apparently so easily? Why did people make their real lives so complicated?

"Yes, sad about Freddie," said Medina casually. "Beaten to death in his own home." Medina turned. Irma looked horrified.

"Why would someone do that?" said Irma.

"That's why I'm here. Hoping you'd know something."

"Me?"

On a shelf above the photos stood a few small, abstract wood sculptures.

"What are those?" Medina asked before joining Irma on the couch.

"My husband carves. He loves taking driftwood from his fishing trips and making something out of the chunks. He spends a lot of time on them," she said with a hint of bitterness in her voice. "He finds the wood comforting."

Medina nodded. This was a good place to start. "I know about your relationship with Freddie."

Now Irma's eyes filled with tears. She covered her face.

"Don't worry," said Medina. "I'm not telling your husband. Adultery's not a Federal crime. A witness told me she met you and Freddie at the Long Beach Grand Prix last year. Would you like to tell me more?"

Removing her hands, Irma's face flashed with fear. "Javier knows nothing?"

"No. And what you say can remain confidential."

The toilet flushed.

Irma cleared her throat. "After I met Freddie here, he came into my store a few times, the CVS on the corner of 60th. He's friendly, what can I say? I figured it was my last fling before kids."

"When did your affair start?"

"Maybe two years ago. It wasn't that often. A few times a month maybe. He knew Javier's schedule, after all."

Ian entered the living room, and when Medina looked at him, an odd warmth enveloped her as if she wanted to hug him, reassure him things would work out. He was so pathetic hobbling in that pink suit, and yet he was so determined to be there, to help. She couldn't help but admire him. Ever since he ran with that gun after Owen, she saw him anew. Medina scooted to make room for him on the couch.

"What can you tell me about Freddie's involvement in the bank robbery?" said Medina back to Irma.

"Bank robbery? No, not him. He'd been arrested once long ago, but not for that."

"That's interesting." Medina flipped pages in her notebook to a blank page and started writing. "For what?"

"His friend Crackerjack and he did something, stealing a car, I think. "

"Does Crackerjack have a real name?"

"I don't know."

"Did he remain friends with Freddie?"

"I heard about him because Freddie got a call about three months ago one evening when we were making love. Freddie let it go to his answering machine, and I heard a man say 'Hey, it's Crackerjack. Give me a call.' When I asked Freddie about him, Freddie just said Crackerjack was a good buddy he once was arrested with long ago."

"And why did Crackerjack call?"

"I don't know. We didn't get into it. We were occupied."

"So as far as you know, Freddie wasn't bank robbing?"

"No, he was fine, except…." She paused.

"What?" said Ian, breaking his silence.

"I couldn't get a hold of Freddie for about a week—even his cell phone didn't work. I saw him Sunday night, and he was really happy. He said next time my husband went fishing with his buddies to June Lake, we were going to go to Cancun. I didn't believe him until he showed me a couple of thousand dollars he pulled out of his pocket. I asked where he got it. He said 'drivin'.'"

"Isn't that a lot of money for driving?"

"I thought so."

"Is that the last you saw him?"

"Yeah, but when my husband mentioned Freddie was real sick, I called. He didn't answer. I was worried."

"You didn't go over there?"

"I couldn't get away."

"Too bad," said Ian. "Maybe you could've taken him to the hospital."

Irma looked at him angrily, and from an eye, another tear fell.

"And where was your husband Monday night?" Medina asked.

"With me. Why? You don't think he had anything to do with it?" Irma looked down as if considering for herself. "No, Javier doesn't know. He's too busy with his own stuff. Between the store, his friends, his fishing, and his wood carving, he's happy."

"Not a lot of time for you?" asked Medina.

"No one said marriage was a rose garden." She looked at them honestly. "As you two probably know."

"Can't say I've been married," said Ian. Medina kept quiet.

Back in the car as they headed out, Ian said, "Seems to me specializing in married women as Freddie did would lead to being beaten to death one way or another. It's only ironic that Owen did it." Ian looked at her curiously. "Have you ever dated a married man?"

She shot him a look. "That's an asinine thing to say," she said.

"Sorry. Didn't know you were so touchy."

"I'm not touchy."

"Anyway, I always thought it was guys that had affairs," said Ian. "Are married women in general that unhappy?"

"I've never married, either," said Medina. "Seems like it's an ownership thing. We're a consumer society, so men and women have to own each other. Once people have someone, though, they want something else, the newest model year."

"That's cynical."

"I've worked with enough guys to know. Add that to my bad relationships, too, and I see how people work," said Medina.

Ian glanced at her as she drove. "Bad relationships?"

She smirked. "I don't understand men's strange thinking."

"I don't get women, so I guess we're even there." He looked out the window. She wondered if he knew about her affair. She wasn't that obvious, was she?

He turned to speak. "I wonder why he took the name Klemma. I don't get it."

"It may be random."

"I just wonder about these pseudonyms still," said Ian. "No one's figured them out yet?"

"I talked to Rick about them. 'Owen' is too popular. Zetta may be related to the letter Z. If so, Z is the last letter, so what is she the last of? There are a lot of Navarres in the world, and Klemma, that's unusual, but no leads."

"Where're we headed?" Ian asked, as if now disoriented on the city street.

"A clothes store. You need clothes. I don't want to go to your place in case Owen is watching for whatever reason."

"Can we get clothes later?"

She nodded. "You must be tired. You can probably use a nap," she said.

"Yeah."

"So I'll take you to my place."

"Sounds good."

"I still need to get to the office. So I'll drop you off and then go."

"Excellent." He smiled.

He wasn't such a bad guy.

Her cell phone rang. She saw it was Rick, so she didn't answer through the car's speakerphone. Not on the freeway yet, she pulled to the side of the city street and took the call.

"Aleece, it's Rick."

"Rick, I thought I'd pop in a little bit later."

"Could it be sooner than later?"

"What?"

"We're just assessing the situation here. A lot of details have come in. I look forward to ascertaining the whole perspective. We'll see you soon."

This didn't sound like the normal Rick. Ascertaining the whole perspective? "Who's 'we,' Rick?"

"So we'll just hang tight until you're here."

"You can't talk, is that it?"

"Excellent," he said.

That meant only one thing. Someone else was in the room with him. Probably Wexler, the Assistant Special Agent in Charge—his boss in Westwood.

"All right," she said. "See you soon."

She hung up, but she had to consider what Wexler wanted. She was off the case, so why the hell would he make a special trip out to West Covina? She sensed Wexler was about to fuck up her life.

As they pulled onto the freeway, Ian tried to be casual and seemingly unconcerned even though Medina was lost in thought. "So was Rick inviting you to a birthday party or something fun?" he said.

"Birthday party?"

"You're on vacation still, right?"

"Oh, the phone call," Medina said. "It was just Rick wanting to talk to me before my vacation."

"Something serious?"

"I don't know. Probably not—but nothing to worry about." Everything about her manner, though, said he should worry. Just his luck.

He knew enough not to push her right now. He was too tired to argue, anyway, and he just had to hope it wouldn't impact following up the leads they got today.

As she pulled off the freeway in West Covina and moved down a suburban street, Ian fought falling asleep. It was as if his body was betraying him. A quick nap, he hoped, should help. They'd be at her house soon. To keep himself awake, he tried to guess which house was hers. The street had large homes, minimum three bedrooms each—far different than his street—and they passed kids wearing backpacks, coming home from school. Why would a young single woman have a family-sized house? Wouldn't a condo work just as well? Her house wouldn't have much landscaping and be rather plain, he figured. They turned into the drive of a white ranch-style house with a particularly green lawn with mower marks and an elaborate garden with many flowering plants. This was her place? Yellow mums edged the walkway. His mother loved mums. He wondered how his mother was. The loud buzz of a leaf blower broke his thoughts. A thin Asian man emerged from the side of the house, turning off his machine. He was perhaps in his fifties, and when he saw Medina, he bowed.

"It looks great, Mr. Taboroki," said Medina, exiting the car. "You're an artist."

"Thank you, Miss," he said.

Ian emerged from the car and felt dizzy, so he grabbed the car door with his good arm to steady himself. The feeling passed quickly, and Mr. Taboroki looked at him with curiosity, glancing at his pink outfit. Ian shrugged and answered the question that had to be on the man's mind. "I'm an actor friend of Aleece's," he said. "I'm in that new musical, 'Pink Iron,' about a guy desperately needing a job, so he dresses as a woman to be a female fitness instructor."

"He's kidding," said Medina instantly. The man smiled and nodded quickly as if to say funny, funny. Mr. Taboroki pulled the leaf blower off his back and moved toward the dented pick-up truck parked at the curb in front of the house. Two lawn mowers with bags stood in the back. Of course Medina wouldn't be doing the lawn and garden herself, not with her schedule, Ian realized. Besides, in L.A., did people ever do their own lawns?

Ian looked more closely at her house, a long box with aluminum windows and asphalt shingles. She had a big picture window covered by drawn lace curtains, and a front door of natural redwood with a small archway of stained glass toward the top. A grand and gnarled lemon tree glowed like an ambulance of yellow fruit. "You have a pretty place."

"Thanks." She smiled. "It's convenient."

Of course she would see it as practical, yet the house betrayed another side of her, a warm one.

After he limped inside, the quiet and darkened coolness felt as good as Carlsbad Caverns. With the throbbing of his leg, side, and arm—all together in a symphony of bass drums—and a sense of utter exhaustion, he hoped she'd just show him his room as quickly as possible.

If she had a guest room, that meant she must have guests occasionally. Parents? Siblings? Friends from other states? No one he knew his age had a guest room.

"This way," she said, brushing past.

The room was painted a light blue, and the double bed in the corner had an ornate wooden headboard and plenty of fru-fru pillows on an elaborate bedspread. There was even a stuffed toy moose with soft yellow antlers. The walls had framed posters, the kind with cats or stark black-and-white landscapes that you get at Aaron Brothers Art and Framing.

"Nice," he said, not knowing what else to say.

"I'm off to the office," she said. "Shouldn't be too long."

"Okay."

"If you're up before I get back, I'll leave you the keys to my other car. My fridge isn't stocked with much, so you might want to hit Vons, which we passed. You need some cash?"

"No. And you have two cars?"

"One's the FBI's. I'll stop by Target and get you some clothes."

"I don't have enough for that."

"Pay me back later." She nodded as if she believed it. "You look about a 32 waist, 34 pantleg."

"You're a good observer."

"I pride myself on it."

He nodded. He looked for a clock and found one on an open roll-top desk, a gold-edged clock in an obelisk of wood. It showed just after two. Only two? With his physical problems in addition to their running around, he could call it a day. Still, he felt anxious as if he had much to do today.

"That call from your boss—sounded important. Is there anything I can do?"

"I don't see how."

"Be honest. Tell me what happened."

She sighed. "I'm betting Wexler is there, about to make things extra bad for me."

"Is there something you can do to stop Wexler?"

"You don't stop a tank."

"When I direct, I tell my actors to guess the other person's agenda. What are they after and how are they vulnerable?"

"Wexler's not vulnerable."

"He is if you can get in the way of his objective. What's he want?"

"I'll think about it."

"Definitely," he stated. "And a computer? For my email?"

"In the next room. Click on Guest. There's no password for Guest."

"So you have other guests. A boyfriend?"

"Sleep well," she said and shut the door.

He sat on the edge of the bed and removed his shoes. He looked out the window. An emerald lawn in the back stretched to a pinkish block wall, much of it covered by thick vegetation. He glanced again at her expensive desk and clock. While only a couple of years separated them, she was an adult, he realized, and he was a kid—an old kid maybe like Klemma. She had a career, and a good one, one she loved and was good at, and had two cars. He was not only out of the university without his doctoral degree, but also he had no clear future, no money, and no credit card that worked. He'd wasted his time in theatre when, at best, he'd be merely a workman-like director and even worse as a teacher. He wouldn't make a great living.

He flopped down on the bed thinking he still liked theatre. If he hadn't gone for a Ph.D., though, he might have found a better calling by now. With a better calling, he might even be married and be starting a family like other people his age. Humans have stages to go through, he thought, including the reproductive stage. He should be off reproducing. More so, he wouldn't have been in the coffee shop when the bank got robbed. His life could have been great, but he was so fucking ineffectual.

He stood again and stripped to his underwear, incredibly sore. He had to pull his pink sweatpants off by stepping on each pant leg and lifting each knee as best he could.

As he stared at the cottage cheese ceiling before closing his eyes, he knew none of his past shit mattered now. All that mattered was finding the three remaining captors. What if he found Owen, killed him, and then died? Would his life be complete? Probably not, but he was too tired to figure it out. As his eyes closed, all he knew was he had to succeed.

CHAPTER NINE

On her way into the office that mid-afternoon, Medina became more and more angry. What was Wexler up to?

She considered the dead Pasadena officer, Sergeant Bradford—was she going to be made a scapegoat for his death and be put on administrative leave? How would that help his career? Maybe it was just personal.

She realized she was driving too fast. She needed to calm down, so she turned on her car radio. George Thorogood's voice popped on, singing "B-B-B-Bad to the bone." Classic rock, not calming. She pushed the button for the classical station. George Gershwin's "Rhapsody in Blue" played.

When she was young, her dad loved the Mexican stations, especially the love songs in Spanish, but her mother preferred something else. She played classical piano on their upright in the living room. She was an elegant woman, worked as a piano teacher from the house, and from her, Medina had learned a woman could be smart and do most anything.

While her mother loved Bach, Medina loved Gershwin, and now the string section and a few subdued horns wound around each other like vines that knew where to grow. The whole horn section strode in and, moments later, a piano announced itself as smoothly as a suitor at the door. The piano rose in intensity, and the other instruments withdrew as if in awe. Medina could picture the pianist's fingers stretching, moving upwards, as the notes crisply kissed the air. The whole Pittsburgh Symphony Orchestra, with symbols bashing and the cascading piano crashing, melted together in a firework of music. Her fingers drummed in time with the beat. The music enveloped her with a sense of all-is-right in the world. Her life, her work, her soul were now on track again. She could feel the smile on her face.

Then it struck her where Wexler was vulnerable: in the public eye. He needed all the positive press he could get, but what if that turned sour?

That reminded her: the day before, she'd received a call from

NPR, a call she hadn't returned yet. Normally such matters were handled by a public affairs spokesman in Wexler's office, but NPR's interest had to do in part with Medina being a woman, so the spokesman cleared it for her to talk. Maybe she could get a National Public Radio report on her side. A national audience could be rooting for her. Once she parked her car in her office's lot, she called NPR right back, still in her car.

"Steve Inskeep's office," a woman answered.

"Steve Inskeep, please. It's Aleece Medina of the FBI returning his call."

"Mr. Inskeep's on the air, but may I put you through to his assistant, Jay Hazuka? I know he wanted to talk with you."

"That's fine," said Medina.

"Ms. Medina!" came the next voice. "Jay Hazuka here."

"Hello," said Medina. "I'm returning Steve Inskeep's call."

"We have a few questions about your case and your role. If you don't mind, could I record you for possible use on air?"

"Yes. That's fine."

"Great. As I understand it, you're in charge of the Busty Bandit case?"

"That's undergoing a transition now. However, I'd been on it since the first robbery a month ago in Monrovia."

"And there's been two deaths involved recently, I understand."

"Six total. There were two at the bank alone, then an exceptional South Pasadena police detective, Anton Jones, was killed in the line of duty. At the hospital, another police officer and a nurse both tried to stop our suspect and died. Then one of the robbers was murdered, which we're investigating. We've been gathering a great deal of information, and we're moving ahead."

"Are you getting close to apprehending your suspects?"

"I can't comment on that now."

"We're particularly interested in your role. Many people think of Jody Foster in *Silence of the Lambs* for their idea of a female FBI special agent, but the reality of J. Edgar Hoover's formerly all-male force may be different. As a woman in the FBI, you must find yourself in—"

"Excuse me, I'm happy to talk about this, but I see my cell phone's running out of power. Would you mind calling me back in, say, five minutes at the number you called yesterday? I'll be in the office in a couple minutes. Your call can pull me out of whatever meeting I have when I walk in."

"Certainly. Or I could call later when—"

"Five minutes will be fine."

When she walked into her office, Cynthia, the receptionist, said, "Rick asked for you to go right to the conference room."

Medina looked down the hallway toward the conference room. This was the moment to act.

"Watch it. Wexler's here," said Cynthia.

"I know. He's up to something."

"You should tell him what Alanis Morissette sang, 'I see right through you.'"

"It wouldn't do a damn thing," Medina said. "Who's with him?"

"I'm not supposed to know," said Cynthia.

"Who? Fess up."

"Toffer, an A-Dick from Westwood."

"I know Toffer," said Medina. An ADIC was an assistant director in charge, two steps in rank above what Wexler was. ADICs were always politically ambitious, and he must be getting close to retirement age, too. He might parlay his notoriety into, say, top brass at the CIA or even one of the high-paying and cushy jobs as head of a Las Vegas casino security team. It only made sense Toffer wanted to attach himself to this case.

As Medina walked down the hall, she glanced back at Cynthia, who held a thumb up.

As she turned the corner, Medina could hear Rick had broken from his usually soft spoken voice to say sternly, "Over the last twenty-four hours, my team has gathered a great deal of information, and Aleece Medina has cracked the case wide open."

"With three deaths?" said a voice she didn't recognize. "We just feel something is way off with the entire unit here in West Covina."

When Medina opened the door, Rick stood, jacketless in a light shirt and striped tie, looking furious, but Wexler in his gray pinstripe suit looked happy, as if he'd been anticipating this moment all week. The other man, Toffer, about the size of Napoleon, appeared just as pleased, more colorful in his beige shirt, rust-colored jacket, and red tie. His smile and salt-and-pepper hair reminded her of a Wall Street guy getting a golden parachute.

"What's wrong? What's going on here?" said Medina.

"Sorry to call you in during your vacation," said Wexler. "An odd time to have a vacation, no?"

"Not after you yanked me off finding the Busty Bandit," she said. "I have to blow off a little steam," she said, looking right at him. "Mr. Toffer," said Medina right to the man.

The man looked surprised. "We hadn't met before, but, yes, Ms. Medina." He smiled, stood, and held out his hand. "I'm Jerry Toffer." Medina shook his hand.

"Friendly, first name basis, eh? You like to smile as you swing the axe, is that it?"

Both men smiled. "As you may know," said Wexler, "You've handed us a beehive of problems with the Busty Bandit case. A half-dozen dead. It seems as if replacing you isn't enough."

"According to whom?" said Rick.

"I'm glad you asked that, Mr. Okinowa," said Toffer. "It's according to me. News organizations keep asking how this can happen? Is this being bungled somehow? With these tough economic times, the Busty Bandit is being celebrated now, a kind of Bonnie Parker, and the FBI is looking inept."

"So you're saying it's a media thing, and you're going to fix it," said Medina.

"Yes. This West Covina office is the problem. It's just not your unfortunate tenure on this case, Agent Medina, but I'm looking above you," said Toffer, now looking at Rick. "Perhaps in your culture, Mr. Okinowa, individualism doesn't count, but responsibility is always individual."

"His culture?" said Medina. "Are you thinking Chinese railroad workers?"

"Excuse me, Aleece, but I prefer another angle." Rick moved forward and leaned against the desk to look at Wexler and Toffer. "We have the lowest rate of cold cases west of the Mississippi," he said. "We have the lowest turnover, and if you're thinking of transferring or downsizing me because of what anyone else would be proud of, well, Mr. Railroad Barons, to quote MLK, a man can't ride your back unless it's bent. Mine's straight, and I will fight. An injustice anywhere is a threat to justice everywhere."

Medina smiled. This was Rick.

Toffer, however, frowned and then his eyes became steely. "I came here with a few options, but it's clear by both of your attitudes that we have some sort of renegade field office here."

"How did the playing field tilt suddenly? We're not J. Edgar's men?" said Medina.

"Jeez Louise," said Wexler, who, having been stationed in Texas years before, stuck with good ol' boy phrasing even if he'd grown up in Connecticut. "I knew you'd bring up the woman card."

"I didn't say that. You did. You know my record."

"First, you have to admit I let you have this Busty Bandit thing. You asked for it, and I gave it to you, and now it's biting me in my butt."

"I don't control the criminals, and neither do you. The murders are all by one man whose code name is Owen. I won't be the scapegoat for this."

"Your decisions and Agent Okinawa's," said Toffer, jumping in, "have led to these unfortunate circumstances. The public is angry."

"This is bigger'n both of us," said Wexler, waving his hand like God.

Toffer stood as if to deliver the coup de grace, but there was a knock on the door, which swung open. Everyone's eyes snapped to the woman in maroon. Cynthia smiled warmly and said, "Aleece. There's a Jay Hazuka with National Public Radio on the phone. He wants to continue your conversation with him?"

"About what?" said Wexler. "How come he's not using my spokesman in Westwood?"

"Because it's about being a woman in the FBI. It was cleared by your guy."

Wexler and Toffer glanced at each other.

"I can assure you," said Toffer, breaking in, "that what's happening in this room right now has nothing to do with you being a woman. The buxom woman has grown, and that's not a bad thing." He didn't realize his double entendre, which made Cynthia mime growing breasts as she exited.

"Tell Mr. Hazuka I'm coming," said Medina, catching Rick's nod.

"I can fire you right now and then you couldn't speak to NPR about anything."

"No, it'll give me much more to talk about."

"Or you're not fired but ordered not to talk with him," said Toffer.

"He already has most of an interview. If it's cut short, he'll know something is up and make it a bigger story than you want."

"How about this?" said Wexler. "I think we've all been reacting to the stress of what's been happening in all the wrong ways. What do you say, Jerry? How about Medina is back on the mission? It'll help us all."

"I'll go with that," said Toffer. His gray eyes took her in. "You can still take your vacation and start when you come back. But you'll be taking orders from us, is that clear? And I'd prefer that when you talk with NPR, you make it short and reveal little. I'm not happy that you're involved with the news media. Agents aren't trained to be in the news media."

"If I draw more people into a career with the FBI, that can't be a bad thing," said Medina. What she didn't say but which Wexler's scowl made clear, was that the people she'd draw would be women, and that, to him, would be a bad thing.

"Go take your call," said Wexler.

As she walked to her office, she only then noticed how her heart was racing. She'd pushed herself farther than she expected. Still, she was realistic. When she returned, she'd be given smaller and smaller tasks to do, and calls to Westwood wouldn't be returned quickly, and soon she'd be out of the loop. She'd be asked about her other cases and forced to deal with them. She really won nothing.

She entered her office, a small room with a view of the freeway. She glanced at the photo of her father in uniform on her desk to remind her of that people can be honest and honorable. She took her call. When she spoke with Hazuka at NPR, her enthusiasm nonetheless had drained. "Yes, being a woman in the FBI affords, in theory, chances to make a difference. The way I look at the world, nothing is perfect, but, rather, society is in a balance. On one side is the sense of peace and safety and people are inherently good. On the other is chaos, violence, and people can seem like animals."

"And how do you see the balance—more good than evil?" Hazuka asked.

She recalled Hamlet's thoughts on good and evil: There is nothing, either good or bad, but thinking makes it so. "The line between good citizens and criminals sometimes is thin," she told Hazuka. "Too thin. Good people can do bad things. For instance, people can be infused with a sense of entitlement or power and then can be very greedy—or very peculiar. They upset the balance. I try to help keep things in balance."

"FBI agents are the good guys?" he asked.

"Good guys and *gals*."

"Yes. So what do you like most about the FBI?"

She paused to consider. She really liked the people in West Covina, even the male special agents, who didn't scheme to roll over her or each other as in the main office in Westwood. "You know what I really like?" she said. "Every day is different. I love that I don't know what my day is going to be like—there's always something out of the ordinary, a new bit of information that takes me to a new place. I'm tested physically and intellectually. Very satisfying." She felt better now, remembering why she joined in the first place.

"So it's a wonderful institution—no problems?"

"All large institutions have their politics."

"Sounds like there's a story there."

"My co-workers are fine, but, face it, the FBI is a macho culture. I've had to deal with harassment at times, especially when I was first assigned in Dallas. Even so, I love what I do, even if some people in charge continue to have male-centric blinders on."

"This is very interesting," said Hazuka, which made her think to be careful. She thought of Wexler, and she knew this was a minefield. Her career could come to a halt in a moment if she said the wrong thing.

"Can you be more specific?" Hazuka said. "What happened in Texas, or, without naming names, what kind of problems do you have now with, say, the FBI as a large institution?"

"Actually, we're getting away from the central subject," she said, "which is what's it like being a woman leading the difficult case of the Busty Bandit? My colleagues in West Covina are fabulous, led by a brilliant man named Rick Okinawa. We as a team are determined to follow this thing through. I am only part of a devoted team."

The interview did not go on much longer, and Hazuka ended saying it might take a few days before they edited the interview and turned it into a story. As Medina sat in her office alone, thinking about what she had said, she recalled Dallas, her first assignment. She was the only female special agent—the only woman beyond the secretaries. In those days, Medina constantly caught snippets of conversations about her makeup, about how she might like to get drunk with them, even about the type of panties she might wear. That first month, one of her supervisors called her to discuss an upcoming undercover case, and he wanted to discuss it at a nearby restaurant that night because he just didn't have time right then. She agreed. It was a semi-fancy Italian restaurant, and from the way he acted when they walked in, with his nodding to people he clearly knew, she sensed he was treating this as a date. He didn't sit across from her at the corner table, but rather at ninety degrees next to her. He did not want to get to the details of the case right away. He drank two gin gimlets in short order, and once he was relaxed, he told her how pretty she was.

"Please," she said. "I'm feeling uncomfortable."

"I'm feeling… good." He did, however, start to talk about the case, asking her if she'd mind dressing like a prostitute for a sensitive assignment.

"I don't feel comfortable with that," she said. "My specialty isn't undercover."

"Mine, neither," he said. "We're a small office. We're a do-everything kind of shop."

"Are we worried about prostitutes?"

"Actually, we're trying to get to a particular guy big into drugs. We've tried a number of ways, and we have a chance for you to be a part of a high-priced escort service for a night. We have a man on the inside who'll let you in. Your bra would be wired, and once you see any sort of evidence of drugs, you'd call in the SWAT team. We've got your back."

"Can I think about this?" she said.

"Sure. Would you like meat?" he said, pointing down toward the menu. She noted the ambiguity.

He ordered a good bottle of wine, and he was adept, smelling the cork, sniffing the wine before he tasted the small amount that the waiter poured.

She said, "I'm not ready for undercover right now."

He paused. "Really? You're not a team player?"

"I'm new, and I don't think it's appropriate to put me on something so big."

He was grinning ear to ear. He took her hand. "I'm glad you're honest, honey. He kept holding her hand, pulling it to chair level. "I know you'll be a big asset to this department," he said. "I'd been pushing to have more women in the force, as women can do many things as good as men, if not better."

"You believe that?" she said.

He nodded. "I also believe you're ready for something big." He gently pulled her hand underneath the table and placed it on his crotch. She sensed his erection in his pants.

She immediately leapt up, knocking over her wine, which cascaded around his bread plate and onto his lap, causing him to leap up and knock his glass over. His neighbors, if they were adept, noticed his wet crotch and what was beneath it. Laughter erupted.

One male colleague called out to the supervisor, "Was it the undercover prostitute routine?"

Thinking about this now made her furious. She'd been twenty-seven and naïve, but now she'd found this office, and it was better. Still, Wexler, her previous boss from San Francisco and almost as bad, was in her life again, like a virulent virus.

With a knock on her door, Rick entered, carrying a clipboard. "They left. Sorry about all that, but it comes with the job."

"Yeah, I know."

"May I sit?"

"Please." Her office, like the others, was small, but it was far better than the bullpen arrangement, all agents in one big room with dividers, that she had had in San Francisco.

Rick looked about awkwardly as if gathering his thoughts. He seemed to be staring at Medina's few framed photos on a shelf. One was Medina and her sister mugging for the camera only last year.

"Is this the part where you tell me I've got twenty-nine other cases without Wexler's nose in them?" said Medina.

"No. I want you on this. I'm just hoping you might cut your vacation short. Maybe come back in a couple of days," he said.

"Love to," she said, wanting to say she'd come back today, but she had Ian in her house. She needed to talk with him first and figure out a way to get him elsewhere where he'd also be safe. She needed to think this through.

"So can you at least update me on what our team's found—even if I can't use it?"

"Sure," he said. "First we found that some calls on Freddie's cell phone came from a payphone at Sixth and Alvarado downtown, which happens to be right by the entrance to the Red Line."

"The subway," she said. "That's not what you'd call a high-rent area. Who might it be?"

"We're assuming it's Owen calling Klemma, so Owen must live around there."

"If you're a struggling actor like Owen, it's cheap rent," she said.

"We also looked into Freddie Liu's record, and he was arrested with another man ten years ago for auto theft, and Liu spent six months in county prison. He's had a clean record ever since."

"Let me guess," said Medina. "His partner had the nickname Crackerjack."

Rick looked surprised and looked at the clipboard he'd brought in. He nodded. "Yes. His real name is Bruce Worrell."

"And where does Bruce Worrell live?" said Medina.

Rick flipped a page. "Hmmm," he said.

Medina swung around to her computer at her desk, opened a certain database, and typed in his name. "He lives in Van Nuys, is employed at Baba's Auto Paint, and can be presently found in the

Men's Central Jail—for why, it doesn't say. I happen to know he contacted Freddie about three months ago."

"Impressive. How do you know?"

"A lead from his address book."

"We've been working on that, too, and found a few more people in there," said Rick. "Women he had short affairs with. None of them had heard from Freddie in years and didn't really help us."

"Any more on his nickname—Klemma?"

"No."

"How about Owen being an actor? Any leads there?"

"No. We even found the ad agency that's produced Tide commercials for the last few years, and no one recognizes him. At this point, we're thinking he's never been an actor."

"Maybe he's a wannabe. Maybe he's attended acting classes."

He nodded, then seemed to lose himself in thought. "Those fucking guys. My culture? Like I wasn't born here or went to Alhambra High School. Those guys are dinosaurs—and we're depending on them?"

"Let me ask a favor," said Medina. "Even though this is supposedly a day off, let me go interview this Bruce Worrell."

"Why not get back on the clock now?"

"I have my reasons."

Rick considered, then nodded. "Go ahead. Call me about Worrell when you're done."

"Absolutely," said Medina.

The Men's Central Jail was a straight shot west from West Covina—Interstate 10 to the Vignes Street exit and a couple more turns. Housing over five thousand inmates, it was the largest jail in the world. She was there in twenty minutes, and with another fifteen in arranging her interview, Bruce Worrell was being sent for. When Medina signed in, she noticed that a woman earlier that day had signed in to see him, a Vicky Yadegari, who had nice curlicue handwriting.

She stepped into the visitors room to meet Crackerjack. Typically, nicknames were part of the gang process, and the process also often brought scars from fights, time in jail, and death. In the chair on the other side of the window sat a bearded white man in his mid-thirties with blond curly hair. He had a slight belly and looked like a guy who loved being a couch potato on weekends, not someone who did time for crime, whatever it was.

"I need to ask you about Freddie Liu," she said after introducing herself and showing her badge.

"He has the Feds involved? What'd he do?"

"Die," she said. "As well as participate in a bank robbery."

"He's dead?" He looked truly surprised and saddened. "How'd he die?"

"Beaten to death."

"By an irate husband?" He shook his head sadly. "I kinda figured that would happen. But he stole from a bank too? That doesn't seem his style."

"That's why I'm here. You were arrested with him."

"That's long ago. He was clean. He's a good guy."

"Why did you call him three months ago?"

He looked at her with a smile. "Is that what this is about?" He laughed. "Well, he was being nice and set me up."

"For what? To help in his robberies?"

He shook his head, laughing. "No. A date. I wanted a date. Heck, I might only have talked with him every couple of years. I lived in Van Nuys and he lived in Highland Park, and we just never really saw each other, but every now and then we talked. One day I started thinking to myself, 'Is this it?'"

"Is what it?"

"Life, you know. My job kept me busy, and I pulled a lot of overtime. I didn't need the money. I just didn't have much else to do. And one day I thought, you know, I should settle down."

"And you called Freddie to get you a date?"

"Yeah. I knew he always saw married women, but I got to thinkin' maybe he knew someone nice who was divorced. I wanted someone my age but without a kid. I figured a divorced woman might like someone like me. I know I'm no prize, but I'm nice. I'd love her."

"And did Freddie set you up?"

"Yeah, to my fiancée now, Vicky."

"Vicky Yagedari."

He looked at her and said, "You know her?"

"No. So why're you here? Anything connected with Freddie?"

"I'm here thanks to real estate values. Vicky and I wanted to buy a house, but do you know how expensive houses are, even in the Valley now? I had some savings, but not enough for a down payment. So I painted a car for a guy—a car that needed painting in the middle of the night."

"A stolen car," she said. "Did you do this thing often?"

"Never. I never needed the money, but now I did. It paid well every night. Wouldn't you know I'd help out a guy under investigation. It got me six months here. So—Vicky and I will rent for a while. This place has shown me what's important. Hell, I don't care if I live with Vicky in a trailer park in Lancaster. If you find that one person, that's what counts."

Medina said nothing but simply looked at this doofus in a prison uniform. There was someone for everyone.

"Why did Freddie like married women so much?" Medina asked.

Bruce started laughing. "Funny story," he said. "True story. Shortly after we had our run-in with the law long ago, Freddie came out to the Valley where I lived, and we hit a few clubs near me, dance clubs. Freddie said the Valley had the best girls. He wasn't a good dancer, but he said if you wanted a nice suburban girl, you had to dance. That night he picked up this fine, tall chick—Celeste, I think her name was—who was teaching him all the moves. After a while, she was all over him, tongue down his throat. I thought they were going to do it right out on the floor. Thing was, Celeste wasn't eager to go anywhere. So he got her a little drunk and then asked if he could use my place. I gave him my keys, figuring I'd give them an hour. That was the deal—an hour. Well, when I got to my place, I heard screaming. Freddie was yelling, 'Get out, get out," and she came running out of the house, fully dressed but crying. I gave her a ride back to the club."

"So what happened?" Medina asked.

"Celeste was a guy in women's clothing. She—he, whatever— kept telling me in the car it's not her fault. She was born that way— she knew she was a woman. She was really nice I thought—though very confusing for me. It's a weird world, that's all I can say. Anyway, Freddie said married women were women. He stuck with them ever since."

"Thanks," said Medina.

"My new philosophy is: find your love, keep your nose clean, and stay happy till you die. That's the deal as I see it."

She nodded. She supposed she had felt similarly after she'd gone off to Biola University, a Christian college, and fell for the wrong guy. Even the thought of her volleyball coach made her stomach churn. She wished that part of her life could be zapped like a bad e-mail.

"You married?" Bruce asked.

"No."

"A good-looking girl like you? They're not beatin' down your door?"

"Not if you're FBI."

He laughed. "You gotta good point there."

CHAPTER TEN

Ian felt driven to awake the way a terrier barks and lunges at a bigger dog. He blinked, trying to orient himself. A black cat intensely stared at him from a poster that bore the words, "Le Chat – Café Noir."

Where was he? He pulled the multi-colored flowered quilt off himself, and in doing so, made his arm with the cast throb. The room's windows, with its curtains open, overlooked a pixel-perfect green lawn with a flowering fruit tree. That's right, he was at Medina's. He checked the clock. It was six—a.m. or p.m.? The outside had a deep afternoon color. Good. It'd only been a few hours. He could think again. He needed two things: Medina's computer and his prescriptions.

He stood, only in his underwear. He remembered his dream. He'd seen himself at a computer keyboard searching through a database. For what? Ah, the unconscious mind was an amazing thing.

He knew he should shower, but he had too much to do and was far too aching to wrestle with that problem. In the attached bathroom, he gave himself a sponge bath, and with a bottle marked "eau de toilette," he spritzed twice.

It took much longer to dress himself back in the pink sweat suit than undress. His leg and side now pounded again. Vicodin and Naproxen would be good to start with. His prescriptions were by the sink, and he took one of each.

In the kitchen, he found no coffee but many different boxes of herb tea, including Cozy Chamomile, Mint Medley, and Sweet Dreams. Medina was a tea drinker? He figured she'd smash coffee beans with a hammer and eat the chunks unbrewed. She didn't seem a Cozy Chamomile kind of gal.

He noticed her windowsill above the kitchen sink—the only place in the house that seemed truly eclectic. It was filled with oddities. A miniature gray Grecian urn stood next to a tall wooden cat apparently carved from driftwood, which appeared next to the bottom half of a broken green glass vase. Stuffed into the top of the vase was a doll-sized torso of a young woman in a lacy dress. Her ceramic head that featured earrings and red lipstick dangled on a gold chain from one of her arms, and her figure was familiar, perhaps a stock character. Nearby, a fifty-cent-sized ceramic dish held a pink plastic wind-up mouse and two green pebbles. All these things meant something to Medina, something revealing he'd never know. We are what we keep.

From the mantle, he picked up an ornate miniature hope chest. He flipped open the top and found inside a ring with a single square gem—a rock on a ring. He pulled it and examined the one-carat princess-cut diamond, the kind he once considered buying his last girlfriend, Pierra, before he found out how expensive rings were. Medina must have been engaged once. When he'd been shopping for a ring for Pierra, he'd asked about the return policy in case she said no.

"If she says no, bring it back. Small restocking charge," said the diamond dealer. "You can also bring it back if woman says yes but breaks the engagement. The ring is yours. Bring back. Small restocking charge."

"What if I break off the engagement?" he'd asked.

"She gets to keep the ring. That's the rule. Break her heart, she keeps the rock."

Medina had kept her rock. Her fiancé must have broken the engagement.

The box, too, contained a gold chain necklace, and as he pulled it out, the end of the chain revealed an elegant sparkling pendant in the shape of a heart. Two miniature gold candy canes were welded to form the heart, and a channel inside the canes was studded with small diamonds. He put everything back the way he found it. He felt deeply guilty now.

He looked back in the open cupboard and the boxes of tea. Fuck tea—he wanted coffee. He would get it later at a Carrie's or Starbucks.

Back in the hallway, Ian eyed his choices of closed doors. Did she say the next room over from his bedroom was where her computer was? He opened it to find the home office. A gorgeous 21-inch monitor stood on the large cherry wood desk. As he walked closer, he saw it was an Apple iMac. In comparison, all he'd been able to afford was a used laptop with an older version of Windows. He touched the mouse, and the large flat-panel screen flashed on, revealing a plain screen with two choices: "Aleece" and "Guest."

He'd used Macs at UC Irvine. He clicked on "Guest" and up

came not a default aurora borealis as he expected, but rather a photo of the Earth and moon taken from a satellite. The photo showed a bluish ball with shifting white clouds, half cast into deep-black darkness so that it was only half a ball. Above it and floating to the left was a smaller and ochre half-ball moon. The icons were at the bottom of the screen. Ian gently moved the mouse with his cast hand. At least he had his fingers free and he could click and type. He clicked on the Safari icon, and he was brought to Google by default. There was no point in researching "Owen." He'd have millions of hits.

The search word "Klemma" brought up over 200,000 hits—much better—but it still was ludicrous to attempt to scroll through, so he thought of adding another search word to narrow down his choices. Perhaps Klemma, too, was a city. He added "city" to his search word "Klemma," producing just over three thousand hits. The screen showed a number of people's names associated with cities. Klemma was most notably a person's name.

Ian researched the history of the name. The name was always female, a variant of the male name Clement. So why did an Asian man have the name Klemma? So odd. The first year it was a popular name—in the top 1000—was 1887, and it was the only year it was in the top thousand. Why use such an old name?

This was getting him nowhere, so he went back to Google to try "Navarre." Ian had never seen the name spelled, so did it have one R or two? He tried the single R first, and there wasn't a lot—a mere 22,000 hits—and listed were websites in different languages: Spanish, French, and something that said, "Zadnjih 10 komentara koje je napisao Navare." Whatever that meant. Again the FBI analysts had their hands full in sorting these names out.

Ian noticed Google asked, "Did you mean Navarre?" showing two Rs. He tried that. Now he had over three million hits. At the top of the list was Navarre Beach, Florida, which said was on the Gulf of Mexico. Texas was on the Gulf of Mexico, too. Was there a Zetta and Owen in a Gulf State, too? If so, what would that mean? It might be how they came up with the names, and nothing more. His head spun. No, he told himself. He believed the names had meaning.

"Klemma" bugged him anew. Why? There was something familiar about it. He remembered the Neil Simon play he almost liked, *Proposals*. It was far too sentimental, but that was Simon. Wasn't the main character named Klemma? He wasn't even sure that was the right play, so he typed the search words "Klemma Neil Simon," which did not bring up anything significant. How about "Clemma" with a C? He put in "Clemma Neil Simon" and that brought up, first thing, a *Washington Post* article about Neil Simon's Proposals and how he created the character of Clemma the maid, his first major black character.

If Clemma was a popular name for black women, Ian thought, why would an Asian man use it? Maybe Navarre, who seemed to be the intellectual of the gang, had seen the play. Where was the play playing?

Ian researched that next. It was appearing in many cities in America, many community theatres, in fact. He went through them. There was a big review for the production at the Old Log Theatre in Excelsior, Minnesota, by the *Minneapolis Star Tribune*. The reviewer, too, thought the play problematic. "While full of Simon's brand of comedy, it too often strains for humor, to the point of idiocy," wrote William Randall Beard. Ian had to concur.

Ian had never heard of Excelsior, Minnesota. He researched the theatre and discovered it was a 655-seat theatre—large and under Equity union auspices—and on "ten acres near the shores of historic Lake Minnetonka." He'd never heard of Lake Minnetonka either. There were great pictures online of the theatre. It looked like a fun place.

He went to Mapquest to give him a map of where the Old Log Theatre was. Up came a graphic showing the address to be between two bodies of water: St. Albans Bay and Excelsior Bay. That must be on historic Lake Minnetonka. Ian clicked on the appropriate button to get a more comprehensive view of the area. He then saw the names of two nearby towns: Navarre and Orono.

Ian felt extremely lightheaded, and he stood and paced the room. He remembered Navarre the woman had used the name "Orono" for Owen and now Orono and Navarre were towns on Lake Minnetonka. The FBI analysts couldn't make this connection because they didn't have this information.

He also remembered Navarre the woman had called "Owen" a "meany," words that were in the title of a John Irving book, *A Prayer for Owen Meany*, a book he'd read in an English class in college. What significance did this have, if any? Here were allusions to both a play and a book. Might Navarre be an English teacher? Maybe that was a stretch, but it simply made sense to him. English teachers liked using allusions the way kids love sprinklers. And perhaps the woman who called herself Navarre was from the area. Her accent seemed Canadian, but Minnesota was close to Canada. How did the name

Zetta fit into this? Ian scanned the names of the cities around Lake Minnetonka. There was no Zetta.

He researched the history of Lake Minnetonka. The lake came to be after the receding glaciers 11,000 years ago left chunks of ice that melted and became a lake with over twenty-two square miles of surface and 125 miles of lakeshore. The first people there were the Sioux, Cheyenne, Iowa, and Ojibwa. The lake was named Minnetonka after a Sioux name meaning "Big Water." All his research, however, showed no city of Zetta, which frustrated him. Even so, he was curious about this lake whose first Europeans were two fourteen-year-old boys, Joe Brown and Will Snelling, who had explored from Minnehaha Falls, up Minnehaha Creek, to the headwaters of the lake.

The biggest city on the lake, according to the map, looked to be Wayzata—a strange name. When he looked up Wayzata's history, he discovered the name derived from the American Indian word *Waziyata*, which had a mystical connotation to the Sioux, whose god, "Waziya," was their god of the North. "Wayzata," meant "North shore." Then Ian gasped again. The word was pronounced "Why-zetta." Zetta was part of the lake after all.

So here he had it: four names connected to the same area. He imagined Navarre coming up with them. Ian swung his good arm up in the air. Eureka!

He'd outdone the FBI lab. Ian gave a little dance, which wasn't much. "Yes! Yes! Yes!" He pounded the computer desk with his good hand to make sounds, too. Even though he didn't particularly like musical theatre, he nonetheless began to sing from *Oklahoma*. "Oh, what a beautiful mornin'. Oh what beautiful day! I got a beautiful feelin' everything's goin' my way."

That's when he noticed Medina standing in the door, staring at him as if his DNA helix had just snapped.

"The nap did you good, I see," she said. She held a big bag from Target.

"I got you two pairs of jeans, three knit shirts, a sweater, a few long-sleeve buttoned shirts in solid colors, socks, and two three-packs of Target brand boxers."

He never wore jeans. He liked khakis or pressed pants, but no matter, he knew in that very moment what he really needed: Medina herself. Yes, it might seem crazy. Yes, he knew she might not reciprocate ever, but he hoped she'd see he was right for her. They were going to find Owen and the others and slam them away, and what would they have when it was over? Each other. Medina was simply the one. She was the B in his BLT.

"What?" she said.

"What do you mean what?"

"You're looking at me oddly."

"I'm in awe you bought me clothes. Thank you! I should give you a hug."

"I don't need a hug."

"Sure you do. You're smiling."

"You're a talented guy, I'm learning. And I'm back on the case," she said, smiling more. "It may be for twenty minutes," she said, "but your idea of finding Wexler's vulnerability worked. Thank you."

He held out his arms, beaming. He stepped close, and they hugged. Yes!

"Oh, what a beautiful day!" he sang again.

"Please, you're breaking my ears. And why were you singing in the first place?"

"You gotta see this," he said and pulled her by the hand to the computer. He showed her everything he'd learned, and she listened, nodding often, getting more and more excited. "Impressive," she said a couple of times.

When he was done, he said, "The problem is there are more than a dozen towns around the lake, 125 miles of lakeshore, and, best I can tell, over a hundred thousand people live near it. If we include the greater Minneapolis and St. Paul area, that's millions of people. So it's not likely anyone would just run into Zetta or Navarre. So what do we do?"

"You did a great job."

"We should go there," he said.

"There's that we problem again. Now that I'm back on, Wexler or even Rick won't let you tag along. Then again, if Wexler doesn't assign the Minneapolis branch to do all the looking, he and his boss, Toffer, will otherwise push me out. This is like asking to be shoved off the case again. "

"Wouldn't your boss Rick help you?"

"Once I tell him about this, he'll have to tell Wexler. It's the protocol."

"So we have to tell?" he said.

She considered for a moment. "Worth considering," she said. She also told him about her interview with Bruce Worrell, a.k.a.

Crackerjack, which proved to be a dead end other than explaining Freddie a little more. He had nothing to help finding Owen.

She grabbed his clothes in a sweep of practicality. "Let's get you in a bathtub and dressed in something better. You smell like a whore house."

"That's not nice."

"I go with the truth. While you're bathing, I'll make dinner."

"And why a bath?" he said. "I like showers."

"I don't want you falling, and you have a cast on your arm that can't get wet. This is safer."

"I could use help getting in."

"You're fine," she said.

"I'm fine," he said back.

"What about your bandages on your leg? We have to change them. Let me look at those first."

He relented and pulled off his pants so that he was in his underwear. He sat on the edge of the bed.

With a short fingernail, she raised the white medical tape on his leg, then pulled fast.

"Yeow!"

She pulled four more pieces off. His bullet wound wasn't as bad as he'd expected: a round hole that looked like a crater on the moon, a few stitches on one side, and black-and-blue skin around it. Nothing festering. Same with the exit wound on the other side.

"Lookin' good," she said. "Let's have you sit in the tub and soak a little. Don't get your arm cast in the water, okay?"

"I'm fine," he repeated.

While he was in the tub, Medina flicked on the local TV news in the kitchen while she prepared dinner for them. She didn't have much, but she had a frozen chicken breast, some flour tortillas, lettuce and other fixings to make tacos. Her mother used to make this when time or ingredients were little. She realized she hadn't made dinner for a guy in a while. Was he *a guy*? No, not that way, but she was getting to like him.

While Medina shredded lettuce, on TV a young woman stood with a microphone in front of a wooded area. "We are here in Eaton Canyon, just north of South Pasadena where the Busty Bandit's henchman, code-named Owen by the police, started his bloody rampage."

"The police didn't name him," Medina said to the TV.

"The burned-out hulk of a Toyota pickup that Owen may have stolen was found here," said the newscaster, whose name, "Wendy Wedner," now appeared on screen. "Owen may be hiding out here in Eaton Canyon where there is the occasional cabin—and there are many suburban homes nearby. Police are going door-to-door, and the net is getting tighter." In the upper corner was Owen's masked face from the shootout at the bank.

"Good," said Medina, but as if seeing a chess game, she knew what Wexler would do next, and now she had information that he didn't have. She called Rick.

"I may be incommunicado for a couple of days before I return," she said. "I may be going on a trip."

"Related to the case?"

"You have to know, Rick, Wexler and Toffer are going to edge us out anyway, right?"

"Yes."

"So I'm in a gray area here. Let's just call these personal days. You've always helped me, and I think I can help us both."

"Am I going to have to disavow any knowledge of your actions? This tape will self-destruct in five seconds?"

"Something like that."

"I'm not a good disavower, so just be careful."

"I'll call when I can to see if you have anything more on Owen. Between you and the police, you'll get him, I just know it."

"Have a good vacation."

When Ian was dressed, they sat at her dining room table, but she'd used her better placemats, her less-chipped china, and sheets of paper towel for napkins.

"Impressive," said Ian sitting down.

She couldn't tell if he was being serious.

"First let's go over everything we know about Navarre," Medina said. "We know Navarre took her name from a Minnesota city by Lake Minnetonka." She wrote on a napkin with a pen the word, "Navarre," underlined it, and added a bullet underneath and the words "Lake Minnetonka."

"She seemed liberal to me, perhaps a Democrat, the way she talked about the rich and poor. It sounded like she was going to donate her share to a cause."

"What cause?"

"Owen suggested a gay community."

"So she's gay?"

"Maybe."

"You never told us this before."

"I didn't remember it."

She added a bullet and the word "Gay" with a question mark. "Was she Zetta's lover?"

Ian cringed. "God, I never thought of that. But no. Zetta's son was her motivation, and I sensed Navarre was helping her."

"Zetta's son?"

He'd explained how he'd overheard Zetta's declaration of love. "At first it sounded like Zetta had loved me—a love that, as she said, 'defied description, every heartbeat, every cell.' But that didn't make sense. I'd been selected as a hostage because I was convenient, not because she loved me. Then Owen told me the night he shot me that Zetta had a son. This whole bank robbing seems to be for her son."

Medina put down her pen. "You never told me this. Didn't you think it was important?"

"I only put it together recently."

"Robbing banks for her son doesn't make sense either. For what? To send him to a private school?"

"I don't know."

Medina picked up her pen again. "All right. Let's keep Zetta a separate issue for now. What more do you know about Navarre?"

He explained his English teacher theory and, sharply turning, added, "She might have had a bowel problem. Owen was mad at her for clogging up the toilet."

"The toilet was clogged when we got there. Maybe she doesn't eat enough fiber." She added "English teacher?" and "Low-fiber diet?" as bullet points.

"I don't know. Or it could've been a tampon."

"It was fecal matter. What else do you know? Was she reading a book, for instance?"

"A newspaper. She was reading a newspaper, which is why the money was wrapped in it." Ian pictured the newspaper as she had held it up—the color picture, a man's arms raised in victory, the very stance that brought Owen back to him. Ian shivered thinking of how brutal Owen had become. He wanted Owen, and to do so, they needed Navarre. "She liked sailing, I think. She said the boat was a twelve-meter boat, the one that won in a regatta."

"Did she use that word, 'regatta'?"

Ian nodded. "She tried to tell Owen about what it's like to sail. Navarre seemed to love sailing."

"Yes, yes, yes!" said Medina. "We've got her!"

"What?"

"If you loved sailing, lived on a lake, and got money—"

"She'd buy a boat?"

"Exactly. A nice big one."

"What should we do?"

"Want to go to Minnesota?" she said.

CHAPTER ELEVEN

As the plane circled in a holding pattern above Minneapolis/St. Paul, Ian stared downward from his window seat. The place looked like Winnipeg, his home town, which was odd because Winnipeg was smaller. Still, everything here looked heavily forested, as if houses and trees got along just fine. Many of the trees were bare, it being October. There were red- and orange-colored trees spattered like paint here and there and many evergreens. Water splashed the landscape, too, everything from small ponds with what had to be rowboats, to a connected series of lakes with sailboats near a downtown area. There were skyscrapers. Were they above Minneapolis or St. Paul? All he knew was that the Mississippi River separated the two. The plane swung around to the suburbs, straightened out, and slowly descended; a river appeared, rich with trees on both sides.

They'd taken an early flight out at 8:00 a.m. and would arrive just after two. While they had waited in the Delta lounge that Medina had access to—she was a frequent flier—she had sat herself at a desk and hammered away on her laptop, then made a few calls. She had returned with a smile on her face.

"I found a sailboat dealership in Wayzata who sold a C & C 99 yacht two days ago."

"They were open this early?"

"A two-hour difference there."

"Sold to whom?"

"A woman named Rebecca, who fits the description of Navarre."

"Do they have her address?"

"He's looking for the paperwork. She paid cash."

This had to be Navarre. "How do we find her?"

"The dealer knows where it's docked—with him still. It'll be our first stop," she had said.

Now Medina glanced out the window and said, "Pretty. I like the changing leaves."

Ian looked at her and thought pretty too. She was so relaxed—gorgeous, even. He wished he could tell her how much she meant to him.

She returned to the airline magazine that seemed to captivate her most of the flight. She'd been in fact rereading an article, underlining sentences. This woman took her reading seriously.

"A good article?" he asked.

"Yes, about the history of Minneapolis, but it mentions Lake Minnetonka. It became the playground for the rich mill owners in the first part of the twentieth century, but anyone with a little money built summer cabins around it."

He moved slightly closer to look. There was a photo of grain elevators, now the Mill City Museum of Minneapolis, with a neon sign on top that said, "Gold Medal Flour." He said, "By the way, you have a strange doll body above your kitchen sink, her head dangling on a gold chain."

"That's a non-sequitur." She seemed to consider what he said, however. "You're talking about Columbina."

He clapped his hands. "That's why she's familiar. She's that character in commedia dell'arte—the often-very-smart character."

She nodded. "Yep. I had a great history-of-theatre class at UCLA."

"Columbina was often the only functioning intellect on stage. Interesting you chose her."

"Are you trying to analyze me?"

He smiled. "She's beautiful. Like you. Where'd you get her?"

She looked at him anew. "A little shop in Rome."

"A honeymoon?"

She cranked around in her seat. "What are you getting at?"

"I mean, I couldn't help looking at all your cool stuff on that mantle, and I happened to open a little treasure box."

"You had no right!"

"It was right there and so beautiful, so I opened it. I saw your engagement ring. I'm sorry… So you didn't marry?"

She turned away from him to get back to her article, but by the way she blinked her eyes, she wasn't reading it. "This has nothing to do with our investigation," she said, "and I prefer not to talk about it. This is not why we're here." She looked at him again. "You got me?"

I wish I had you, he thought. He smiled, but she only shook her head.

"Okay," he said.

"Besides, we're landing."

They were approaching the ground. Ian gripped his armrests the way barnacles held ship hulls. He hated this part. He held his breath, imagining the wheels locking up, the plane's nose-diving into the ground, the plane swinging sideways until it fell off the runway and burst into a ball of flame.

"You okay?" asked Medina.

Gritting his teeth, he nodded. They passed over a freeway, the trees came closer, and, at the last second, the ground leapt up and touched the wheels. The plane rolled quickly and easily down the runway, slowing down.

"Toothpaste," said Ian. "I hope I remembered my toothpaste."

After they collected their bags, Medina patiently walked with him as he limped toward the shuttle train that would take them to the rental cars. She'd reserved something at Hertz.

"You're getting better with that cane," she said.

"I'm good at things," he said. "Maybe I'll become Bat Masterson."

"Who's that?"

"A marshall and gambler in the Wild West who used his cane to good advantage."

"That's you? A wild guy who spends his money recklessly and pulls in crooks?"

"Yes, someone who gets his man. Or woman."

"The Busty Bandit?"

He let it hang.

Their car was ready on the third floor of a parking structure. The air was crisp as they followed the stall numbers for their rental. Glad he wore a sweater, Ian said, "So what did you get?"

"Guess."

"A Crown Vic, the kind police use."

"You really don't know me." She pointed to a silver Volvo C70 coupe, a sporty car.

On the way, Medina clicked on the radio and found the NPR station. Terry Gross of "Fresh Air" was interviewing an author.

"Can't you find a classic rock station?" Ian asked.

"You like elevator music?" she said.

"Oh, and National Public Radio is better?"

"Of course it's better."

"Don't you like the Who?"

"Teenage wasteland."

"How about Joni Mitchell?" he said.

"I've had enough with clouds," she said. "It's NPR."

She kept it on the talk station. It was her car.

They took Interstate 494 from the airport, and about twenty minutes later, following the screen of her GPS unit that came with the car, they took exit 19B for Wayzata. The areas on either side of the freeway had a lot of trees broken by a car dealership, a nursing home, a diner, a bait shop. As they went down a hill, he saw the lake, a large expanse of blue surrounded by trees.

Downtown Wayzata was a mere seven blocks long. Its tallest building was two stories, yet this wasn't some dinky little farm or logging town as Ian was used to in Canada. Wayzata's main street, called Lake Street, had bright lighting on quaint, old-fashioned poles. For a few blocks, there were trendy shops and restaurants on both sides of the street, suggesting this was a small, rich community, and the blue bay opened up to their left, leaving only one side of the street with stores.

The lake didn't have water skiers, as Ian imagined it would have in the summer. It was October, and the water had to be cold, but there were three sets of white sails—sailboats—out on the water.

"A cute little train station," said Medina. To her left, near lakeside, stood a white wooden train station the size of a cottage.

"I'm from a town like this—Winnipeg."

"And I'm not. I grew up mostly in apartments in Latino L.A. Not a whitebread place like this."

"None of us get to choose where we're born."

"I've had to fight for everything I've wanted."

"And I'm fighting now."

It was her turn to let it hang.

Lake Street veered left, but the semaphores were down and blinking red, and a train blasted its horn. Soon a train with forty-nine cars—he counted—kept them from moving. Finally, the last car came, a red light on the back. The semaphores lifted, and they crossed railroad tracks. Ian thought about how the last car of a train used to be the caboose, where the brakeman and conductor rode, but those jobs weren't needed anymore—all electronics now. More and more, he thought, electronics were taking over. Would there eventually be robots doing live theatre? No. While electronics were certainly used in the booth—each lighting and music transition preset, and the sounds and music were all digital—the stage was all human. And people would still kill each other and rob banks, so Medina's job would be around. There was change, and there was no change.

The road became Shoreline Drive, but there was no shore, just swamp on either side of the road, plus the railroad tracks.

"Nice little houses," said Medina, and she pointed. The swamps had given way to residences. A mansion stood on a carpet of lawn that stretched to a tennis court and then a covered dock on the shore. Soon they crossed an isthmus, where the lake was on either side of them. Connected to either side of the isthmus were long docks holding many expensive boats. It looked like Millionaires' Acres.

"More upscale than Winnipeg," he said.

"The shop should be coming up soon," said Medina, looking at the screen of her GPS.

Sure enough, after they passed two more mansions, one with an old-fashioned windmill, they approached a large parking lot whose sign said "Sailors World Marina & Boat Club." The office was in a light-colored two-story structure, which looked like another house, not quite a mansion.

They parked in the lot and stepped out. As Ian hobbled toward the building, a man was locking the front door, his dark briefcase at his feet.

"Are you Mr. Woodrup?" Medina called out.

The man, tall in white pants and a yellow short-sleeve shirt, looked underdressed for the cool night air. Ian imagined the place was like Canada, getting ready for what would soon be a leafless, white, and frozen winter. The man turned with a big used-car smile. "Are you the Smiths? For the thirty-six-foot Catalina?"

"No. I called you from Los Angeles. Aleece Medina with the FBI."

"Oh. I left you a voice message earlier."

"About what?"

"The boat's been picked up." He looked at Ian curiously, noticing the cane and cast. "Hazard of the job?" asked the man.

"You might say that," said Ian. "That was stolen money your boat buyer used," Ian said. "I think we can seize the funds, can't we, Special Agent Medina?"

Medina looked at him.

"Yes," Ian said for her. "Unless you can help us locate this boat."

"I have no idea," Woodrup said louder. "For all I know, she hauled it to another lake—over eleven thousand lakes in Minnesota, you know. Plus Lake Superior up north is as huge as an ocean."

"But she bought it here," said Medina. "My guess is she lives around here." Medina had what seemed to be an eight-by-ten photo, and she showed it to the man. Ian leaned in to see. It wasn't a photo but a sketch based on his description of a skinny woman with long hair and red fingernails with roses, and wearing a dress. It was from an elevated point of view—probably because it was also based on a bank robbery photo from a security camera.

"That's her, and she was new to me. Lots of rich folks live around this lake," said the man. "The C & C is a cruiser, meant for, you know, cruising the islands, Puerto Rico to Aruba kind of thing."

He unlocked the door, and they stepped inside, where he flicked on the lights. It could have been a travel agent's office except the posters on the walls were all of sailboats, tumescent with wind-filled sails. One poster showed people in down jackets and the words "Big Island Frostbite Regatta." Mr. Woodrup found a sales brochure of the boat in a file in his desk.

"Don't you have to have a lot of paperwork on this kind of sale— for the IRS? Her social security number?" said Medina.

"It wasn't a new boat, but used, and I had it far too long takin' up space. I sold it for under ten thousand," said Mr. Woodrup. "Should I be calling my lawyer?"

"How might we find this boat or woman?" said Ian.

Medina glared at Ian. He wanted to give an eyebrow lift that said, "Go with me on this. It's called acting." Even though he had several questions, Ian realized he'd better back off. She's the boss.

"What paperwork do you have?" she said. He opened a drawer, found the folder, and pulled from it a bill of sale. Medina scanned it and then said, "Rebecca du Maurier? Twelve Manderly Drive, New Hope, Minnesota?"

"Seems like a good name."

"Fake. An allusion to a novel."

"New Hope's real at least."

"What about the towing company? Maybe we can find the boat that way," Medina said. "Companies must specialize in moving big boats."

"It was just a guy with a brown pickup and a trailer. Never saw him before. I didn't chat with him because I had other customers. I'm sorry. I didn't expect I was supposed to grill him. You're the experts," said Mr. Woodrup. The man only took one of her looks before he said, "Start asking in the spring, assuming she starts sailing it on this lake. People will notice. Then again, maybe she took it elsewhere. There's a lot of water on Earth."

Ian's heart sank.

Mr. Woodrup handed Ian the brochure, then shut his desk and regrabbed his briefcase. He gestured toward the front door. They all walked out, leaving Mr. Woodrup to lock his door.

Walking toward their car, Medina said to Ian, "What the fuck were you doing back there?"

"Helping,"Ian said. "So what do we do now? Or are we just, as you might say, fucked? Do we call it a day?" The anger whooshed through him. He'd trusted Medina's style, and look where it got them.

Medina glanced over to Mr. Woodrup, who was headed for a dark new VW Beetle. "Thanks again," Medina shouted to him.

"Sorry about the bad news," said Mr. Woodrup. "I guess you don't have one of those FBI crystal balls, eh?"

"I wish we did," Medina said. "I'd love to know where she'd be tomorrow."

"Tomorrow?" he said coming close to them. "Tomorrow?"

Ian glanced at Medina.

"I forgot," said Mr. Woodrup, "but there's the year-end Big Island Frostbite race tomorrow. Maybe she'll be in that—the biggest race of the year."

"What time's it start?" asked Ian, surprised, wondering how the man forgot the biggest race of the year.

"Nine, I think. At Big Island. Hey, I just sell these things, I don't sail 'em."

"Hold it," said Medina. "If her boat's a cruiser and large, it's not a racing boat. Why would it be in a race?"

"For fun. It's open-class sailing. If you have a slower boat, such as the C & C, you get time shaved off your score."

"How do we get to Big Island?" said Medina. "Is there a bridge?"

"You have to boat there," said the man. "And I have no rental boats."

"Where could we rent one?" asked Medina. "Any boat."

"Boats N' Breezes might still be open this time of year. Course it's closed now, but it'll open in the morning. Go farther down this road. Veer right onto North Shore Drive. You're heading toward Orono."

Ian nodded, realizing the irony of that statement and, he hoped, the truth. Where was Owen/Orono now? Suffering, he hoped. "Will we recognize the C & C 99 because it's big?"

"Easier still," Woodrup said, "she has numbers on her sails. Huge numbers: 2254."

"Thanks," said Medina, whose look suggested to Ian that things were falling into place.

Ian grinned, happy again, but as he looked at Medina more close-ly as she opened the car door, her face showed no more sign of emotion. She could be like a poker player when she wanted to, keeping him wondering how she thought.

CHAPTER TWELVE

Seated in the hotel tub with the shower on, Medina shaved her legs with a man's disposable razor. They had been cheaper than the pink ones. Would today's findings lead anywhere? Think this through, she told herself. The boat was sold to a woman of Navarre's description with the pseudonym Rebecca du Maurier. She probably lived near the lake but not likely on the lake; otherwise she would have taken the boat immediately after she bought it. She may or may not be in the race in the morning. If not, what was the next step?

She dialed the water to be a touch hotter.

She wondered if satellite photos of the area might show a big boat standing in a lot. Then again, there were so many trees in the area, a big boat on a trailer could be easily obscured. Plus she really wasn't officially working. She didn't have the FBI resources at hand.

She stood, rinsed her legs, and thought of how Ian had pretended to be an FBI agent so adeptly. He didn't actually show a badge or anything so it's not as if he was impersonating outright. He's in theatre, after all. For him, it was probably an exercise. Technically she wasn't an agent there, either—not on the clock—so she was pretending, too. They pretended together.

She knew what was on his mind. What if he knocked on her bedroom door one night—would she let him in? Being honest, she realized she might. She could use a little comforting, and Ian wasn't the usual guy. He could be sensitive. Of course, he could also be clueless like most guys, but he wasn't bad. She felt good with him. That wasn't something she'd felt in a while with a man.

As she turned off the shower, she heard the room phone ringing. Who knew her here besides Ian? She walked quickly for the phone, drying herself with a towel on the way. She sat on the bed and answered, "Hello?"

"It's me," said Ian.

"Hi." She glanced in the mirror and saw her hair over one shoulder, her posture straight, the towel in her lap, her breasts free. If she'd been more concerned with fashion, she might show them off—an asset. With her free arm, she grabbed her opposite shoulder, giving her a sense of cover. In the mirror, though, she looked silly and let go.

"Have you figured out how to set your clock radio?" he said. "Is the switch in the front supposed to be on Auto or on On?"

"I haven't looked yet. I always have the front desk give me a wake-up call."

"Hotels still have that?"

"Yep. Is that it?"

"Why? Are you busy?"

"Is something on your mind?"

"You mean related to the investigation?"

Even though she was the one to suggest it was the end of the conversation, she realized she should give the guy a break. He seemed to want to talk. "Find anything good on TV?"

"One of my favorite filmed plays, *Wit* with Emma Thompson is on, but I've seen it a few times."

"What other plays do you like?"

"Lots. Offhand, *Copenhagen* by Michael Frayn. *Noises Off* by Michael Frayn, which is the world's funniest play. *Skylight* by David Hare."

"Any female playwrights?"

"*How I Learned to Drive* by Paula Vogel, *Wit* is by Margaret Edson. Let's see, others?"

"*Wit*. I think I've seen *Wit*. What was it about?"

"A woman professor with late-stage Ovarian cancer. She's a John Donne scholar and says in the beginning, 'It is not my intention to give away the plot, but I think I die at the end. They've given me less than two hours.' And in those two hours, you hear her incredible life and dealing with disease. Who'd ever expect to laugh about ovarian cancer?"

"I did see the film version. Emma Thompson," she said. "The woman dying is still relatively young, and so she questions whether she's made the right choices.

"Yes," he said. "I often wonder if I've made the right choices."

She said nothing at first, then, "What do you mean?"

"Haven't you questioned whether going into the FBI was the right thing?"

"Nope."

"Even with Wexler?"

"Even with a handful of assholes like him."

"It seems like once you're on a path, you can't stop. I like my path," he said, "but when I'm dying on my bed like her, will I find I made a difference?"

"Before then, you're wondering what's on TV and will it make you laugh."

"Ha! I like your sense of humor, Aleece."

"Thanks."

"You want to walk or get out and do something?"

How fun it'd be to do something more tonight. But what kind of message would that send? "I don't think so," she said.

"Oh?"

"I'd better say good night."

There was silence, then he said, "Sleep well." He hung up.

She turned to the wall that separated them as if she could see through it. She liked his oddness. Except nothing could happen. If there was one thing she'd learned in being an agent, it was that the big problems people got themselves into were often because of acting on desire, pushing forward without pause. She hadn't paused in college with her volleyball coach, a married man. She would never do something so stupid again.

Goodnight Ian. Another lifetime.

Later, dressed in a long white T-shirt that said Knott's Berry Farm, she looked at the clock radio next to her bed. 9:37. That meant it was 7:37 in Los Angeles. She dialed Rick's cell phone.

"Aleece, what's up?" he said, answering in a near whisper.

"Are you asleep or on a stakeout?" she asked.

"The latter," he said.

"I'm in Minnesota."

"Doing what?"

"Vacation, remember?"

"That's right. Too bad you're not here. We're watching Metro station at Sixth and Alvarado, near where we think Owen lives. It's a long shot, I realize, but I want to do something before Wexler's group gets up to speed. It'd still be great if we solved it."

He was really saying that he was doing everything he could to win this for her. Still, she didn't want to tell him what she was doing, even if she was feeling guilty about it.

"A big guy like that should stick out among the masses," Rick continued. "We might be able to find Owen."

"I hope it works," she said, remembering what she wanted to ask. "That fecal matter found at the house. Any results?"

"Nothing that can help us now—why?"

"It might give us clues about Navarre. It's done on *CSI* all the time. Like, say, a certain mosquito found in the fecal matter that comes from a certain bay in Lake Minnetonka."

"All we know is the fecal matter belonged to a person who liked corn, but not a lot of other roughage—a meat eater. DNA from the embedded human cells showed it was from a male, not from Navarre as you thought, and it doesn't match Freddie's DNA, so it has to be Owen's."

"Oh," she said, though a bit disappointed it wouldn't help her with Navarre. "I may be here through the weekend, but I should be in mid-Monday."

"You'll tell me the moment you're back—or if you have something?"

"Yes," she said, and she liked his implied consent. There weren't many guys like him.

CHAPTER THIRTEEN

The radio blasted on, playing the news on National Public Radio. "Twenty-three have been killed in a massive pileup on an Interstate in Tennessee. Freezing rain and fog brought driving conditions—" Ian whapped it off with his good hand. Hadn't he set it for a regular buzzing alarm? The radio was a surprise. So was the news. Nothing worse than waking up to death.

He was able to dress himself more easily now, even if he still needed his cane. He could bend better. His side was particularly sore this morning—must have slept on the broken rib.

At breakfast, Medina and Ian said little—not that he was mad at her, but he was not a morning person, and he needed more energy to be charming. Her hair was in a ponytail, and she wore her pink Pink Iron sweats and had matching running shoes. He'd never considered her as a person in pink.

"What?" she barked at him.

"Did you get hijacked to a Barbie Store or something?"

"I like my gym. Did you bring the sweater I bought you?" she asked. "We're going to be on open water."

"It's up in my room," he said, "but I'll be warm enough."

"Right," she said. "If it weren't for women on this planet, guys would probably be extinct by now."

"It's not that bad. I anticipated. I'm wearing two shirts," he said. His dark button-down long-sleeved shirt fit over yesterday's shirt.

"Get your sweater."

"Okay already."

Later as they walked out into the parking lot, the sun rose, a half ball in a watercolor wash of orange. He glanced at his watch. It was seven sixteen. The sun was ascending exactly when scheduled, and this simple fact outweighed the earlier news of the cars piling up in Tennessee. If people didn't believe in destiny, here's one case of it.

"You think we'll be able to rent a boat?" he asked.

"Renting on the day of the race isn't likely, but I'll take a canoe, even. There has to be a boat somewhere."

"Maybe I don't understand what we're doing. How're we going

to arrest anyone in a canoe? Do we yell out, 'Slow down, we have to paddle'?"

"The island's far off-shore. We have to get close enough to see the boats and racers, even with the binoculars I have." She patted the blue purse around her shoulder. "If and when we see Navarre is there and figure the logistics, I can call for assistance."

"Did you call the boat rental company?"

"I just got a message. Said it opened at eight."

"So we'll have to wait."

"I'm good at that," she said.

They were a half hour early, yet people were already at the docks preparing their sailboats—some scrubbing the decks and others stringing their sails. It wasn't clear who was in charge because nobody was in the office, even though the door was unlocked.

"Anyone wearing a nametag?" said Ian.

"That would be nice, wouldn't it?" said Medina, and she gestured toward the docks. They walked onto the two-plank moorings, the sun low and sparkling off the water like billions of diamonds. Lately he had an itch under his cast, but he knew he wasn't supposed to stick a pen or anything under it to scratch it. The breeze was strong and very cool, however, and even with the sweater, Ian wrapped his one good arm around himself. It must have been below fifty degrees. Even in Winnipeg, he often underestimated how warmly he should dress. Stupid.

Ian noticed a teenage boy in a blue windbreaker and jeans gesturing to two people, an older couple, in a small sailboat. As he and Medina stepped closer, the boy told the couple, "You need to be wearing your life vests at all times. It'll be wavy out there today."

The man pulled hard on the strap of his wife's orange vest. "Okay?" said the man.

"Good luck to you," said the boy, who now turned as he saw Medina and Ian. "Can I help you?" he said.

"Any boats to rent?" Medina replied.

"It's a busy day, what with the Frostbite race," said the boy.

"We don't need a sailboat, but a motorboat."

"Like a Whaler? We're out of everything. People like to watch the race, too. Maybe I have a small pontoon boat. I think one cancelled."

"Can you check?" said Ian.

"Yeah, sure." The boy looked at Ian again. "Sports accident?" asked the boy, pointing to his cast.

"If beer bonging is a sport," said Ian with a grin.

The boy seemed extra impressed now and stepped forward, but then he saw something happening at the end of the dock with another boat and stepped toward it. "By the way, my name's Mark," said the boy. "You're going to have to wait until I get these boats off. I'm the only one here."

After a half-hour of sitting at a wooden picnic table on the grassy bank of the shore, Ian said, "Maybe he forgot us."

"It's after eight." She stood and Ian followed. They found Mark helping insert sails into a boom.

"Any other boat rental places around?" said Medina.

"Not this time of year," he said. "Give me a few more minutes, and I can help. Really." Mark looked like he cared.

"Okay," said Medina.

Minutes later they were in the office. Mark looked over a chart on the wall. "I do have that small pontoon boat. Want it?"

"One of those square things?" said Ian.

"It floats," she said. "We'll take it."

"The pontoon boat is this way," he said, taking them out the side door to the docks.

Tethered at dock's end, past a number of large cruisers and sailboats still there, bobbed a floating toy block of a boat, a rectangle that featured padded white fencing as if to keep a toddler from falling into the water. At the rear was a pilot's seat with a steering wheel, and behind that, attached to the rear, was a small outboard motor. There were a couple of other molded plastic chairs on the boat, too, a few in the rear, one at the front. Mark jumped casually onto the boat, and the boat rocked like a see-saw. Once on, he reached out his hand to Ian. "Give me your hand," he said. Ian let the boy help him. Medina then jumped on, and Mark took them across the blue non-skid plastic surface to the rear. He pointed to the outboard engine. "You know how to start this?"

They shook their heads. The boy then showed them how to prime the engine by squeezing the bulb on the rubber line that connected the square red gas can to the engine. He pulled the engine's cord just as on a lawn mower, and the motor sputtered to life. Ian nodded, having mowed plenty of lawns in Canada as a kid.

"You guys have caps?" Mark asked.

"Caps?" said Medina.

"Baseball caps. There's not a lot of protection from the sun, just this little awning," he said, batting the square of blue material on thin aluminum poles over the pilot's seat.

"We don't have caps," said Ian.

"I can sell you a couple," said Mark, pulling two out of his bag, embroidered with the company's logo. "Twenty each—I can put it on the bill."

"All right," said Medina.

"You want to buy a tank of gas or will you refill it before you get back?"

"We'll take a tank," said Medina. "Put it on the bill."

"And how about a map of the lake?"

Medina's mouth dropped. "Are you going to sell us the pontoons separately, too?"

"I'm just trying to be helpful," said the boy, looking hurt.

"Yes, we'll take a map," said Medina. "Where's Big Island?"

"If that's the only place you're going, then, heck, the directions are easy. We're in Crystal Bay, and you have to go off to our left, that way." He pointed out across the blue water. There were just trees—no island or any bigger part of the lake.

"Trust me," said the boy. "When you go down that way, you'll see a bridge, and you go under the bridge into the next bay. Keep going straight."

The boy then held up the map. He pointed at something the shape of a giraffe bending over. "This is Big Island. You go around this hammerhead here and swing around. The race'll start here." He pointed to a bay.

"Can I buy a windbreaker?" said Medina. "This guy forgot to bring one."

"I have my shirts and sweater," said Ian.

"We don't sell windbreakers," said the boy.

"How about yours?" said Medina. "Thirty bucks cash."

"This old thing?" he said. He quickly took it off. Medina handed him the money.

"Can you shove us off, too?" she asked the boy. "I can't both shove and drive."

"Do you mean pilot?" asked Ian. "Have you ever done this before?"

"What talent do you need to point straight ahead?"

"I know boats. You can push us off, and I'll sit at the helm," he said.

"I'm paying for the thing. Can't I drive?"

He said nothing.

"You're getting mad?"

"No, you bought me the windbreaker," said Ian.

"We only go five miles an hour, right?"

"No, no, by all means, you drive."

"I can't believe you're getting upset."

Medina turned to the boy who shrugged his shoulders as if he were witness to many arguments, and he didn't want to get involved. He shoved them off and said, "Good luck. Should be a nice day."

"Thanks," said Medina.

Ian shook his head. He should be like the boy. Stay neutral. He caught Medina staring at him. "Just because I have the expertise with boats? Drive already." Under his breath, he added, "What the fuck."

"You're back to channeling David Mamet."

"Better than channeling J. Edgar Hoover."

"I'm driving," she said, and she set the engine into gear and pulled the throttle to full until the engine sounded like very loud bees. The boat, despite the engine noise, only gently pushed ahead.

Ian shook his head again and sat on the chair up front so he wouldn't have to be near her.

Soon, with the lapping of the small waves against the flat front, the sun on his face, and the fresh pine smell on the wind, Ian rather liked the lake. To one side, a huge mansion stood, perhaps that of a billionaire, just off a beach. The houses around here were something. Then he realized the sweeping green lawn in the front was a golf course, so the place had to be a country club. Its stately main building was the kind he only imagined on the East Coast.

A bridge came up—plenty of room for their boat. Medina ably steered and looked happy doing so. She grinned. He nodded his approval.

Once they went beyond the bridge, the lake was much larger, with waves that had white caps. The boat bobbed more. The wind made him cold. If Medina hadn't bought him the windbreaker, he imagined he'd be frozen. He figured he was Canadian, though—he'd been through worse.

Another twenty minutes, they were coming around what had to be the far end of Big Island. From the water, it was just all trees with a small gravely shore.

Further around the bend, in the distance, a congregation of sails appeared like a small flurry of paper airplanes against green. "Boss, de plane, de plane," said Ian, eagerly standing. He turned to look back at Medina, catching her smile.

They were similar in a way. In fact, as he scanned her shaded face, the wind gently rocked her ponytail. Gorgeous.

"What?" she asked.

"What?" he said back.

"It looked like you were going to say something."

"Really?" He moved his chair closer to her. "I suppose it was a fleeting thought. It fleeted." A horn blast came from across the lake, and they looked for the source.

She reached into her purse and pulled out a compact pair of binoculars, brushing aside a pair of handcuffs.

"You come prepared," he said, "A purse like no other. Might make for a fun weekend in Vegas."

"Anyone ever tell you you're odd?" She raised her binoculars to look.

"What do you see?" he asked. As she silently stared, he heard another horn blast from the direction of the sailboats. She said nothing but handed him the binoculars. The bobbing of their boat made it hard to see well. Everything went up and down, including a large buoy with a flag. Nearby was a motorboat with another flag. That must be the starting line, and the sailboats were all behind it, aimed in various directions. In less than a minute, another horn blast could be heard. The sailboats were trying to align themselves in the direction of the starting line. Ian surmised the horn blasts must be the countdown to the start. On one small boat nearest the starting line, he could see wild gesturing by the man at the tiller. The captain was probably shouting to slow down. By the time there was what sounded to be a shotgun blast, the boats were all facing the starting line. Two in front were the first over. They must have raced a lot to be right there.

"Can you see the sail numbers?" Medina asked.

It was hard to be steady enough to see. He handed the binoculars back to her. "Once we get closer, maybe it'll be easier."

The pontoon boat at that moment went up and down, and a wave crashed over the bow, spraying him. It felt cold on his face, but at least he had the jacket.

The boats were partially headed toward them but aiming to their right side. Ian noticed one boat was larger than the others. "May I have the binoculars?" he said. Medina handed them to him. While it was harder than ever to keep the binoculars steady, Ian could read the sail numbers. Two two five four—there it was. Ian was sure that the long-haired woman at the tiller, white fleece pants and a blue zippered and high-collared fleece jacket, looking boldly ahead, was Navarre. She appeared much more fashionable than he remembered her. She looked better. An older short-gray-haired woman sat next to her—an aunt?

Ian felt elated, and said, "I see her. We got her!" He now examined the crew members, four large men in gray sweats, the kind of guys who looked like an ad for the Mafia—big guys. Their combined muscle and weight could probably turn an oak tree into toothpicks. They looked like a lot of muscle for Medina and him to take on. Medina did have a gun, didn't she? He hadn't seen sight of her gun on this trip. Maybe she couldn't get it on the plane without declaring it and making their journey an official mission. "Look on the windward side of the boat, the upside," he said. Ian returned the binoculars to her.

She looked and grimaced. "Shit," she said. "Sailors haven't been that big since the Bounty."

"So what do we do? Do you know karate?"

She frowned.

"You went to FBI boot camp, right?" he said.

"Yes, where we were given a most powerful tool. She reached inside the pocket of her sweatshirt where she pulled out a gun. She had one after all. Then she pulled out her smart phone. She started typing on it, then nodding, then dialing some numbers.

"Are you calling your boss in L.A.?"

"It's too early there," she said and put the phone to her ear.

"Yes, is the chief in? It's Aleece Medina from the FBI." As she waited, she said to Ian, "I've learned to go to the top. It's the Wayzata police."

"Hi, Chief. You don't know me, but I'm Aleece Medina, special agent with the FBI, L.A. Division, West Covina R.A. I can give you my credential number in a minute. I'm here in Wayzata technically on leave, but I've run into a suspect that I need help with. I'm looking to make a warrantless arrest with probable cause, out here on the lake."

She listened, nodded, then said. "Ah, the sheriff." She turned to Ian. "He's connecting me with the sheriff's office." In a moment, she gave her basic information again and what she needed.

Ian watched, impressed with how sure and calm she looked and speaking her jargon. He wished he were writing some of this down. It'd be good for a play someday if he ever decided to write. Whatever sense he had earlier that he could do what Medina did, he now realized how he was deficient. Movies especially made it seem that the lone professional took on a squad of monsters, and between accurate punches and sharp shooting, one person could do it all alone. The reality was she knew how to call and get action.

Medina gave her credential number, adding, "You will? Thanks…. Yes. My SSA is Rick Okinawa." She went on to explain the fact that the suspect was in a sailboat race. She turned, looked behind her, and nodded. "Yes, I see it. Lakeside Yacht Club." She was looking at what appeared to be a white house, a pavilion, really, on a tiny island, surrounded by boats tethered to a freshly mowed lawn—at least that's what it seemed from Ian's seat.

"Wonderful, wonderful," she said. "I'll call you back in a few minutes, once I've talked to some officials here. Thanks." She put the phone in her pocket.

"I'm getting sheriff's cars and a boat. We'll be okay."

Medina looked again through the binoculars toward the starting line. "Let's talk to the officials there." She steered a course toward the starting line boat. One of three men in the boat held up a bullhorn and said, "Please move away. This is a boat race, and you are interfering."

"There are no boats we're interfering with yet," said Medina. "They'll see our business in a sec," and she kept heading toward them.

The man in the bullhorn repeated, "Please move away."

"No!" shouted Ian as loud as he could. "We have an emergency!"

"That's the spirit," said Medina. He looked back to see if she was being sarcastic, but she was giving him a thumbs up. As they pushed closer to the boat, Medina said, "Take over driving, will you? I'll be at the front to talk with them."

Ian moved quickly to the helm, pleased. Perhaps she understood that boats didn't behave like cars. There were no brakes. Using a boat meant knowing when to reverse the motor in advance.

The men in the speedboat stared at them. They all were older, dressed in white shorts and blue windbreakers that said Lakeside Yacht Club. When they were about ten feet away, one of the men, the one with the bullhorn still in his hand, said, "Emergency?"

Medina had her wallet out, showing her ID card. "FBI, sir."

"What do you want with us?"

"We need a person on the C & C 99, sail numbers two two five four."

Ian brought them in so gently, the boats only kissed. One of the men reached out and held their boat.

"It'll be a couple of hours until they're back here," said the official at the steering wheel. "Which person?"

"The one at the tiller right now," said Ian.

"Dottie?" the three men said in unison.

"You sound amazed," said Medina.

"Everyone loves her," one official said. "She's not in trouble, is she?"

"Just need her for help on a case."

"She's a good helper," said one of the others. "A professor, you know."

"What kind of case?" added the last.

"An incident in Los Angeles. What's Dottie's full name?" asked Medina.

The one with the bullhorn looked puzzled. "You don't know?"

"I have my reasons for asking," she said.

"Darlene Lundberg—don't know a middle name."

"Okay," said Medina.

Ian nodded, impressed how little information Medina gave out while she took in much more.

"She gives great parties," said the man with the bullhorn, "to help us on our fund drive. I'm still not clear why the FBI—"

"She may have witnessed something," said Medina.

"Did she even go to Los Angeles?" said the man at the wheel. "I don't know that she travels much."

"Well then, she can clear up a few things," said Medina. "A sheriff's boat is supposed to meet me at your clubhouse," said Medina.

The third man, the one who was the tallest and had the grayest hair, jumped on their pontoon boat and directed them toward the clubhouse, away from Big Island. "I'm the Commodore," he said, shaking Medina's hand.

"How soon until the first boats cross the finish line?" she asked.

"Over an hour," he said.

During the slow journey over, Medina phoned the Sheriff's department back and updated them.

As they skimmed closer to the clubhouse, the white pavilion house came into view. It had a bell tower—or was it a lighthouse?—and a second-story deck that held outdoor furniture and Webber grills. The place was a mini-mansion and stood on a small, separate island that was about three hundred yards from shore. A sign over the grand front door said, "Lakeside Yacht Club." The island had no shore, but, rather, a concrete wall that allowed boats to float right at its side. Tethered to the island, which had a perfectly mowed lawn and no trees, were small boats, most of them sailboats. The man directed them to an open spot. They tied the boat up and jumped onto the island.

"We'll watch from the lawn until the time comes," said the Commodore. He had a larger pair of binoculars, and from the steadiness of the shore, Ian could see the race much more clearly than before. They sat, as it was going to be a while.

Twenty minutes later, a white cigarette-shaped boat sped toward them, its huge outboard spitting a large white wake. As the craft buzzed closer, the word "Sheriff" became visible on its side. Two uniformed officers in dark pants, tan shirts, and blue caps stood and tied their boat to shore. Medina ran toward them and Ian followed. She turned and said, "I'm sorry, Ian, but I need you to stay with the Commodore."

He was disappointed but understood.

Less than an hour after that, the Commodore stood. "Here comes the A-class," he said, and rounding the bend were sleek, long boats, close to the water, with six-man crews that moved in unison from one side of the boat to the other as the sail shifted at the turn. Three boats were very close to each other, and Ian watched how the crews worked in tight precision. As one of the boats crossed the finish line first, the Commodore shouted, "Hurray, Bullworth!" He turned to Ian, "I taught that kid everything I know. Well, he's not a kid anymore but one of the great surgeons of Wayzata."

"How soon should Dottie's boat come around?"

"Soon."

What happened next was a silent movie seen through the Commodore's binoculars. Dottie's boat rounded the corner, and all on board looked gleeful. The older woman next to Dottie, ecstatic, leaned over and kissed Dottie long and hard. Dottie's partner? Everyone on board raised his or her fists in celebration.

The boat crossed the line, and once it was clear of other boats, the sheriff's boat sped in quickly. Ian thought it all so anticlimactic—no one jumped off the boat, no one shouted in panic, and no guns came out. The large men simply looked at each other, puzzled. Everyone on board nodded to whatever Medina told them. The men pulled down the sails, and once down, one of the officers tied the speedboat to the sailboat, towing the latter past the island another two hundred yards to the shore where two Hennepin County Sheriff cars stood. Once everyone was on shore, the police frisked their suspects, and the officers found large knives on two of the men. All were taken off in handcuffs into the cars' back seats, three people to a back seat.

"How do I get to shore?" Ian asked the Commodore.

"You can't get there from here," said the man, who then slapped Ian's back. "Come on, I'll take you. You'll like Dottie."

CHAPTER FOURTEEN

As elegant as a store manikin in a sports shop, Dottie stood next to one of the sheriff's cars, raised her handcuffed arms, and straightened the collar of her fleece jacket. Her long, black painted nails sparkled with gold flecks and contrasted her thin white fingers. She glared at Medina as if expecting an apology.

"There's a huge mistake here," said Dottie. "And handcuffs? Where's the benefit of the doubt?"

"Standard procedure," said Medina, directing Dottie into the back seat, following one of the handcuffed husky male crew members from her boat. He had a particularly long neck as if always trying to look over the horizon. A second man, even heavier and with disheveled blond hair and an untended beard, followed her in.

Medina then sat in the front passenger's seat as a muscular young deputy who looked as if he stepped from the pages of the *Farm-Fed Journal* entered the driver's side.

"Really, now," said Dottie, wedged in the middle of the two men like sliced turkey between two large buns. "Why can't we chat in the yacht club's bar like civilized folk and get this over in twenty minutes."

"You're innocent? All the video footage I have of you in the banks is wrong?"

"I'm talking about these men," said Dottie. "They're just sailing crew. They know nothing of my travels, and their knives aren't weapons. On a boat, you never know when you need to cut a rope."

"Excuse me, but I don't get this," said the man with the long neck to Medina. "Dottie's one of the nicest people around."

"Gentlemen, who we have here is one of the bigger bank robbers of Los Angeles—part of the Busty Bandit gang."

The man looked even more puzzled and scanned the area closely outside the window. "The cameras have to be here somewhere."

"What're you talking about?" said Dottie.

"It's one of those reality shows like *Punked*."

"No, no, my friend," said Medina, who felt a swell of satisfaction. "This is real."

"You're a robber, Dottie?" asked the heavier man. Dottie merely smiled and shrugged.

In the car next to them, the other woman, gray-haired, looked like a spaniel off to the pound.

"And the woman?" asked Medina.

"Catherine's my housemate. She knew I went to Los Angeles, but she doesn't know why exactly. You need to talk only to me."

"You're already under arrest," said Medina, "and the others are under investigative detention. We'll question everyone downtown." She knew that Catherine and the men would be released, and weapons charges would be up to the locals.

Movement outside caught Medina's attention. With only a light limp now, Ian moved quickly off a dock with the Commodore. Medina realized there was no place for Ian in the cars. She'd better tell him.

Dottie gasped when seeing Ian. Medina stared at her, and Dottie said, "Is that young man okay?"

"Remember, what you say can be used against you," said Medina, underscoring the rights she'd read to her on the dock.

"I just hope he's okay," Dottie said.

"Why? Because Owen hurt him? And you brought in Owen?"

"I'd better wait for a lawyer," she said.

"I have to talk to the young man you recognized," Medina said and launched open the passenger door. She held up a finger to the driver and said, "Just give me a moment, and then we'll go." She hurried toward Ian, who walked quickly toward her, too, as if his lottery numbers had been called.

"Hey, we did it," she said.

"Yeah. Did she confess?" said Ian.

"Bean spilling doesn't happen so easily. Maybe later today."

"Can I help?"

She merely shook her head.

"Why not?" he asked.

The Commodore swept in, arms out, and said, "So is this it? I can go?

"Actually," said Medina, "Ian needs to get back to the Sheraton."

"You need a ride, guy? How about after the race is over?"

"I should be with you," Ian said to Medina.

"You can't go," she said trying to remind him he wasn't FBI. "Who knows how long it'll take to process these people, book her, and more."

"Ah," said Ian. "Of course."

She smiled, pleased.

"Except don't you need me to confirm it's her?" said Ian.

"She confirmed you already."

"Oh." Disappointment settled on his face.

"Maybe there's a great show on HBO or something," she tried.

"Yeah."

"Are you ready to roll?" said the Commodore. "We need to get back to the other boat."

"What about our pontoon boat?" said Ian.

"Oops," said Medina. "Can you take it back?" She reached into her pocket. "And here're the car keys. You have transportation after all."

The Commodore frowned, confused. "So you don't need a ride?" he said to Ian.

"Just to the pontoon boat," Ian said.

"That's easy enough," said the Commodore.

Without her expecting it, Ian impulsively hugged her. It felt too long, too intimate, too awkward, and she cleared her throat. He pulled back and grinned as if he expected more. Why do guys have to be so complicated?

"See you later, then," she said.

"No problem," said Ian. He stared, still waiting. For what?

She nodded.

Ian gave a short wave, and he walked off with the Commodore. She returned to the waiting cars to head downtown. Before they left, standing outside of the car out of earshot, Medina called Rick and explained about Dottie and the circumstances.

"This is major," said Rick. "Congratulations. I'm impressed and proud. Of course, Wexler and Toffer are going to think you're a renegade and probably write letters of censure."

"And hold up my pay and any promotion?"

"Maybe if we can get them in front of reporters announcing this capture, basically taking credit, they might calm down."

"So I still have a job?"

"I have no better agent—but I do worry about the toll this has been on you."

"I'm fine."

"Keep receipts. We'll reimburse you, even if this was your vacation. You'll interrogate her in downtown Minneapolis?"

"Yeah. County jail."

"I'll have to alert the Minneapolis field office, and undoubtedly someone from there will meet you, too."

"Fine."

"After you've questioned this Dottie, then I don't know. Hang tight. Maybe I'll fly out. Wexler's likely to demand you come back. One way or another, we'll get Zetta and Owen."

"Yes. So nothing came from your stakeout?"

"Nothing besides my wife going crazy with the kids for the last day. I owe her big-time."

Medina nodded. Most of the men in her unit had families and wives who cared about them.

"Later," she told Rick. She hung up and realized she hadn't mentioned Ian at all. She'd have to send Ian back. He'd have to see he was done.

The Sheraton was just off the freeway on the way to downtown Minneapolis, so they stopped by where Medina ran to her room and grabbed her case files to use in her interrogations. Twenty minutes later, they were in Minneapolis, whose skyline was an electrocardiogram of brown brick and glass. Where the freeway ended, they took a right turn and sailed on city streets. In another few blocks, after going through the most modern-looking city she'd ever seen, with buildings connected on the second story by glass tubes, the officer driving pointed to something very old looking, a grand, block-wide brownstone building with steep green roofs. Gothic looking, the building sat like a stern grandmother at a beer keg party full of young people.

"That's City Hall," said the muscular deputy. "The sheriff's office and jail's in here. Hey, if you need someone to sit in on your interrogation for safety reasons, I volunteer. I like this FBI stuff."

"I'll keep that in mind," she said.

Handcuffs clinked from the back seat. She turned to look. The three suspects in unison had leaned forward, like penitents on a pew, to see their destination.

She realized she needed to interview Dottie and Catherine ASAP as she didn't want any local agents muddying her efforts. Locals— and usually the men—often got involved just to be involved, upsetting the delicate balance she liked in interrogation. It was their territory, so she knew she had to hurry.

Casting a thumb to the back, Medina said, "Can you process them quickly and get me a room?"

"May I sit in?"

"If you stay quiet."

"As a mouse." She took in City Hall. "An impressive building," she said.

"Ortonville granite. Built over a hundred years ago," said the man, "but the jail's been updated over the years. We'll get you an interrogation room in short order."

Once settled into a clean small interrogation room that featured acoustic tiles on the walls, Medina reminded the young deputy to ask no questions. Medina started with the crew member with disheveled hair and beard in hopes of finding some information for leverage with Catherine, then Dottie. Medina had to be quick because she might only have a half hour before local FBI showed up—and Wexler and others may be flying from L.A. soon, too.

"I'm taping this," said Medina to the crew member. "Please state your name for the record."

"Scruffle Seaton."

"Scruffle's your legal name?"

"Stanley."

When she was a kid, her family had a dog, Scruffle, a terrier mix with crazy wiry fur. "Okay, Scruffle. How did you meet Dottie?"

"From the GLBT Pride Boat Cruise last year."

"What the heck's that?"

"You know: Gay-Lesbian-Bi-Trans. The Pride Boat parade's this wonderful mixer with drinking and boating for those blessed with a difference. Real fun."

"Dottie's gay?"

"She lives with Catherine, doesn't she?"

The deputy laughed, but she shot him a look, and he stopped.

"I can't assume," said Medina. "Do Dottie and Catherine have financial problems?"

"Who knows these things? I don't even know if my sister does. People don't announce that. Do you?"

"Sometimes you can tell."

"They have great parties—shrimp cocktail, ice statues, liver paté, open bar. They seem to be doing all right."

"What's Catherine do?"

"She's an artist, a painter—runs some department at some art school in Minneapolis."

"Which art school?"

"God knows."

"Officer?" said Medina turning to the deputy. "Is there a big art school here?"

He nodded. "The Minneapolis College of Art and Design."

"That's it," said Scruffle. "I hardly know Catherine and Dottie, frankly. A few parties, some conversations I couldn't follow about Republicans, and I crew for Dottie occasionally. I get paid."

It was clear that Seaton didn't know Dottie very well. He was there to crew. She let him go. Medina brought in Catherine.

Catherine sat in her chair slightly forward, hands folded, as if ready to conduct a faculty meeting.

"I'm recording this, please state your full name."

"Catherine Valesco."

"Valesco? Sounds Spanish."

"I was once married to a Spaniard. It's the name I started my painting career with, so I've kept it."

"And you left him for Dottie?"

"What bearing does this have on why you've arrested Dottie and detained me?"

"Dottie's a bank robber in Los Angeles."

"That I'll never believe."

"And I have 'reasonable suspicion' to detain you. After all, you're living with Dottie, are you not? As if you're a married couple?"

"I don't like the disdain in your voice."

"I have no disdain. I like gay people."

"I'm not gay," she said with sharply. Medina had run into this before, partners in crime having sex but swearing they weren't gay.

"Listen, I could care less," said Medina. "Gay or not—doesn't matter to me. My beef is about the six people killed so far, thanks to this robbing spree. You two have lavish parties, I hear. And you have this big, beautiful sailboat. Do two faculty members of lesser colleges really bring in that kind of money?"

"There is no such thing as a lesser college. All education is important. What's more truthful is that corporations in America have killed higher education, first impoverishing professors. Did you know out of 1.5 million professors, a full million are adjunct, and the average adjunct makes just twenty thousand a year?"

"Fits my point."

"We're not adjunct."

"Has Dottie been to Los Angeles?"

"Yes, not to rob banks. She went there for an English conference. You have to be mixing her up with someone else."

"We found her through robbery videos."

"Our colleges and universities have become corporatized, and so has our justice system ever since Karl Rove took focus on stocking state supreme courts with Republicans. Look how it worked in Florida, with that state's supreme court giving all its electoral votes to George W. Bush in the 2000 election."

Medina glanced at her watch. This woman loved politics and was going to chew up too much precious time.

"How does any of this connect to Dottie?"

"Dottie and I have become caught up in the machinations of the FBI's need to have bottom-line success. Is this not true? We are little rubber dots caught up in the gears of justice."

"I think you two had bills and a certain lifestyle, and Dottie went to keep the cash flowing."

"I should hold off speaking more until I have a lawyer."

"Right now you're just detained. If you can clear things up, then you're on your way. Do you have financial problems?"

"We're fine. We're not like the administrators of our schools who get huge raises while the poor faculty don't even get cost of living anymore. There's been a redistribution of wealth from the scholars to the administrators, to the 'consultants,' the PR and marketing firms, the law firms—"

"Is that what Dottie was doing, redistributing the wealth?"

"I am no longer talking."

While Medina had plenty of more questions for Catherine, and probably could get her talking without a lawyer, she didn't fight it. "Call a lawyer, and you can talk to the local FBI, who are coming in." Time for Dottie.

When the deputy led Dottie in, Medina felt a surge of joy. She'd dreamed of being face-to-face with one of the leaders for months. Careful, Medina thought. Bring her in slowly. This part of the process was like being a good fisherman—as her mentor at the FBI Academy at Quantico once explained. It was one tactic. Don't reel in your suspect too fast or the line will break. Be friendly at first. Don't bark out questions. People said a lot more, often unintentionally, if you showed empathy. It was important to start correctly and establish concern. In fact, she wouldn't start recording right away.

Dottie no longer had on the fleece jacket. "I love your blouse," said Medina. "Is it Anne Klein?" Medina didn't know many labels, didn't care for them, frankly, but Dottie had to be concerned with fashion if she wore this sailing.

Dottie eyed her suspiciously, then looked at Medina's own clothes. "Cute sweats," she said.

"Not as elegant as your sailing clothes," said Medina.

Dottie ran her hand down her white sleeveless top that had a crepe front and black turtleneck. "This is Anna Sui. I love her style."

"I was going to say," said Medina.

Dottie looked more at ease. "Ask away," said Dottie.

"I have to record this, as you probably know."

"That's fine."

"I just wanted you to hear what we have so far." It was important not to appear desperate for information, but rather to make it clear to Dottie that she was in a tough spot. "You're on video robbing the bank. Photos show you kidnapping Ian Nash, whose testimony is lengthy, and we have physical evidence tying you to the house on top of Mt. Washington."

"Do you?"

"Bleach doesn't clean everything." Dottie didn't need to know they didn't have a lot, just Owen's fecal matter, some hairs, the panties from the dryer, and some fingerprints that yet may tie Dottie or the others. "I also have you saying today that you recognized Ian Nash. He recognizes you. You bought the boat with cash, and the list goes on."

"Yes," said Dottie, whose shoulders now slumped. "It doesn't look good."

"I'm here if you want to explain. If you cooperate with me, I may be able to help you."

"May I refuse to answer questions if I don't like them?" said Dottie.

"Yes, but no matter what, you have to submit a swab from your cheek for DNA profiling—which you can do now while we wait for your lawyer."

"Or we can chat a little, if we want," said Dottie.

"So you don't mind that we begin without an attorney present?"

"For now it's fine. I've studied this interrogation scenario, by the way. I did my research. People don't realize books can tell you a lot of things."

"Yes, you teach English. Where?"

"Normandale Community College. I leaped into teaching late because my first career was in computers. I was a computer engineer at Control Data. Ran my own group."

"Was that your absolute first career?"

"After my stint in the Air Force."

Medina nodded, remembering Ian's explanation of "MITO procedures" and his suggestion that this person may have been in the Air Force. Ian had his strengths. "From Air Force to engineer to English—those are major changes."

"Yes. My first spouse didn't like my leaving the lucrative world of computers to be an English teacher."

"A huge salary cut, I imagine," said Medina. "Because of that and perhaps because of the corporatization of higher education—is that why you robbed banks?"

"Corporatization—I see you've been talking with Catherine. She feels that American education was once the best in the world, and it's been killed thanks to state and federal defunding of higher education and then corporations swept in to pay the bills and run things."

"What about you two? Too many credit cards? Too many bills for big parties and boating?"

"We're fine—and Catherine knows nothing of bank robberies, which you probably learned."

"It's hard to believe. Where did she think this big boat came from?"

"I told her it was a steal." Dottie winked. "She knows my passion for sailing, and I said it was a great buy. I do all the bill paying in our family, so she truly knows nothing about money."

"Two teachers' salaries buy all you have?"

"We don't have young kids. And maybe this is where we should wait for my lawyer."

Medina felt her jaw tighten, but quickly relaxed it. Time was tight, but Dottie didn't need to know or see any signs of tension. "That's fine," said Medina. "Your lawyer—she'll be here soon?"

"Yes, a she—you guessed right. Good. Must be hard being a woman in the FBI."

"It has its upside, but we're not here for me."

They each smiled. Medina thought about how some people did not like a gap in conversation, that it brought tension and a space they wanted to fill. Dottie being a professor probably filled spaces.

"Ever read *History of Sexuality: An Introduction*?" Dottie asked. "Philosopher Michel Foucault presents sex as a form of discourse. He also asserts that sex pervades all aspects of a person's life."

"Interesting," said Medina, thinking how Dottie indeed was a talker. So was Catherine. Which one was alpha?

"You becoming a female FBI agent is an act of sexual discourse," said Dottie.

Medina did not react.

"Is that the way you are in bed, too?" said Dottie. "Blank-faced? Sex is the key to our personality, you know."

"You want to hear the kind of jail term you're looking at? Cooperating can bring it down."

"Can't talk about you, can you? Careful about risking yourself. However, as Foucault says, sex should not be kept under a veil. Something tells me you've cut that part of your life out, your sexuality. Am I wrong? I'm sensitive to these things."

Medina tried to show nothing, but she felt her stomach fall away. Was it that obvious? This was stupid—and not like her at all. The crooks never got the best of her—but they also didn't talk Foucault. "I was an English major as an undergrad," Medina replied. "I read a little Foucault, a brilliant mind. But I'm not here for that."

"Don't you miss English as a subject? It encapsulates all other subjects—sociology, psychology, math, physics—everything goes into literature. And stories are about the stupid things we do."

"Such as buying boats with stolen money?" said Medina, bringing the conversation back.

Dottie looked at her hand, seemingly lost in thought. She twirled the wedding ring on her left hand, a gorgeous gathering of many small diamonds. "I suppose I won't get to sail on that marvelous boat again, at least in this lifetime," said Dottie.

"Depends on how much you help. Perhaps after a while you could get something larger than what floats in a prison bathtub."

"I feel like Ophelia being pulled down into the water by the weight of her dress." She smiled, and the wrinkles in the otherwise smooth skin of her face showed someone who grinned more often than frowned. This wasn't Medina's usual robbery suspect who lived a life on the edge, had a violent childhood, was young and mostly stupid.

"I take it you were the brains of the operation," said Medina.

"My friend needed help."

"Zetta?"

"Yes."

"What's her real name?"

"That I won't divulge."

"Why?"

"I'll tell you a story, and it's really a story of the FBI. Zetta was once one of my students—and someone very dear to me. Very dear."

"So Zetta's gay? You had an affair."

"Why would you assume that?"

Medina said nothing, realizing she should just let Dottie talk.

"Zetta had been married and had a child, a boy we'll call Billy. Her husband beat her, so he became an ex-husband—and she became my friend. One day, right in front of a Target store and witnesses, the ex-husband snatched Billy and sped off in a Camaro."

"How old was Billy?"

"Five."

Dottie's chair scraped back, sending out a sharp sound. She continued: "The ex-husband, who had been living out-of-state, may have taken Billy beyond Minnesota's borders, so the FBI was called. The FBI wasn't helpful after the first couple months. Three years go by. Still nothing. So my friend tried a few private detectives. They're expensive. One had a lead, but it would take him out of state. In fact, he prided himself in his record of solving parental kidnapping. It takes a lot of money. My friend needed the money and asked me. I didn't have the money to lend."

"And did you tell Catherine any of this?"

"I told her about the kidnapping, but I didn't keep her up-to-date with my interest in helping Zetta."

"Why not?"

"Catherine's a worrier."

"And maybe you thought Catherine would be jealous?"

"Heavens, no. Zetta's a good friend, and Catherine doesn't care. Also, Zetta's been deeply focused on her son."

"Love can have different paths," said Medina.

"Catherine has been a great path for me," said Dottie. "When Zetta came to me, I had to find another way for her to get money. I know I may be self-incriminating here, but the fact was I could use more money, too."

"So you did have debts," said Medina, keeping her rising enthusiasm at bay.

Dottie shook her head. "The truth is Catherine and I are aging, and our schools are donating less to our retirement in the name of cost savings. Catherine's right—any savings seems to go to salary increases for administrators. Add that new professors are getting NO benefits, no health care, no retirement, no educational benefits, no offices. We faculty are being relegated to the status of agricultural workers."

Medina felt more hope, realizing Dottie seemed to want to explain for elucidation's sake.

"You're saying you had a good reason," said Medina.

"I'm saying in higher education, what professors get is not fair, but the students have it worse. They have to bear large tuition increases. Many of my students don't have parents who went to college, so there's no role model. Students who need the community college system are being shut out, and yet you should see how thirsty they are to learn. English isn't an easy subject, yet when we go over *Hamlet*, for instance, they ask such great questions. They sense the corruptibility of those in power. I've yearned to set up a scholarship fund to help students."

"Interesting. Where would you show the income from?"

"Colleges don't ask such things. It's not like a mortgage. I'd give them money for a scholarship fund." Dottie paused as if considering what she was about to do. "Yes. Zetta and I had a mutual need. Then I bought a good book, which happened to be true facts about bank robbery in L.A. written by an ex-FBI guy. I learned the pitfalls of bank robbery and how to do it right. L.A. seemed like a good place, too, far away from this town. I thought we had done it right until I met you."

"I suppose that's a compliment."

"It is."

"Tell me, how did you find Freddie Liu and whoever Owen is?"

"You haven't found Owen or his real name—interesting. Freddie didn't tell you?"

"Freddie's dead—killed by Owen."

Dottie gasped, covering her mouth. Again, she became silent.

"Beaten to death, very bloody," said Medina. "So who is Owen?"

Dottie shook her head. Her eyes filled. "We should have never hired Owen. My instincts were right, but Zetta... Well, there was an attraction there. Let's just say Zetta was wrong. I'm so sorry to hear about Freddie."

"Owen's killed five other people, too, including the detective I was working with and Ian's nurse. Owen was after Ian. You unleashed something terrible, a blood bath."

Her manila folders next to her, Medina opened the one with photos and silently laid eight-by-tens of the bodies of Jones, the two young people killed at the bank, the hospital nurse, and Officer Bradford. "We need Owen's real name."

A tear rolled down Dottie's smooth cheek, and Medina pulled a tissue from her pocket and offered it to Dottie, who took it gratefully and dabbed smooth skin.

"Tell me about Owen or who the detective was that Zetta hired, where she went."

"I can't. I need my friend to get away with her son, which I hope has happened by now."

"When's the last time you spoke to Zetta?"

"What I have and have not heard is for another conversation. I need you to make a deal with my lawyer." Again she smiled—slightly—showing Medina that Dottie was not someone to be intimidated.

Dottie again twirled her ring, and Medina thought of Dottie's use of the word "spouse" earlier. Who speaks that way? Also, if she were in the Air Force, had she been in a flight crew? It wasn't until the mid-nineties that women could fly in the Air Force. And then Medina realized something, and she looked at Dottie's neck, covered by the turtleneck. She thought of Lester, a guy in one of her training classes at Quantico. She thought of Catherine insisting she wasn't gay. Then there was the fecal matter found in the toilet—maybe it wasn't Owen's. "Are you and Catherine legally married?" she asked.

"As a matter of fact, yes."

"And not in Canada." In Canada, same sex couples could legally marry. Dottie said nothing. "You're a man, Dottie, aren't you?"

"Why would you say that?"

"An acquaintance of mine, Lester, had been born Amanda. She'd undergone a sex change to be a man, and is in the FBI as far as I know."

"I haven't undergone a sex change, but I am not a man. Just because the body had said one thing, doesn't mean— Let's just say I've always felt a certain way, and my leaving engineering and my previous name, Don, straightened things out for me."

"You just haven't had an operation. Do many people know?"

"A lot of my transgendered friends know about my past. My son and daughter know. My former wife certainly does. I'm not ashamed of it. In fact, I'm proud of what I had to do. I've learned a lot about people from this time. To answer what you're asking: my employer, my students, my neighbors just know me as me, Dottie."

"And Catherine?"

"Of course she does. According to the law, we are husband and wife. I didn't have that kind of surgery, but I did get rid of my beard through electrolysis." She rubbed her face. It must have taken hundreds of hours for the painstaking hair removal. "Heck—I like women. And Catherine and I are fully legal, thanks to my other name, Don. Bush's America had nothing on us." Dottie stared into Medina's eyes. "So this doesn't disturb you?" said Dottie.

"You seem like a good person—who has done something wrong with banks and bystanders."

"Can you offer me a good deal?" said Dottie.

"This is a federal crime, so it'll be up to the Department of Justice to prosecute and offer a deal. However, I'd say no death penalty. If you plead guilty, I'll highly recommend parole and will testify how helpful you've been."

"My lawyer will be here soon. Bring in the DOJ. They can negotiate, and then I'll talk."

CHAPTER FIFTEEN

Freshly showered, Ian stood naked in his hotel bathroom when the phone rang in the next room. He wiped the remnants of shaving cream off his face and answered.

"Hey, so you made it back fine," said Medina.

"Yes. So, did Dottie fess up?"

"Fess up? You've been seeing the wrong movies."

Her voice sounded upbeat. Ian knew things had to be good. "Tell me already."

"Come down to the hotel bar. I'm here. The news is better in person," she said.

Ian dressed and hurried down. When he sailed into the Reserve Lounge, she was at the polished counter. She looked at him in a way he had never felt from her before, as if he were a main meal. He sat next to her in one of the two open seats. Having changed out of her sweats and into black pants, a stylish white tank top, and amber earrings, she looked worthy of a magazine cover. He had guessed that she could look this good. She grinned so much, her whole body radiated cheer. "Tell me more," said Ian. "Tell me about Dottie."

"I'll let you order first."

"No, I'm not thirsty. Stop torturing me. What happened with Dottie?"

As he said that, a short balding bartender brought in a giant pink drink for Medina, "Your strawberry margarita with Sauza Anejo tequila."

"The anejo has flavor," she told Ian. "Sure you don't want something?" Medina brought the drink to her lips.

He shook his head, and the bartender left. "Spill away. Good news?"

Medina nodded, took her first sip, then fully explained the story of Zetta's son's kidnapping. "Dottie wouldn't reveal Zetta's real name, however," said Medina.

"The motive's interesting," said Ian. "Zetta robbed banks because, essentially of the FBI's ineptness in finding her son."

"You make it sound like the FBI didn't want to help. Do you know how many kids are abducted by parents each year in America?"

He shrugged. "Hundreds?" When she didn't answer, he reconsidered. "Thousands?"

"One hundred and sixty-five thousand last year. Even though it's a federal crime, parents still do it. Every agent could spend every waking hour on this crime alone and it wouldn't be enough."

"I don't mean to make you defensive."

"Sometimes it feels like there's a tsunami of evil. Is there something in human DNA that can't accept the Golden rule—treat other's like you'd like to be treated?"

"Exactly." He liked her this way, philosophical. "When you think about it," he said, "about why Zetta robbed, why I was taken hostage—hell, why we're even in Afghanistan—it's all about rationalization, isn't it? Zetta's husband kidnapped his son because he rationalized he was doing something good. Catholics and Christians in Ireland all those years killed each other because they rationalized it was something necessary. It's enough to make Jesus throw up."

"I'm not getting into religion tonight."

"That's a banned topic?"

"You like to argue, don't you?"

"What about Owen? Who is he?"

"His real name is Chad Litt."

"That's a real name?"

"What he was born with, Dottie didn't know, but he's an actor and uses the name Chad Litt. They found him at an actors' studio on Robertson Boulevard. That should help the FBI a lot. Plus we know a few more things about him that Dottie gleaned. Litt was raised by a unloving uncle in Nebraska—apparently better than Litt's abusive dad. She's not sure what happened to Litt's parents. Litt worked in the merchant marines before heading west. He certainly thought he was a ladies' man and was frustrated when Zetta didn't return the interest. Oh, and by the way, Dottie is transgender."

"What?"

She told him what Dottie explained, including that Dottie had been a computer engineer named Don and left a marriage to live as a woman and teach English. Dottie had said she'd lived too much of her life trying to please others, and this is finally what she wanted.

"So she's a transvestite?"

"Yes, I used that word at one point, but Dottie said she doesn't think that way. She's a woman and happens to have a penis, and she says not to think of gender as so black-and-white, man/woman. She said many other cultures, including some American Indian tribes, have a variety of in-betweens—and they are cherished for it."

"I don't get it. Then again, now that I think of some actors I've worked with, I can see it." He then realized the bigger issue at hand. "So how do we get Zetta and Chad Litt?"

"We have to go back to L.A. tomorrow. I have to meet with Toffer while Wexler's on his way here."

Ian felt his gut turn. "What do you mean? I thought we were going to see this through. We're so close."

"It's out of my hands," she said. "The Westwood guys are completely in charge. This has high-ranking oversight, so you should be happy."

"You thought I'd like this?"

"We have to go, Ian. That's that."

He shook his head. "What if I want to stay here?"

"Ian. Please. This will get solved, I promise. I want you to come with me because Chad's still out there, still dangerous."

"You think he's coming here? You think he's still after me?"

"I don't think either, but we did our part, and we have to go back."

"This isn't like you. If you're not on the case then this will fall apart again. It's thanks to you it hasn't."

She gave him what he considered her agent-in-charge look. "We need to leave in the morning. Wexler will be here, and he's taking charge yet again. The resident agency is in full gear, too."

He stared out at the view of the changing leaves outside. Ever since he'd woken up in the hospital and she was there, he'd worked and cooperated with her. "Isn't there another option?"

"No. I realize you're upset."

"And I don't mean to sound ungrateful, but this is no time to let the bureaucracy crush us."

"It won't. Let's celebrate," she said. "Things are happening."

As he looked at her, she did not seem entirely convincing. "I know you want to continue this," he said.

She shook her head. "I like what I do, and this is the time I have to play along. I'm back on the company clock. They're paying our return fares."

"Is this the normal protocol? You'd think they'd keep you on the case."

"Nothing about this is normal—but as a woman, I've had to deal with this kind of macho bullshit occasionally. They won't fuck it up, though. This will be solved."

His anger, he realized, wasn't going to help him. It never did. He knew he had to sell her somehow, and David Mamet's play *Glengarry Glen Ross* about ruthless real estate salesmen came to mind. In directing a student production once, he'd learned a lot from the charismatic Ricky Roma. The main thing wasn't to be direct. Be indirect. Just sell himself subtly.

"Are we okay?" she asked.

"Yeah," he said, thinking of how Ricky Roma could toss out a theatrical and bizarre statement to keep a potential client wondering. "I'm like a mushroom," said Ian, waving his arm with a flourish. "I live on humidity in the dark."

She frowned but didn't question him. "We'll get Litt soon, which is what you want, right?"

"Yes, but we're the committed ones—the ones who can see it through."

"For this last part, we need more manpower. Let Westwood deal with it."

"But they're cutting you out completely?"

"Let me get you a drink. What do you drink?" said Medina. "Or can't you drink if you're taking pain meds?"

"It's only high-dose naproxen," said Ian. "Nothing narcotic."

The short guy behind the counter at the other end strode over as if he had radar for orders. "Something more?" said the bartender.

"What do you think I drink?" Ian asked Medina.

"A gin gimlet for the man," Medina told the bartender.

"That's an old geezer drink," said Ian.

"It's the new martini," said the bartender.

"Guys in the know drink it," said Medina.

"Hard to believe," Ian said.

"And another margarita for me, too," she added, pushing her empty glass toward the bartender.

When the bartender brought the drink over in a martini glass, placing it before him on a round Sheraton coaster, he stared at the dandelion-hued beverage. A wheel of lime was impaled on the side.

"Thanks," he said.

"Taste it," she replied.

He lifted it, and he smelled the lime, which reminded him of a lime tree he once had outside an apartment door. He sipped the drink. The sharpness of the alcohol kissed the crispness of juniper and citrus. He nodded and realized Medina might know him better than he did. This could be his drink.

The bartender set down another strawberry margarita for Medina. They raised their glasses in unison. Ian glided his in near hers, and they clinked.

"Cheers," he said, placing his hand on her shoulder.

She smiled and placed her hand on his.

"I mean it," he said, looking at her hand. "It's something I could get used to."

She smiled and said nothing. At that moment, a waitress came up to Medina. "Your table's ready." Medina stood, and he looked at her more closely. Her shape radiated through her close-fitting top.

"We're eating?" said Ian.

"Sure. You hungry?"

"Always."

At that moment, a drum and cymbal burst in—apparently from a synthesizer—because a young man at a keyboard in the corner began playing a spirited piano introduction to a song he recognized and loved, "Captain Jack" by Billy Joel. People moved onto the small dance floor. Ian said to the waitress, "Excuse me, Miss?" When she turned to look at him, he said, "Would it be okay if we came in, say, ten minutes after a dance?"

"Absolutely," she said.

"Do you dance?" he asked Medina. He couldn't believe he was saying it because he didn't dance. Still, it felt right. He needed to make a move.

She smiled and stood. He took her hand with his cast arm and moved her to the dance floor, and he pulled her close, pretending he could dance. It seemed to work. The young man sang, but the words washed over Ian, who simply felt Medina's hands in his, her body against his, and he sensed her breath against his neck. They moved in tandem.

Medina pulled back to look into his face. She looked concerned. "Is this good with your leg?"

"It's feeling better all the time. Exercise is good, right?"

"You can slow down slightly," she said. "Listen to the music and move to the beat." He didn't let her criticism get to him because she was smiling. She seemed impressed with him. He slowed down. She nodded. He was getting it.

But Captain Jack will get you high tonight

And take you to your special island

He rubbed her back with his good hand. He felt in control. This was going well. And the singer sang:

So you play your albums and you smoke your pot

She said in a whisper into his ear, "Have you ever tried pot?"

"Hasn't everyone?" he said, wondering if she had some. Was this her turn-on? When he was a teenager, the rumor was that the police had the best pot—maybe the FBI did, too. "You have any?" he said.

"No. I was just referring to the song."

"Oh."

"Have you smoked it more than fifteen times in your life?" was her next question.

"Actually, no. It makes me sleepy." He didn't want to be sleepy—just sleep with her.

"That's good," she said. "You can't join the FBI if you smoked more than fifteen times in your life."

"Really? You can have a drug-ridden past and be in the FBI?"

"Not drug-ridden—just pot and less than fifteen times."

"Huh," he said, thinking. "Why fifteen? Why not sixteen? Or ten? I wonder how they came up with that."

"Probably a committee. They ask you such questions when you're connected to a lie detector. You have to take a polygraph to join the FBI."

"Interesting," he said. Not that he ever had any intention of doing such a thing. "I know you have secrets—we all have secrets—so did you have to divulge them during the polygraph?"

She laughed and her earrings jangled. Her earrings were strings of delicate amber beads.

"No, really," he said. "What came out during the test? What kind of things would I have to talk about?"

"Well, okay," she said, looking at him, then holding him closer while dancing . "I did a stupid thing in college. I'd gone to a Christian college, and this was after a Christian high school."

"You were a good girl."

"Yeah, and then I—" She broke it off, looking slightly upward as if someone walking on a higher floor might be the very guy she was thinking about.

"It's okay," he said.

"The truth is I fell for my volleyball coach, a married guy." She laughed and blurted, "I can't believe I'm telling you this stuff."

"You had sex with him?"

She looked at him. "Kind of clinical, isn't it?"

"I should have said 'made love.' When you're a teenager, everything is about love."

"I was a great volleyball player," she said, "A good spiker. I could really hammer the ball into a pocket."

"I bet."

"Our team was going for the championship. Anyway, he told me he loved me and was going to leave his wife. I was eighteen and believed him. He was older than me—by seventeen years—but people said I acted older than my age. Even before anything happened, my friends on the team made jokes about us getting married. He was caring, sweet, funny…" and she looked off again. "And then one night during an away game, well, things happened."

"And it felt good?" Ian said softly.

"I was a virgin, and it was like that first taste of vanilla. But then his wife figured out our affair somehow—maybe he left my phone number on a piece of paper or the way he looked at me at games when she was there. It gave me my first hint that women could be good at detection. Shit hit the fan, to say the least, and next thing, I'm kicked off the team and…." She gave a guttural sound. "People started looking at me funny as if I'd put another nail into Christ. I was being ostracized. Professors started grading me hard, and, what was going on? There's nothing like the social network at a Christian university."

"What did you do to fight back?"

"Things just got worse. I missed him and I couldn't believe he wouldn't talk to me. Then I couldn't believe that some of my friends wouldn't talk to me. That's when I realized God was bullshit. I quit that school and finished at UCLA where I was honors the whole way."

The song ended.

"And so end's my story," she said.

"What happened later? A better boyfriend? Live with anyone?"

"UCLA happened, which led to law school. Law school brought Mario, but a two-lawyer, two-ego family wouldn't have worked. Let's say I'd been willing to try, but Mario found Vanessa. I then found the FBI."

"Was Mario the guy with the engagement ring?"

"Yep." She pulled away. "I think we should eat dinner." She didn't look happy anymore. They walked from the bar toward the restaurant as the musician started playing a more contemporary song, something Ian heard on the radio a lot lately but didn't know by whom. Medina looked at the ground, lost in thought. Ian realized he shouldn't have brought up her secrets, but it certainly gave him a better understanding of her. He needed to change the topic if he was going to save the night.

"What'd your father do?" he asked. Family seemed a safer topic.

"A cop."

"Sergeant Medina?"

"Captain—until he was killed—shot. Captain Medina."

"Sorry to hear. I mean, not sorry to hear he was captain."

"I know what you mean."

The hostess recognized them. "You two looked cute dancing. I wish my boyfriend danced."

"Thanks," said Ian.

"Your table's still ready." They followed her.

Once seated, Medina smiled and said, "Sorry. I didn't mean to get all maudlin."

"It's not horrible by any means. Everyone does stupid things in relationships."

"Let me hear about yours, then."

"Like what?"

"What about your girlfriends?" she said. "What drove the last one away?"

"Pierra?" His stomach twisted at how Pierra had left him. "She was hung up on a guy from her past. She'd talk about how he'd carry her naked into bed in a room with candlelight all around and—I mean—I hated hearing about that."

"Wasn't she just telling you what she wanted to be more romantic?"

He paused. He'd never thought of that. "Well, there were other things she did. It just didn't work."

"If you don't want to talk about it, that's okay. I talked about my past."

"Pierra and I were engaged, but she just seemed hung up on her previous lover is all. I couldn't have a life of her pining after him."

"So you left her." It was a statement.

"She left me, actually. She was just messed up."

"And you blame her. I bet your previous relationships went the same way."

Why was she saying this? The sinking feeling he had when girlfriends told him all was over came roaring back. He had to look away.

"And you blame them," she said. "You blame your instructors for your being ousted from the theatre program. Best I can tell, you blame your parents for things. Don't you ever take responsibility for your actions? I mean, really. Yes, you were a hostage, you can blame Chad Litt, but that doesn't mean you have to blame your fucking life on others. Grow up already."

He sat there, astounded. She may as well have shot him as Owen had. What gave her the right?

"Ian, you are smart. You are good looking, but you carry around so many chips on your shoulders, you may as well be the whole Keebler elf clan. You think you're as good an investigator as me, right?"

"I never said that. But I am good at things."

"You have talent, I grant you, but look how many mistakes you've made, how many people've died because of you. You think we're on a fun jaunt to Minnesota and aren't we doing a good job? We'll show Wexler, right? And maybe the head of the FBI will give you a medal?"

That was exactly what he'd hoped. What was wrong with that?

She was shaking her head.

"And you're perfect now?" he said. "Do you know how hard it is to break down your defenses? You may as well be a stealth bomber for all your armaments. Everything you do shouts out that you're not relationship material, but I've seen your house. I've seen your pink sweat suit. There's a part of you that's soft, and that's wonderful. I cheerish it. Okay, so I have some chips. So do you. We're both vulnerable, Aleece, and that's a good thing. We come with ruts, but we smooth them out for each other."

"You want me to smooth them with you?"

"I'd say smooch, but that's a whole other thing."

"Yes it is." She took the napkin from her lap and dropped it on top of her menu.

"Wexler is on our side, don't you see?" she said. "And if I know one thing, it's this: shit always comes down when you least expect it. Not from Wexler. From where you least expect it."

She stood. "I think I drank too much. I'm sorry. You could be a likable guy if you'd only learn a little tact and responsibility."

"We're not having dinner?"

"You can blame me. I'm not feeling good. Let's just restart in the morning, okay?"

And she walked away, a little more sure-footed. Just like Pierra.

And he realized something else. He had to fix things. Everything. The first place to start was with his parents. He needed to see about flights to Canada.

◆

Medina awoke in her hotel room—alone—twisted in her sheets and blanket, and tried to focus on the clock. It was after ten. She never slept this late. What day was it? Oh: Sunday.

Her head pounded. She untangled herself, sat up, then flopped back down. She realized she should have taken aspirin before bed, but she'd been happy to just crawl into bed and put an end to the day. As she tried to reconstruct the conversation with Ian, she couldn't remember the exact dialogue, but she knew he'd pissed her off. She shouldn't have told him about James, her coach. Sweet James, the asshole. What had she expected from Ian? Compassion? But she'd opened the door to his curiosity. She'd exposed herself. When she wanted him to reciprocate and be vulnerable, he became defensive. Typical—just like all guys.

Dragging herself to the bathroom, she splashed water across her face and looked at her face—blanched and still tired-looking. She was just in her panties and a sweat-drenched sleeveless T-shirt.

In the shower, she kept the water cold. No pain, no gain. What about Ian? Thankfully, she hadn't followed her desires and slept with him. That would have been a mess. True—she'd liked him. And even if he wasn't vulnerable last night, she liked that he was often funny, liked it that he was attracted to her. Yet this case wasn't over. It would have been terrible to have involved herself with a witness with the case still open. Even so, she'd better apologize to him.

Her cell phone rang as she toweled herself off. Before she answered it, she tried out her voice: "Red leather, yellow leather, red leather, yellow leather. Zanzibar, testing, testing," she said, trying Ian's trick. She flipped open her phone: "Hello?"

"It's Rick. Good news. Did I wake you?"

"I'm fine. So what's going on?"

"Are you getting ready to return?"

She hadn't done a thing yet. Her head throbbed. Hangover. "I'm nearly ready," she said.

"Things are happening," he said. "The Minneapolis crew's great. There are not a lot of private detectives in the Twin Cities. They guessed right away who Zetta had hired to find her son. He's been out of town, too, which only reinforces he's the guy."

As she put a little Blistex on her lips, she said, "Uh huh."

"The detective's answering service says he's due back today. Can you talk to him before you go? Wexler's delayed, so I can put you on it. I don't care what he says. It's your case, after all."

"Thanks," she said, holding back a need to shout hurray. "You have a name and address?"

"Yes. Private detective Joseph Moore," and he gave her the address. "I'm going to fax some information to your hotel. Right after you interview him, call me, and then you need to get back here." Her heart fell again.

"Absolutely," she said. They agreed to talk later. She hung up, then considered calling Ian. She stared at her phone. He should know, but she should apologize, too. Best in person.

In the bathroom, she brushed some color into her cheeks. After she dressed, she turned to leave. An envelope had been slipped under the door—a Sheraton envelope. She picked it up, exited the room, and was opening the envelope when she arrived at Ian's door, which was open. A maid vacuumed the floor. The bed was made.

"Where's the man in this room?" Medina asked.

The maid turned off the vacuum. "Perdoneme?" said the maid.

"Donde esta el hombre?" asked Medina.

"No esta."

"Gracias," Medina said and opened up the rest of the envelope. Written on Sheraton stationery was, "Aleece, I can't thank you enough. You've been a generous person, and whatever I said last night to make you mad at me, I'm sorry. It's clear I have issues with authority or perhaps just not being cognizant enough to leave things alone—or both and more."

Yes, but not leaving things alone had been great for finding leads.

His letter continued, "I ended up calling my parents last night. Long story short, they loved hearing from me, and they urged me to come up. It's probably better for me anyway—safer. They arranged for an early morning flight. I'm off to Canada."

That was fast.

He ended with, "Good luck on finding Zetta and Chad Litt. I wish I were there for that, but as you inferred, it's not my job, bye." He signed his full name, Ian Nash, being formal.

She felt as empty as a drunk's whiskey bottle. She wondered if Ian had really just returned to Los Angeles and made up Canada as a way to save face. What did she expect from her being so honest with him? Well, she hoped he really did go to Canada.

As she drove toward the private detective she was to interview, she realized how she really missed Ian. When she returned to Los Angeles, she had to find Chad Litt before anyone else did.

CHAPTER SIXTEEN

Up in the air, Ian stared out at the white swirly blanket of clouds below, which obscured everything. He knew, though, that Canada would be a short stop. He had to get back to L.A.

During the night as he had tried to sleep, Ian relived how Owen, i.e. Chad Litt, had smashed through the car window, dragged Ian out, and kicked him repeatedly at the house where Jones had just been murdered. In his dreams, Ian had created new questions for Litt, such as, "I don't get you—why are you so angry? Why are you killing people?"

Litt had laughed and just said, "There's a meanness in this world." Now Ian realized his brain, even when sleeping, was working on the case, trying to figure out Litt, trying to figure out the man's motivation and where he could be found.

Later, he dreamt of Medina at the hotel restaurant, surveying him with bedroom eyes, then flinging him to the floor and kicking him, too, as she told him off again, and he'd jolted awake once more. How could violence and love be so intertwined? This seemed wrong—which is why he focused on Medina's last statement: that he'd blamed his whole life on other people. It was his duty, his responsibility, to fix that.

He also realized he'd ruined something wonderful with Medina. Take responsibility. Could he fix his relationship with Medina, make it even something better? He doubted it. He could see, however, how everything had been going so well on both the case and with romance, and then he had to open his mouth once more. What was wrong with him that he deserved this?

Then again, his life so far hadn't worked well. He had to step up to the plate.

If he resolved it all, would that take him to a better place? Maybe. He knew if he wanted to be back in good standing with Medina, he had to do a few things well and quickly. So now he was off to Canada. He had so much to do—hours to go before he'd sleep.

Two hours later, he deplaned, pulling his wheeled carry-on bag up the jetway in Winnipeg. His parents sounded fine on the phone—

his mother crying, even. Still, could all those years of problems go away? If he could apologize and repair some of the previous damage, that would be good. Still, part of the problem was them, and if they didn't recognize anything, would it be for nothing? He had decided in Minnesota, though, that he had to be like the people in AA and meet those he'd wronged, apologize, and not expect anything back. Just take responsibility. He'd try it.

His stomach was queasy, yet he continued to move quickly toward the terminal. Would they really be there?

As he passed the customs inspector, who waved him through, he could see on the other side his mother, short, blond, built like a penguin, jump up and down. "Ian! Ian!" And there was his father, tall, gray-haired, an oak with a few bends, smiling, standing next to her. Ian grinned and waved with his cast and moved even faster.

"Oh, my, your arm," said his mother.

"Yeah, I got a little hurt."

She hugged him tightly. He yelped as she managed to press on the wrong rib. "I'm hurt there, too," he said.

"And you're too thin. I hope you can stay a while because I'm feeding you."

He let her statement go.

"Good to see you, Ian," said his father, and Ian shook his outstretched hand with his left. Dad, in a coat and tie, was always the formal one.

"Have you had lunch?" said his mother.

"I had the plane's snack box," said Ian.

"Nonsense, we're having lunch here at the airport," said his father. "It's good food—and always fast."

"You're too thin," said his mother. "Didn't the kidnappers feed you well?"

"It was only for a couple of days," said Ian.

"Have the criminals been caught?"

"Some of them, not all. Let's get seated, and I'll fill you in completely."

They found a restaurant with a streetcar theme and grilled food. Once seated and they'd ordered, Ian gave them more details than he had on the phone—the drug he'd been given after being kidnapped, the escape, working with an FBI agent, and his beating at the house, and near murder at the hospital.

"And why would you want to go back to Los Angeles after that?" said his mother. "You can stay with us, right Murray?" she said to her husband.

"It'll give us a chance to catch up more," Ian's father said. "You can get a job here and move to your own place when you're ready."

"I still have to help in L.A. to solve this all."

"We'll talk about it later," said his mother. "This is a heavenly day. Later, Philly and Uncle Paul are coming over, and tomorrow the twins fly in. I hope you can stay until Thanksgiving. It'd make this year so special, and know who's coming?"

While Canadian Thanksgiving was more than six weeks earlier than America's, he couldn't do that. "Ma, I told you I have to leave tomorrow—the next morning at the latest. I have a lot to do in a short time."

"I thought you were just being polite," said his father.

"I have to get to L.A. I'm on a schedule."

"How about one more day?" said his mother. "Then you'll make Thanksgiving."

"Thanksgiving is what messed us up the last time."

"Was that it? Your father and I never really understood."

"Communicating is part of our problem," said Ian.

"Problem?" said his father.

"No, no—it's my fault. We can talk later. I'm happy to come for a longer time soon."

"That would be wonderful," said his mother.

"I should have such a jet-set life," said his father. "I'd love to afford that."

Ian let it go, even if finances remained a big question mark for Ian. His father's thoughts always seemed to find a freeway from his brain to his tongue, and in the past, Ian would not let even the smallest comment go. Once the food arrived—Ian had ordered a steak— his mother said, "So, are you seeing someone?"

"Ma, I was just kidnapped."

"I meant before the kidnapping."

"There's someone I have my eye on," he said.

"Tell us about her," she said.

"She works for the government," he said.

"That's good," said his father. "Government jobs are steady and safe."

"She carries a gun," he said to dispute him.

"A gun!" cried out his mother. "Don't tell me you're dating a policeman, policeperson, whatever."

"She's a woman. FBI." It occurred to Ian that so much of his and his parents' relationship was getting a rise out of each other. Maybe it was their form of affection.

"FBI?" gasped his father.

"What, there are no actresses for you to date in Los Angeles?" said his mother.

"You'd rather have me date someone else who had little money or job prospects?"

"What's wrong with someone who doesn't own a gun?" said his father.

"Can this policeperson have babies?" said his mother.

"She probably can have babies."

His father gasped. "You want your pregnant wife carrying a gun?"

"She's not my wife. We haven't even dated." He leaned forward. "She won't even see me."

That silenced his parents. They looked at each other frowning. His mother looked up and down—her way of processing, he knew—and she spoke: "Is it because you were kidnapped?"

"Ma, sometimes you two…" He considered his options now. "Listen, let's sit down and have some lunch. Let's just catch up. I want to tell you all what's happening with me—to me—about me, if you'll listen. I came to make peace."

"My blood sugar's a little low," said his father. "This is a good idea."

"I love you, my dearest," said his mother, grabbing his chin to stare right in his eyes up close.

"I love you both, too," said Ian, and he meant it.

Medina drove downtown to private detective Joseph Moore's residence, several blocks beyond City Hall. Moore's condo was on the second floor of what appeared to be an expensive building on the west bank of the Mississippi River. Tall windows for each story went floor to ceiling. At street level, an elegant Italian café bristled with brunch business. The building itself was wedged between the huge Mill City Museum and the wildly modern Guthrie Theatre, a round blue bagel. The area must have required a good income to live in.

As she stepped into Moore's building, she was stopped by a glass wall and door. To be buzzed in, one had to look up a resident's code and punch it in on the keypad by the speaker. She found Moore's name on a list. She noticed the camera. He could undoubtedly see who was there and pretend not to be in. In his business, strangers might mean trouble. Those with badges, more so. She did not buzz.

She hurried to the backside of his building to see if there might be another way in. She did not find any back door, but she did get a view of the Mississippi, which was not exactly "mighty." The river was perhaps a mere hundred yards across, and beyond the other side were trees and what appeared to be a ten-story concrete six-pack of beer. She recognized them as old grain elevators, storage units for wheat. Above it was a neon sign that read "Pillsbury's Best Flour." This was the old milling district. Just to her left, a mini-Niagara Falls spewed water over a ledge that dropped perhaps twenty feet. At one time, as she knew from the airline magazine she'd read in flight, the falls had been the source of the power for the mills. The Twin Cities sprang up thanks to its milling, and at one time it was the flour milling capital of the world. The view was as picturesque as the magazine made it.

Because she could not get into the building, she returned to her car, which gave her a view of both Moore's lobby and the building's garage door that led into a parking structure. The second floor had all its blinds down, so if that was his unit, she couldn't tell if he was in or not. She had to assume he wasn't in, still yet to return from out of state. While she waited, she grabbed the extensive fax about him that Rick had sent to her hotel, and she read. He began his police career as a patrolman, then over eight years, moved up in ranking to detective. When he quit—it didn't say why—Moore became a private investigator. For the last twelve years, according to the report, "he tended to work for the Who's Who of the Twin Cities: the Daytons, Pillsburys, Crosbys, McMillans, and more." He even once worked for Prince, Minneapolis' most well-known rocker. Clearly, he was expensive—enough to motivate a regular person to rob banks to pay his fees. His file also noted he'd never been married and, from his birth date, he'd be fifty-eight now.

She kept looking up as she read, not wanting to miss anyone. People came to sit under the orange umbrellas of the café's sidewalk seating, but no one had yet entered Moore's lobby or garage. She read on. Moore owned two Jaguars, a Bentley, and an Aston-Martin. She nodded—the guy clearly loved his toys, and perhaps he had extralegal ways of making money.

Ninety minutes later, a Jaguar sat in front of the garage door as it rolled up, and the car drove in. Medina dashed from her car and rolled on the ground under the descending door. The car rolled on, so he hadn't seen her. Brushing herself off, she walked up the ramp and heard a car door close. She jogged the rest of the way, finding Moore, a man in black, in front of a door into the building, selecting the right key. His longish gray hair was styled, worthy of a senator.

"Mr. Moore," she said as pleasantly as if she might be a neighbor.

"Yes?" He smiled, probably because she was younger and female. From the tailoring of his tight-fitting silk shirt, she could see he kept in shape and was proud of it.

She pulled out her badge, her laminated card with photo, and showed him. "I'm special agent Medina." He looked at her ID closely as if knowing what to look for.

He frowned. "Can't you use the front door like everyone else?"

She ignored his question and dove to the heart of the matter: "I'm here on a case that took you out of state—the missing child you were after."

He held out his hand to stop. "I don't discuss client cases. The FBI should know that."

"Even if she robbed a bank to pay you?"

He smiled and shook his head. "Anything else?"

"Lots more."

"Why don't you come in? It's more comfortable." He opened the door, and it led right into his laundry room and, beyond that, the living room.

"Thank you," she said, and stepped inside and into the main room. He had high ceilings, portrait paintings on the white walls, a hutch that featured small female statuary, books, and etchings of old buildings. The art stood out thanks to the halogen spots from the hanging tracks above. It was a room meant to impress rather than live in, a showcase designed by an interior decorator. Beyond the living room stood a state-of-the-art kitchen with a stainless steel refrigerator, a stove with large red knobs, and a high counter with four bar stools. Soft contemporary instrumental music played from built-in speakers. Did the music pop on with the turn of his key? This was a man's idea of a babe trap. It probably worked often enough. The guy couldn't be long from retirement. Did he think that his magic would work until he died?

"Have a seat," he said, indicating his high-backed chairs next to a granite coffee table.

"I need to find your client now," she said, sitting.

"You don't know her name, do you?" He was adept. She'd hoped he'd reveal it without thinking.

"How did she pay you?" she asked.

"Cash, but it's not unusual for clients who want no paper trail."

"We have many of the serial numbers of what was stolen. If they match what they gave you—"

"I don't keep cash around."

"Your bank accounts are being investigated for money laundering as we speak. Your local bank may still have the bills taken in the heist. If you don't help, you may land in jail and your license yanked." She stared directly at him. "Talk."

He looked uneasy, which, for him was probably foreign. "I went into this case legitimately. Her son was kidnapped, and the FBI didn't help."

"You know what I need," she said.

He smiled. "I bet you're fire in bed."

She gave no response. She knew guys like him.

He sighed once more. "Her name is Margery Ingersol. I found her ex-husband Ralph and the boy in a trailer park outside of Lexington, Kentucky. Ralph goes by the name Frank Rogers now—works for one of the stables. I gave her the information yesterday when I found him.

"Just yesterday?"

"She only paid me for past work recently."

What about the boy?"

"Billy."

So Dottie gave the right name after all.

"He looked fine from a distance. Perhaps by now she's found a way to get her son."

"You didn't do that for her?"

"I only provide information. She can take it to the FBI or whomever."

"And who did she take it to?"

"Ya got me."

"What's her cell number?"

"I'll give it to you, but I'd advised her she dump the phone. I told her cells can be traced."

"Thanks. I'll still take it, and I need Frank Rogers' address."

He considered. Then nodded and stepped to his desk, which stood starkly alone in an alcove by the front door, a large painting of a Roman landscape behind him. A spotlight lit the painting. As he was writing the information on a card, he said, "I don't see a wedding ring."

"Who marries these days?" she said.

He laughed. "True. If you get the milk, why buy the cow?"

"That sounds like something you'd say."

"Got milk?" he said with his Tom Cruise grin.

"Your fridge has an old motor."

He laughed. "You might be surprised," he said. "When you're done with this case, let me take you to a play at the Guthrie."

"Something tells me you see the same plays many times." She took the card from his hand and peered at the address. "I've got to catch a flight for Lexington."

CHAPTER SEVENTEEN

Now early afternoon, Ian lay in his old twin bed in his room at the top of the stairs. He was surprised the room was much the same as he'd left it: his old oak desk, his bookshelf but with different books, and his framed Oleanna poster. Mamet's name towered large in dark blue over a crisp black-and-white photo of a man and a woman facing each other, mostly in silhouette, during an intense moment. Under the title it said, "Whatever side you face, you're wrong."

That's the way he felt.

He wanted to believe his plan for apologizing to those he wronged would have a positive effect, and he hoped he could then find Chad Litt, too, if he remained at large. He also wanted to believe that Medina would be ready for him. So far so good. His parents had been happy to see him.

A knock came at his door, and, because the door wasn't fully closed, it swung open. His father entered. "Oh, you're taking a nap. I'm sorry," he said, starting to back out.

"No, that's okay," said Ian, sitting up.

"Your mother's whipping up some dinner. She knows you like salmon."

"We just ate."

"It's for later. You know how your mother likes to cook."

"Yeah," said Ian, sensing his father had something deeper in mind than dinner.

His father sat on the edge of the bed looking at the ground, frowning, apparently gathering thoughts. "You can tell me, can't you? Are you in deep trouble, say with the FBI?"

"Dad, I'm the victim here."

"I know you, Ian—even though I haven't seen you for a few years. Remember as a kid how you were into rockets and I helped you shoot them at the playground?"

"That was fun."

"And I let you keep those rocket engines in your room because you promised you'd never do anything with them without me there."

"So?"

"How about the time when your friend Tom came for a sleep-over? I asked you two what you were up to, and you said 'nothing.' About twenty minutes later, your mother and I heard a loud whooshing sound, and I ran into your room, this room, and it was completely full of smoke."

They each looked over to a corner of the ceiling where a black mark could still be seen in the acoustic tile. "You launched a rocket right in your room."

"It was an accident," said Ian. "We didn't think it'd actually go off."

"You were touching the leads to a battery, and you didn't think it'd go off?"

Ian pictured himself at ten, remembering how he had set the whole thing up to show his friend how rockets worked. Ian nodded. It was his fault.

"I sense you're touching another kind of igniter right now. What's going on?"

Ian noticed a small picture in a small frame at the top of the desk in the corner. While he couldn't see the details from that distance, he knew what it was: his brother Julian catching a Frisbee in the park, a promising future of other great catches ahead of him. Ian remembered the picture in the paper of his brother's car crunched against an oak tree. After racing down a suburban street, his brother Julian had died after his car had gone out of control.

Ian looked at his father on the bed's edge. His dad's deeply creased face was the same distraught look from Julian's funeral.

"I know you talked to your mother a lot about your being taken hostage."

"Yes. I'm sorry I hadn't called earlier," said Ian.

His father looked near tears, as if he had something difficult to say. "The point is that you and I haven't talked about it. After we heard about your kidnapping, your mother and I just felt lost. To have had so little contact with you over the last few years was hard enough, but now to think you might be killed."

"How'd you even hear of it? It was in L.A."

"Canadians in the news have a way of getting attention here."

"I'm sorry. I really am. I thought you wrote me off long ago."

"Never. This is where I've never understood you. You seem to take things the wrong way."

"It's my fault?"

"No-no. See, it's me. I guess I'm a bad explainer. And I suppose I was hard on you because it seemed to be the only way you listened. After Julian died, none of us were quite normal for a while."

"But I wasn't as good as Juilian. He was my big brother and always did things better—including talking with you."

"You've never done something stupid as racing a car."

Ian did not volunteer how his instigating Owen's return nearly did him in and left a detective dead. Instead he said, "Not making up to you and Mom earlier has been stupid."

"Some things take time. Maybe you didn't know how much we've loved you, all of us. I love you."

"Thanks. And I love you."

His father took Ian's good arm and held it. Ian moved forward to give him half a hug. They'd never done even that before.

"Feels good, eh?" said Ian.

"Look at that," said his father, moving more fully onto the bed. "I have to say, I don't think I'm as bad as you've made me."

"I've never seen you as bad."

"I'm not Hitler, no, but I've always sensed you've needed something from me. I've tried to say or show you the right thing."

"I'm not sure about that," said Ian.

"What I've learned is that I cannot make another person happy," said his father. "I couldn't make your mother happy after Julian's death, nor could I help you as you seemed to struggle with it and us. The twins were okay—too young to really understand."

"Plus they've always had each other," said Ian.

"True."

"Anyway, I felt a bit helpless with you and just accepted that." His father ended there. Apparently that was it.

"I thought if I made myself a great career, you'd be impressed."

"You don't need to impress me."

"I can't now. I'm broke and out of the doctoral program."

"I'm proud of you anyway. I'm impressed you called and came up here."

Ian leaned forward and hugged his father again, this time with both arms, as if Dad were the Grand National Bank. His father hugged him deeply back. It felt good. As simple as that? It was.

"Is this all that's brought you up here?" said his father.

"Basically that."

"Anything else?"

"I don't know. I'm kind of nervous about another thing."

"About what?"

Ian told him the whole story with Medina, about everything that had happened once she'd asked him to stay with her. "There's kind of a push-pull thing going on with her," he said, putting words to his feelings. "She's appealing, but when I get too close, she pushes me away. Like on the dance floor."

His father listened well. In fact, that was what Ian remembered most about growing up—his father did not talk as much as listened. Mom did all the talking. "I don't get it. I seem to like strong women," said Ian.

His father nodded. "Your mom's a strong woman."

"So you're saying it's a mother thing?"

His father laughed. "No—your mom's nothing like this FBI agent. I'm saying strong women are great."

Ian told him, too, about Chad Litt, who seemed hell bent on killing him—and on killing others.

"Where is he now?" asked his father.

"At large—in an incredible manhunt in Los Angeles."

"And you want to go to Los Angeles?"

"I'm not going to any of my usual places. It's a city of millions. And if I can figure out his motivation, maybe I can help the FBI find him."

"I worry. Is that okay if I worry?"

"My problem is," said Ian. "I have to work hard at everything always—every grade I've ever gotten, every friend I've ever made, it's taken work. It's like I don't have a natural talent. It's always work. You see?"

"I do," said his father. "Nothing's wrong with work."

"Medina made a point that I've been blaming others, which got me thinking. I've been blaming you or Mom or fate. I have to own up to things."

"You're doing this to get her back, aren't you?"

Ian grinned and shrugged.

"I'm no love expert, but I don't think it's going to work. From what you've told me, she doesn't need anyone. And you—this owning up to things is not as easy as you think."

Ian nodded.

"You may have lost her, true," said his father, "but you still have a future. If you need to get on your feet, let me encourage you to come back. You can even stay here."

"I'm twenty-nine, Dad. Coming back here would feel like I made a major wrong turn. It's why I kept my American citizenship—to have my own country."

His father nodded.

"Anyway, I'm on my mission to own up," said Ian, "and that's part of why I have to get back to California. I have two people to apologize to there—and then get on with my life."

"Do you have the resources?"

"You mean money?" said Ian. "No. I was hoping to ask you for a loan."

His father smiled knowingly, reached for his wallet in his back pocket, and pulled out a gold card. "It's an extra credit card. If you want to go online and see what you're spending," he said, "the passcode is zero one two zero."

"My birthday?" said Ian.

"Yes, easy to remember."

Ian smiled. He really was in his father's mind.

"You can use this for whatever you need. Use it for planes, for food, whatever you need. When you don't need it anymore, send it back."

"I'll pay you back."

"No, it's a gift."

"I insist it's a loan."

"Don't be stubborn. We need to get you on your feet. Consider it your luck changing."

"Thank you, Dad."

They hugged again.

"Don't mention it. Now let me get you to the airport."

"Now?"

"ASAP is now. Of course, you have to eat salmon first." And he did. His mother included his favorite roast potatoes, garlic beans the way he loved them, and canned peaches, the best. Soon, he was back in the air. Next stop, his old girlfriend.

As Medina moved toward her gate at the Minneapolis-St. Paul International Airport, now that she had the new information, she cancelled her flight to Los Angeles and grabbed a flight to Lexington, instead, which made a quick stopover in Chicago.

Once she was in her seat on the plane, her phone rang. She'd forgotten to turn it off, but the plane hadn't left yet. She could see it was

Rick. She had not called him yet on purpose. She wanted to get to where she was going first.

"Hey, Rick," she said brightly.

"Did you finish? What happened? Did you forget to call?"

"I'm sorry," she said.

"What did you find?"

"A lot," and she filled him in on what she'd pulled from Moore.

Rick shouted "Yeow! We're on a roll. I'll get a team from Lexington's resident agency to swoop in on the trailer park. I'm sure there's an outstanding warrant for him on kidnapping. We'll grab the ex-husband before this Margery Ingersol does. We'll grab her when she tries to pick up her son. Is Ingersol the husband's last name, too?"

"Was," said Medina. "Now it's Rogers."

"We'll go to Mr. Rogers' neighborhood and bag the guy."

"And save the child."

"Yes."

Medina took a big breath. "I want to be the arresting agent."

"You've got to get back here."

"For what? Our whole group has been after these people. Let me go to Lexington. Have the resident agency stake out Rogers, and if he leaves his trailer or they can grab the kid, they can do it. If nothing's happening and they can wait for me, so much the better. I'll be there in a few hours."

"One second," said Rick. "Someone's trying to ring in."

She waited. Rick often overruled his agents, but what made him particularly effective was that he liked good ideas and encouraged feedback. He wasn't worried about always having the last word. If she ever became a Supervisory Special Agent, could she be as receptive as he was?

"Good news," Rick said, "Our painstaking work has paid off. A night clerk in a transient hotel near the 6th and Alvarado subway station has identified Chad Litt from a photo. We're now staking the place out."

"It's all coming together."

"Yeah. We've also been checking into Freddie's background and learned he used to drive for a limousine service. We pored through his driving log in hopes he might have driven Litt at some point—especially if it related to an acting studio."

"Yeah, Ian thought Litt was in an acting class."

"We discovered Freddie drove often for a particular acting teacher, Al Halo. The guy's got a studio over on Robertson. Halo may know something, so I'm on my way to question him now. This guy, Chad Litt, isn't in any of our databases, not even in DMV for California. He's still a mystery."

Medina saw the plane's door shut, and a flight attendant, a woman in her forties with her blond hair in a bun, pulled out a sample seatbelt and oxygen mask. Medina would have only another minute on the phone at best. "Rick," she said. "Will you let me go to Lexington? If it makes it easier, I'm sitting on a plane to Lexington."

There was a long pause. Medina felt her stomach drop.

"The plane hasn't taken off?" he said.

"No."

"Why're you doing this to me? You know you should've reported to me immediately. Protocol."

"I figured if you went with me this far, you'd understand. I'm sorry."

"I try to work with you, Medina. I don't get this."

"I'm in pursuit—that's perfectly valid."

"I want you back here."

"Rick, you don't get it. It's us versus them—us versus the criminals, us versus Wexler and Toffer who are using our case."

"So you're putting my career on the line?"

"You hired me."

"Shit," he said with another pause. "Go."

She felt a surge of joy. "Thank you. You won't be sorry."

"I'll alert Lexington you're coming."

"I've called Lexington already. They'll be staking out the trailer park and waiting for my arrival."

"Before I could do it?" he said.

She grimaced again.

"You've never been like this," he said. "You've always worked with me. What's going on?"

"I had to rush to the airport. I'm sorry. And after we found Dottie, it's all coming together."

"We'll talk when you get back."

"Okay." She didn't tell him it was about Ian, too. She needed to make it up to him after telling him off. Solve the case and give him closure.

"All right," Rick said. "Keep doing what you're doing."

Good. There was still hope. "See you," she said.

"Please turn off all cell phones and electronic devices," the flight attendant announced.

Medina pulled the seatbelt across her lap, clicked it together, and tuned out the flight attendant's speech. Where was Ian right now—at home with his parents? She wished she had that number. Rick had a lot of information on Ian now, and she could call him later to get it. One kind of information Rick wouldn't have, though, is did Ian hate her guts? She shouldn't have celebrated with him in the first place. She made a mistake—move on. Get over it. What's done is done. She wouldn't call Ian until much later with good news when it was all over. What the hell—she'd like to see him again. She could work out why later.

She considered where Margery Ingersol was right now. Medina played in her mind a possible scenario: her private detective, Moore, had waited until Ingersol had arrived in Lexington. He probably took her to the trailer park to show her, then returned to Minnesota. She must have come in late because Moore did not leave until the morning, so he had to show her early that day. So what would Ingersol do? Was she hiding nearby ready to grab her kid? Did she have a gun? Did she already do something? What Medina knew of Ingersol was that she liked clear, precise plans.

Ingersol wouldn't want to confront her ex as he might flee again with Billy, and her main goal was to get her son. If she had a gun, she might get the job done, but would she really want to shoot him or even brandish a gun in front of their son? Probably not. She couldn't call the FBI or police because she'd be arrested. What might she do? She'd probably observe from a distance and look for a time when Billy was outside. He'd be eight or nine now, so he might play alone or with friends, and she could snatch him back. Of course, if Ingersol happened to spot someone observing her, she might flee again. If she didn't notice, she'd make her move and be caught. Medina hoped for the latter. At that point, they'd then have three of the four bandits, and the net was swirling above Chad Litt, too. Rick would find him. With all the resources at work, they might solve it all today.

But the queasy feeling in her stomach said things could go a whole other way. Too many times it did.

Ian landed in Los Angeles a little after six p.m. He'd gained two hours going westward. He wasn't absolutely sure his car was back home as the police had promised after he'd landed in the hospital. Even if it was, the window that Owen had smashed was still out.

He'd deal with that later. Plus there was a time factor. He grabbed a courtesy van to Hertz outside of LAX and rented a Ford Focus, which was inexpensive, another item that fell onto the credit card. A few miles in the underpowered vehicle, he figured it was so named because it tried to focus on being a car. It did the job, though. He knew exactly where he was going because he'd driven by the house twice over the last few years in hopes of seeing Pierra from a distance. He wasn't sure if she'd be home or, for that matter, if she'd moved in the last six months. It was a house far in the West Valley, Canoga Park, with a front yard, an attached two-car garage, and brown stucco freshly painted by a guy named Preston, her new boyfriend.

It was just after sunset when Ian arrived, and he walked quickly to the door before he changed his mind. He pressed the little white button and knocked, too. The doorbell had a plate around it in the shape of a heart. Very cute. So this was a love nest? He was surprised he no longer cared. Meeting Medina had changed things for him.

The front light clicked on. The front door swung open. Preston, a tall, wide-necked guy, early thirties with red hair, stood at the door. Ian recognized him because Pierra had described him well and added that Preston was everything Ian was not. "Preston has a practical job, isn't jealous of my work, and doesn't mind my relatives," was the way she put it. Preston was a manager of a tile store in nearby Woodland Hills, and now Ian noticed the front hallway had elegant blue-and-white ceramic tile.

"Ian, right?" Preston said.

"Yes."

"I recognize you from the TV." Preston saw his cast and looked concerned. "Are you okay?"

Ian nodded.

"Oh, man," said Preston. "That must've been scary. We're so sorry. So'd they catch the guys?"

"A few," said Ian. "Looks like it'll wrap up soon."

"That's good." He turned and yelled, "Pierra! Pierra, come to the door." He turned back to Ian. "So what brings you this way?"

"As a hostage, I was drugged and kicked and nearly killed. Beat up badly." He held his cast up again.

"I hope those guys get the death penalty," said Preston.

"There were two women, too."

"Women did this to you?"

Ian looked down at his cast, wondering if "this" was what he meant.

"You know, sometimes I wonder how we live with 'em — women," said Preston. Pierra strode up behind Preston. Her dark hair was longer, wavier, fingering past her shoulders. She wore a low-cut blouse, white with giant orchid flowers all over it. She was gorgeous. "Ian? What're you doing here?"

"Look, they broke his arm," said Preston as a reason, pointing to Ian's cast.

"You okay?" she said.

"Come in," said Preston. "Join us in the back." Ian recognized a slight Southern accent in his voice.

"Thanks," said Ian stepping in, and he briefly explained what happened since his release, including his hospitalization and a trip to Minnesota with "the FBI." He didn't mention Medina's name. He ended with "I'm okay."

"Good to hear," said Pierra, looking like she meant it. Apparently being kidnapped put him in good with her. Maybe he should have been kidnapped earlier. No, Ian reminded himself. That's not why he was there.

"This way," said Preston. "We're having mint juleps—want one?"

Didn't they want to know more of why he was there? "Sure," said Ian. "I've never had a julep before."

"Bourbon, sugar, and mint—good for a hot day."

"Was it hot today?" said Ian.

"Not really. We just like 'em."

Ian followed 'em to the back, but this still felt odd, as if they were expecting him. As they walked through the living room, Ian found the place neat, with a large-screen plasma television against one wall and a sectional sofa in leather that curved around to the back sliding-glass door. It was all the shit that Ian couldn't afford.

Outside, there was a cast aluminum patio set and a built-in gas grill with a tile counter top. For an October evening, it was mild weather. Six-foot brick walls and large trees bordered the back yard; the middle was a rectangle carpet of grass. Wouldn't it be wonderful to be a bird in the Valley? "A comfortable place you have."

"We like it," said Pierra.

Preston handed him a drink in a fresh glass. "Have a seat," said Preston.

"So you were… in the neighborhood?" tried Pierra, sitting down, looking dubious. At last.

"I can only stay a short time," said Ian, "and I thought, well… you know."

"You thought what?" said Pierra.

"Listen," Ian started, having rehearsed his part in his mind in the plane and in the car. He hadn't considered Preston, but it shouldn't make a difference. "I wanted to say I'm sorry about everything in the past. You're a good person."

"I'm confused. Why are you telling me this?"

"I'm owning up to things now, including my past. I almost died, and I realized things."

"So you're apologizing for your behavior," she said. "And what is that specifically?"

"I'm sorry for calling your relatives *crackers.* It's what brought our engagement crashing down, right?"

"You did *what*?" said Preston, now looking offended.

"It was stupid, yes."

"Yes," said Preston.

"It was after a list of other things, too," said Pierra.

"A list?" said Ian. "Well, anyway, I'm apologizing. I was insensitive and I regret it. Truly, Pierra."

She shook her head and told Preston, "He was a workaholic, too. He always brought work on vacations. He was also in competition with me to get his doctorate first." She turned to Ian. "Did you get yours?"

"Not yet," he said.

"I have." She smiled proudly. "I teach at Cal State Northridge."

He gritted his teeth. This isn't what he wanted to discuss. Her degree shouldn't matter to him, but it did. It underscored his failure. He made himself say, "Congratulations."

"Also he always made me go Dutch," said Pierra.

Preston shook his head as if Ian was part of the Weird News, such as the man whose house was overrun with thirteen hundred lab mice.

Ian scoffed. "Come on, now. I grew up thinking men and women were exactly equal, so I was just being equal."

"Oh, man," said Preston, laughing. "What planet are you from?"

"Okay, so I was a bit misguided."

"A *bit*?" said Pierra.

Why was she doing this to him? This wasn't easy.

"This is so odd," she said. "You must have some ulterior motive here. Or are you doing that Alcoholics Anonymous thing?"

"I don't drink that much." He was going to say *I'm astounded you figured this out,* but was he astounded or was he mad?

"I've realized things," he began again, getting back to his main goal. He turned to Preston. "I'm not out to woo Pierra or anything."

"Did you ever woo?" said Pierra.

He faced Pierra. "I came simply so I can move on with my life—and you, yours."

"We're moving on just fine," said Pierra.

"You're still angry with me," said Ian, "and you probably should be. I was a jerk. I'm sorry. I only hope I can find someone as great as you've found."

Pierra blinked, stupefied. "Well…." She reached over and took Preston's hand and smiled. "I hope you do, too."

Ian turned to Preston. "David Mamet talks about how women really have an advantage over us, like we don't know the rules, and I think he's right."

"I gotta agree with you there," said Preston. "Who's David Mamet?"

"He's a macho asshole playwright who Ian fuckingly worships."

"What do you want from me?" blurted Ian. In that instant, he realized what a genius Pierra was. She knew how to manipulate a moment. In comparison, Ian was a slug walking across salt, curling into death. "I mean, what can I say to you dissing Mamet? I like that Mamet is sure of himself and speaks with authority. Do I make fun of Rubén Ortiz-Torres?"

"Who's that?" said Preston.

"A contemporary Mexican artist," said Ian. "She takes her quarter-Mexican blood seriously, as you probably know. She interviewed Ortiz-Torres often for her dissertation on contemporary Latino artists and their relation to European art history."

Preston appeared dumbfounded for a second, then said, "Oh, that guy." Pierra shot him a look. "I'm sorry," Preston said. "I remember now."

"You guys," she said, shaking her head.

"You're smarter than me, darlin'. That's all I can say," said Preston. He slid from his chair onto his knees and kissed her. On his way back to his chair, he leaned to Ian and whispered, "That's how it's done."

"Pierra, you were right about almost everything all of the time," said Ian. "Please forgive me." There. That was the point of his mission.

Pierra stared at Ian, then smiled. "Okay, then." She held up her glass. "Salud."

Ian grinned. "Okay, then." He raised his glass, too, as did Preston, like they were the Three Musketeers. "Salud," they said in unison.

Ian looked at his watch. He could still make it to Orange County at a reasonable hour, check into an inexpensive motel, and be ready early in the morning for his professor. Maybe he could even get insight on Litt.

🩸

Earlier that day, Medina had spoken with special agent Nora Rassmussen at the Lexington resident agency shortly after she arrived. At last, another female agent. They agreed to meet at her hotel in a half hour. They had less than three hours until sunset—no time to waste. They could then prepare for the takedown at the Monaco Estates, a mobile home park. Medina's uncle had lived in such a park in Los Angeles. There was nothing mobile about the homes—no wheels. The homes had to be tied down and skirted. It wasn't a park, either, and she doubted the place Mr. Rogers lived in was park-like or as rich as Monaco. When it came to it, every word of the title was likely false.

Nora was prompt. A tall woman with short reddish hair and dressed similarly to Medina in a suit with a white blouse, Nora had a map of the trailer park.

"Here's lot sixty-two. A car is in the driveway, but, word I got, no one's gone in or out yet."

"Shit. We might be too late," she said.

"We're thinking that, too, but it's only been a few hours. We have the warrant and a stakeout. We wanted to wait for you."

Nora drove, which allowed Medina to absorb the area. They moved quickly down Highway 60 then 62 past a number of small farms and the petite town of Versailles, which had a tall steepled city hall and small houses with front porches near town center.

"Pretty town, Versailles" said Medina. She gave the name a good French accent, 'Vair-sigh,' having studied French at UCLA.

"Actually," said Nora, "here it's pronounced 'Vur-*sales*.' In Kentucky, what good's a word if you don't pronounce all the letters?"

Shortly after Versailles, the homes turned into estates with running white fences that ran up and down the hills like the horses they enclosed. The houses, if they were visible at all, tended to be two stories with columned front porches and windows with accented shutters. This was old rich.

The entrance to the Monaco Estates came after a stretch of a running white wood fence. From the road, it looked as if it'd be for another rich manor, but as soon as they turned in the driveway and rose up and down a hill, a gathering of mobile homes appeared. The homes were on actual lots with well-tended lawns, trees, and space. There was a clubhouse with a basketball court and pool. This wasn't L.A. where mobile homes were five feet apart. Medina realized that with any rich community, the workers had to live somewhere, and this looked much better than Highland Park below Mt. Washington.

Nora stopped and spoke into her handset. "Hey, guys, we're here. Any movement in the suspect's home?"

"None that we can see," came a male voice in response. "The kitchen and living room shades are drawn, so we can't see in there."

"Okay." She turned to Medina. "Should we move in?" Medina quickly played out two scenarios in her head. One was that Mr. Rogers and son were out for that day, and an FBI raid on the home would get neighbors talking and someone would call Rogers' cell phone and alert him. The second was that Ingersol had come already and the FBI was too late.

Medina figured the latter and nodded, and Nora spoke into her handset, "Move closer and surround the place. We'll drive in and knock on the door."

"Will do."

Nora parked behind the car in the driveway, an older Chevy Malibu. Already visible were men moving in wearing blue jackets that said "FBI" in large letters. Nora pulled out her gun, which gave the cue for Medina to withdraw hers.

The home was a modest single-wide, smaller than his adjacent neighbors in doublewides. Quietly, they moved up the wooden stairs to the front door. Medina pressed the doorbell. When there was no answer, she knocked. "Mr. Rogers?" Nora shouted? "Mr. Rogers, it's the FBI."

Nora pulled up her handset. "Does anyone see or hear any movement?" She received a "negative, ma'am" from three different people.

"Send them in," said Medina. She and Nora pulled back as the police moved in. One tried the door, which was unlocked. He flung it open and quickly stepped aside. The aluminum siding of the trailer wasn't going to stop any bullet, Medina realized, but habits were habits.

The agents poured in. A minute later, one came out. "It's secure. You need to see this," he said somberly and he waved for Medina to come.

When she entered, a man sat on a bar stool at the tall kitchen counter, his head on the counter. His face was in a milky cereal bowl. Rogers wasn't going to respond. A small lake of dark blood surrounded the chair's feet. Definitely dead.

Medina turned to Nora behind her. "Tell them to put their guns away."

"I felt for a heartbeat," said the lead officer. "Nothing."

Nora spoke into her handset. "Stand down. Dead body in here."

Medina found herself walking slowly and softly near Rogers as if too much noise would disturb his sleep. From the deep slash in his neck, a good semicircle in the front, he probably couldn't have screamed—windpipe cut. His head must have been held in the bowl for the minute it took him to die. Probably tried to hold his throat with one hand and get whoever's arm with the other. Both arms now hung limply down. The attacker had to be very swift and strong. Wonder if the boy had seen this?

"Did your suspect Ingersol do this?" said Nora.

Medina shook her head. The scene spoke to Medina, and she knew exactly what'd happened. Medina felt stupid for not anticipating it. First, the chain of events occurred earlier than Medina had figured. Ingersol had arrived in Lexington early Saturday. Second, the woman must have known that she'd need help. She came with it—in the form of Litt.

CHAPTER EIGHTEEN

The next morning in Orange County, after he had parked in the Mesa Structure on the UC Irvine campus and was walking toward the drama offices, Ian spotted Professor Cromley walking across the green grass. Perfect.

"Professor," Ian shouted.

The hunched man whose unkempt hair moved with the breeze looked up, absolute panic on his face. He stopped as if on the wrong end of a deer rifle.

"No, nothing to worry about," said Ian. "I just came to explain something."

The professor shook his head, which made the uncombed white hair on top dance, and he pointed toward Studio Four, a tall, square building, very modern like the rest of the campus. The man said, "I have to go."

"I need to speak with you. Just for one minute." Ian used the index finger on his hand with the cast to indicate "one." Cromley noticed his cast. You can't dismiss a cripple.

"Call my secretary for an appointment."

"I'm leaving town today, so I needed to see you now."

"And you fully expected I had the time?"

Ian realized that such a dismissive statement in the past would have enraged him, but today, he only saw it as a hurdle. "Recently I'd been held hostage in a bank robbery. You may have seen it on the news."

Cromley's face became a puzzle. "That was you?"

Ian nodded. "I was beat up severely, too." He held up his cast again.

"It kind of looked like you but I thought, you know…"

So why didn't you call the police? Ian realized, though, that if he said that, he'd alienate the man. He needed another approach. "In your 'Studies In Playwriting' class, you'd talked about how a play was really an illusion and a metaphor for life."

"Yes," said the professor, glancing at his watch.

"And you said that people normally don't change quickly, and

216

rarely over one event, but that theatre has to condense life and make us see things, scene after scene."

"True. Good to see you were taking notes, but I'm late. I'm sorry." He started to walk.

"Professor, wait. One sec. Please. I've been through a lot in a week, and… " In that instant, Ian could feel his own face crumble. In his mind he saw Detective Jones's body, Cuervo's covered body, and the beaten face and body of Freddie Liu. His eyes watered. He had to grit his teeth to save his dignity.

The professor took a step closer and eyed him carefully. "Are you okay? Do you need to see a counselor?"

"I came to see you." Ian felt his eye twitch. "I'm sorry. The week's been crazy. This was probably a stupid idea to come here."

"If you're trying to get back into the program— Really, I'm not the person to see."

"I'm not trying to get back," said Ian. "I came to apologize."

"For what?"

"For being obstinate… and all the other stuff. You and your colleagues were right. I wasn't right for the program."

The man looked wary. "Is this some kind of Mametesque parody of Method acting?" Cromley referred to Ian's disdain of Method acting, where actors tried to replicate real life emotional conditions to create a realistic performance. Big proponents of the Method, first developed by Constantin Stanislavski in Russia, had been Marlon Brando, Dustin Hoffman, Robert DeNiro—and Cromley. In Ian's comments in class, it was false acting—which is the way David Mamet had explained it. Rather than prepare by remembering emotional moments from the past, actors should be open to the unexpected while onstage. Real vulnerability is the most telling.

"Listen, I don't hate Stanislavsky," said Ian. "I just don't like how Method actors misinterpreted him. I'm guilty, too, though, of not listening to the man. Stanislavsky also said, 'The greatest wisdom is to realize one's lack of it.' I seem to have smashed head on into that realization." He smiled. This was the point, and Ian felt good.

Professor Cromley stared at him as if having stumbled upon Virgin Mary's profile on a piece of bread. "But see how Stanislavsky is correct in using life's experiences?"

"Except I'm not acting," said Ian. "This is a true moment—a thousand times more interesting than the best actor, you ask me." Ian shoved his hands into his pockets to make sure he didn't seem threatening. "So I'm sorry," said Ian. "I'm responsible for my dismissal, and I thank you for your classes." Ian gave a small wave and started to walk away. A breeze wafted across his face. He could smell that the lawn had been freshly cut.

"One sec," said Cromley. "You just apologized for what? Being you?"

Ian turned back. "Yes, and more."

"You don't want back into the program?"

Ian shook his head no. "Mamet said that my generation likes to stay in school. It's good that I'm out. I mean really—who needs a degree to be an actor or director? I should have listened to him earlier."

"So this is it? You don't need anything from me?"

"I got it already," said Ian. "Thanks."

Cromley screwed his face, mystified. "Really? What'll you do?"

Ian's first thought was to call Medina, now that he'd apologized to everyone, but Cromley meant what's next for the career. Ian quipped, "Maybe I'll join the FBI."

Cromley stared. "You serious?"

Ian realized he was. He looked at Cromley's belly pack, the small pouch at his waist that was always stuffed as if it held bibliographies on a hundred topics. "I'm good at inductive reasoning, and I'm a good researcher. I've a master's degree, and I've smoked pot less than fifteen times. Heck, the FBI's a possibility."

Cromley frowned.

"It also seems like I'd be doing more good than in theatre," said Ian. "Isn't that what we want, a life with meaning?" Ian nodded, impressed with himself. He'd never put it all together before.

"Life's odd, isn't it?" said Cromley.

"Sure is."

"Nice to see you're okay." Cromley stuck his hand out. They shook.

As they parted, Ian twisted around. "You know, professor. Actually, I do have a question—about character motivation. You were always big on that, yet the man who nearly killed me apparently had never killed anyone before he got involved in bank robbery. He's now killed six people without guilt and then he's been like the Terminator after me. I can't figure out his motivation."

"Do you know much about his background?"

"All I can tell is he wanted to impress everyone in his gang. He seems to want to conquer women and kill men."

"Let's say he was a character in a play and we're given little information on him—as in a Mamet play. You have to agree Mamet doesn't give a lot of stage directions or insight to his characters."

"True," said Ian, wondering if Cromley was going to slam Mamet again.

"What I know is serial killers tend to have been influenced a great deal in their childhood—such as being adopted, being rejected by peers, being in juvenile detention or an orphanage, witnessing violence such as Dad beating up Mom—or a combination of these things. Formative years play a role, but not all siblings in such conditions become serial killers. There's something unexplainable that happens to rare individuals."

"I'm trying to think of a play with such a killer."

"How about Shakespeare's *Richard the Third*? The man was a monster, and he wanted to be. He said early on, 'I am determined to prove a villain.' Of course, there was his physical deformity and the notion he was killing people to get back at God, but I look at it as a symbol of his psychological deformity. Besides, the play doesn't say he's a hunchback. Basically, he was born prematurely and felt inadequate—which may be exactly like your guy. He's trying to prove himself, yes?"

Ian nodded, in awe. "You're right. This guy, Chad Litt, comes across as if he feels inadequate. Maybe if he kills me, it will prove to himself how powerful he is."

"It's always about power. Everybody mocks *Richard the Third* and thinks he can't achieve anything. Richard, though disabled, wants to prove he can reach the ultimate power and be king—and he does."

"Thank you. That's great. And would you mind if I used you as a reference—in case I apply to the FBI?"

Cromley smiled. "Sure. What the hell. As long as I don't have to be a Republican."

Medina examined the front door's strike plate and bolt carefully. No signs of forced entry. With her digital camera from her pocket, she took a few photos for her records, one shot showing Rogers at the counter, his head in the bowl. She imagined Litt knocking on the door one morning, selling something, or saying he was a neighbor, then being his charming best. Perhaps the boy was still asleep or at least in another room. Litt would have chatted away, and Mr. Rogers would have started eating again. Silently, Litt could have pulled out his knife, stepped up behind, cut the man's throat and held him down. In Litt's world, killing was easy. Medina photographed some close-ups, focusing on the neck wound.

She did not document everything. The team would do that. They'd find evidence that could be used in court later, but what mattered most to her now was the boy. He was probably back in sweet Mama Ingersol's hands, no doubt. Litt, Ingersol, and the boy would have left the area as fast as possible. If she were Ingersol, knowing her ex-husband's body might be discovered, they couldn't use the airport, train, and bus stations, which might be alerted and watched. Ingersol would drive. But where to? America was big. Relatives might aid in her hiding. Minnesota was likely. It wasn't a given, but certainly a possibility. Ingersol could easily drive somewhere else.

Medina called Rick and updated him on all that had happened that morning so far.

"Have you gone to nearby gas stations or stores for possible video footage of Ingersol, Litt, or the boy?" Rick asked.

"It's being done now," said Medina. "We're also showing pictures of them at car rental agencies. We'll see what cars around Lexington have been reported stolen, too. What else have you found about Ingersol? There's more now, right?"

"She has no record. She's clean."

"I'm betting she's going to Minnesota."

"I'll get Minneapolis to watch Ingersol's parents' house. We'll alert law enforcement in the states around Kentucky and all the way to Minnesota."

Medina thought Dottie might know more about Ingersol's likes and personality and have a valuable clue. However, she told Rick, "I'm figuring the drive from Lexington to Minneapolis has to be at least eight hundred miles. They're traveling with a kid, so that's at least a fourteen-hour drive. She'll probably split it into two days. In other words, they'll be getting in later tomorrow."

"That sounds right."

"Rick, don't scream, but I've got to get to Minnesota and help there. I want to be there ahead of her. I'm so damn close."

"I expected you to say that."

"Will Toffer or Wexler fire you or me if I went?"

"They've been getting so much press lately, they'll go with what I say. If this works out right, Toffer can retire, and Wexler can get a promotion. Get to Minnesota."

🖤

In the Lexington airport as Medina waited for her flight to Minnesota to board, her cell phone rang. It was a Los Angeles number she didn't recognize, but her instinct said to take it.

"Aleece! It's Ian. How's it going?" His voice sounded bright, and he explained he was using hands-free in a rented car on the 405 in Los Angeles.

"You're not it Canada?"

"I was there for a day, and now I've been here for a day."

"I don't understand."

"I took your advice and I'm patching up my life. Doin' okay, too, thanks to you."

She had the sensation of plummeting on a ride at Magic Mountain where her stomach flew away. She sensed he wanted to talk about what he was doing, but this wasn't the time. She had too much to do. It was just good to hear he didn't resent her.

"You have a cell phone?" she said.

"Time to join the new age. So can you tell me about the case?" he asked back.

"No," she said. "Not just yet. I'm sorry." As she reminded herself, he wasn't a fellow agent; he was no longer involved.

"United Airlines Flight 2864 to Chicago is now boarding," said the booming P.A. system. "Please have your boarding passes ready."

"You're going to Chicago?" Ian said. "Are you at LAX?"

"Elsewhere."

"Oh, you're boarding."

"Not so much that." She was, in fact, moving toward the gate where people were quickly gathering. "I just can't talk."

"So you can't say if you got Zetta or Litt yet."

"I can't."

At his sigh, she felt bad. He cleared his throat. "Why can't you talk to me?"

"I shouldn't have involved you so much before. It was wrong."

"No, it wasn't."

"No, I mean, it comes down to FBI rules."

"We made a good team."

"It's not about that." If only he'd understand. The PA system interrupted, "Blue Grass Airport courtesy telephones to the hotels are located next to Baggage Claim."

"Blue Grass? Are you in Lexington?" said Ian.

"Please, Ian."

"As you've said, 'God is in the details.' The fact you're going to

Chicago, where you're probably transferring back to Minneapolis, suggests something more's happening there, so that's okay you can't tell me."

"If you can just be patient, Ian. Good things—great things—are happening, but it's… sensitive."

"Ah, you're getting close."

"Look," she said. "This is about doing things properly."

"I have done things properly. That's what I'm calling about. When I got to Canada, I saw my parents."

"Final call for United Airlines Flight 2864 to Chicago," came the announcement. "Sorry, can we talk later?" she said to Ian.

"Of course."

She walked toward the ticket agent with her boarding pass. "I'm getting on the plane. I'd love to call you later, if I may. I do like talking with you." *I miss you,* she almost said. "Okay?"

"Let me give you my number," he said.

"I have your number. My cell recorded it."

"Amazing things, these cell phones."

"Bye," she said.

She walked toward her seat, pulling her wheeled overnight bag. Yes, God was in the details. Time to find the final ones and finish this off.

In UC Irvine's main library, Ian found an open computer and hopped on it, where he located the latest news from Lexington. The leading story was that a local man, Frank Rogers, was found dead in his trailer from an apparent slit throat, and his son Billy was missing. The FBI suspected that his ex-wife, Margery Ingersol, had killed him and taken back her son who had been kidnapped by Frank three years earlier. No details were known of her whereabouts or what she might be driving.

So Margery Ingersol was Zetta's name, Ian thought. Ian also knew that she wasn't likely to slice her husband's neck. She had help, and he suspected Litt. Litt was not in any news story anywhere in the country, he soon saw. He had to be with Margery and the boy, going to where Medina was headed: Minnesota.

Using the computer, he also looked up news on Dottie and found the briefest of stories on her arrest for bank robbery, and, seen as a flight risk, she did not receive bail. She was being held in the Hennepin County jail pending transfer to Waseca, a federal prison seventy-five miles south of Minneapolis.

Ian found the next flight from LAX to Minneapolis/St. Paul—less than two hours. He booked it, ran to his rental car, and raced out of there.

At the Hennepin County jail, Medina faced Dottie in a small conference room with her white-haired lawyer, Leblanc Petersen, a Nordic-looking fellow, by her side. In her orange prison jumpsuit, sans makeup and feminine attire, Dottie looked haggard and manly. She was being kept with the male population.

"I've advised my client not to answer more questions until she's been transferred to the female population," Petersen said.

"I'm not the warden," said Medina. "They have their rules. I have no influence."

"A federal agent? I'd be surprised."

"I'll do my best. I want to help, but I'm here concerned for Margery and her son's safety," Medina said.

"You discovered her name," said Dottie. "And she has her son?"

"Yes, and her ex-husband is dead, thanks to your Mr. Litt, who now we've confirmed from this gas station photo is with her."

Medina showed the two a grainy photo of Margery pumping gas with Chad Litt cleaning the side window with a squeegee.

Dottie blurted, "Oh, no." She looked worried.

"Litt is driving Billy and Margery back here, we think," said Medina.

"I'm sure Margery knows what she's doing. She's a smart girl," said Dottie, sure of herself again.

"I'd like to stop this now," said Petersen.

"And how would you feel if I came back in a few days with a photo of Margery dead? Maybe she doesn't do things the way Litt wants. Or her son. Litt killed two people at the bank, then Detective Jones and your driver, two people at a hospital, and now Margery's ex-husband. He doesn't mind killing."

Medina pulled out her smart phone and showed her a photo of Frank Rogers' sliced neck, and his face submerged in the cereal bowl. Dottie gasped. Petersen whispered in his client's ear, and Dottie nodded, then whispered back.

Petersen cleared his throat. "We agree. Time's of the essence. In your notes, I want you to show my client's cooperation."

Medina nodded.

"It's not like Margery will call me here, though," said Dottie. "I have no idea what she'll do next."

"I need to know more about Litt. I must have missed something when you explained before. Tell me again how you found him?"

"Between you and other agents—don't you guys talk to each other?"

"Humor me."

"Margery and I needed to scope out L.A., but the freeways intimidated us. We used cabs to drive us to various banks. Freddie turned out to be our driver twice, and he asked us why were we so interested in banks."

"Hadn't you noticed he was a driver you'd had?"

"Do you ever remember cab drivers? They always just seem ethnic. Anyway, he was curious why two out-of-town women went to banks. I guess he heard our code names for each other, too—Zetta and Navarre. Then he said, 'If you're robbin' banks, let me be your driver.' Said he was working two jobs and needed the money."

"Had this been your plan, find a cab driver, or how did you think you'd find accomplices?" Medina said.

"We were thinking nightclubs. Margery said she always attracted the wrong guy, so why not use it to our advantage? But Freddie figured us out, so we used him."

"And Freddie knew Litt?"

"Yes. He said we should have a mean-looking guy to help, and he knew an actor who looked right and needed the cash. This was Chad Litt."

"How'd you find the getaway house?" said Medina.

"House sitting was Margery's idea. She'd read a story about it in the L.A. Times. Everything fell into place."

"Including Litt killing two people at the bank?"

"Then I knew we were in trouble. This whole thing's become a nightmare." She gathered her long hair on one side of her face and pulled it behind her ear.

"We need to find Margery before he does her harm," said Medina. "Where might she go with Litt and her son?"

"No idea at all."

"What would you do?"

"If it were me, I'd go far north to the Lake of the Woods by the Canadian border—little islands and desolate places to hide," said Dottie. "Or Northern Wisconsin, too—Madeline Island, pretty woodsy."

"Is she close with her parents?"

"No. They had a falling out years ago, and they refused to help pay for finding their grandson. Her father said she should've never married the man she did, the man who stole her son."

"I received a text that Margery called your house and spoke to Catherine, where she learned about your arrest. Catherine told her to hang up, so we lost a trace, but it tells me Margery may be in this area. Where might she hide out?"

Dottie's face crinkled with worry. "I wish I knew. I don't want her to die."

"What about places you went with her that are unusual?" said Medina. "Parties in the woods or something."

"There's one thing," said Dottie. "Maybe it's far-fetched, but her father loved fishing and once took us with him. This was years ago when I first knew Margery, and her father knew me as Don. He liked me."

"Far-fetched I'll take," said Medina.

"We fished at a gorgeous spot at the end of a dock—near the heart of Wayzata. We parked at a bakery right at the end of the main street. And then walked around to a really long dock. It was surprisingly secluded."

"End of Lake Street? Which end?"

"The end where the mini-mall is. It was right next to the railroad tracks. We walked over the tracks, went through some bushes, and we came upon the boathouse. It was like a cottage, where we picked up extra fishing rods. A little kitchen in there, beds in the loft, too."

"Whose boathouse?"

"Her father's boss's. The man's kids used the boathouse for slumber parties, but they must be grown-up by now. Anyway, it was far enough from the main house and had enough trees and bushes to be hidden. The dock was large and had an awning over the two boats. Margery probably doesn't remember it, but there you have it—isolated, yet in the heart of the city."

Medina thanked Dottie and Petersen.

Twenty minutes later, Medina traveled down Wayzata's main street starting at the west end and moved past the train station, past elegant clothing stores, the Bookcase, and sidewalk cafes full of couples. She could picture herself with Ian at one of these cafes after everything was over.

Trees and potted flowers added to the flourish of the street. It was late afternoon on a warm October day, and the sun shone in a golden light. On the lake, sailboats gently bobbed, and speedboats made beelines for somewhere, perhaps the last time for the season. In that Photoshop moment, it felt as if all the people were getting and doing what they wanted.

What about Chad Litt? His need to be ruthless struck her as what she'd encountered rarely but chillingly: a person's enjoyment to be cruel and to kill. She wouldn't be surprised if he'd tortured animals when he was young. Perhaps he hadn't acted on his nature until the bank robbery, and once he killed a few people, he realized he was good at it. Litt probably also thrilled in seeing that he controlled people's lives. He'd already killed seven people and could do more.

Medina focused on finding the bakery Dottie had mentioned. The bakery had to be on the lake side because the railroad tracks were there. The stores soon appeared on that side. Once she hit the Gas-and-Go, the road curved up the hill past the mini-mall, and she realized there was no bakery. Best to ask. She pulled into Starbucks, which was in a building that looked more like a big bank than a coffee house.

The lot was full, and she had to park in the back, near the tracks. She walked past the outdoor tables in the back of Starbucks. Teenagers chatted eagerly, drinking mostly domed drinks full of whip cream. She entered Starbucks and stood in the line. The place was spacious, larger than most coffee shops in Los Angeles, certainly larger than Carrie's Coffee in the Landwest Bank. Music played, Johann Pachelbel's Canon in D. It began slowly, tranquilly, classically with a single violin. Nothing better than the sweet voice of a single violin. Then another violin joined it, a serene sister. The chord progression led to a dancing of notes. Fewer songs on this planet were as beautiful. Then an electric guitar cut in. A guitar? The guitar buzzed and built, betraying the fingering. It was fast. Furious. It was like a skateboarder slashing down a mountain. She hadn't heard this version. There was passion. It made her smile.

When it was her turn, she told the server, a young man, "A grande cappuccino, please." She could use a little more energy.

The woman next to him, in her thirties, looked at Medina, "Want this cappuccino here? No one claimed it. Free." Medina noted the woman's nametag said Manager.

"Thanks." Medina took it. "My lucky day. By the way, a friend told me of a great bakery around here, but I can't find it."

"The Wuollet Bakery and Espresso across the street?"

Sure enough, there was a bakery across the street. How'd she miss that? "My friend said it was right next to the railroad tracks, though. That's why I didn't see it."

"This used to be a bread bakery, churning out loaves," said the woman. "I guess the upscale bakery across the street put it out of business." That meant this was the spot. More luck. The boathouse had to be on the other side of the tracks. "Thanks," said Medina, and she hurried out.

Out in the parking lot, she stepped up to the tracks. Looking first left, then right, the tracks went straight in either direction, bordered by a tall hedge and many trees. Over the top of the hedge, a few hundred yards down, the uppermost peak of a roof showed. That might be the main house that Dottie had mentioned. Still, the hedge was very thick—no way through. She'd have to drive around and find the house. Except with such a thick hedge, surely people on the other side had to have a shortcut. Was there a way through the hedge?

She placed her coffee on top of her car to use both hands in the hedge and walked down the tracks a little toward the house to find a thinning area. A small break in the bushes, tunnel-like, soon appeared. It was like entering a cave. She moved in slowly. As she emerged on the other side of the hedge, there stood a small white cottage with double-hung windows—but there were no signs of anyone through the back windows. A lawn led to the lake where there was a dock and an awning with two boats underneath. This whole area was hidden by the hedge—another world. To Medina's left was the main house, mostly obscured by a number of pines and other small trees. If she could get further left, she might have a better angle to see the boathouse's front. All she needed to see was Ingersol or Litt through a window—that would allow her to call in the police for a warrantless arrest with probable cause.

Medina heard the snap of a twig behind her, and she turned. A large figure rushed at her, and she focused on the extra-large-sized coffee cup in his hand with its lid off. Brown liquid flew right at her. She tried to dodge it, but the hot fluid hit her face—a thousand needles—and she growled and fell into a protective crouch against the hedge, unable to see. She felt a hand or foot pushing sideways, but she went with the roll, twisted around and, still blurry-eyed, found a foot and twisted it, causing the man who had to be Litt to fall into the hedge. He didn't fall down, however. She tried to scramble away but felt her side kicked again and again, and she screamed in pain. Her eyes blinking through a blur, she grabbed wildly and caught nothing. Her head took a blow, and her hands shot up to protect herself. With one more blow, she passed out.

She felt coolness on her face and opened her eyes. Ingersol, her Busty Bandit, sat above her and applied a cool wet cloth. In a white sweater, Ingersol looked angelic, concerned. Then Medina realized her own mouth was taped shut and her arms and legs were bound. She lay on the floor of some sort of storage closet. Fishing rods stood against one wall, and something labeled Marine Wax was on a shelf.

"Chad's temper is a problem," said Ingersol, "but he's right: you could do us in."

Medina tried to respond, but it came out as a series of moans.

"I'm sorry. I can't let my son hear you," said Ingersol. "Luckily he was watching his iPad when Chad attacked you. And luckily you screamed so I could stop Chad from killing you. I don't want you dead, but we need to get out of here soon."

Medina tried to say, "No, listen," but again it came out as just moans.

"We're just working out the details. I don't know how the hell you found us."

◆

"Answer, answer, answer," Ian chanted into his cell phone, now that he'd landed. She didn't answer, so he left a message. He looked off, trying to picture where Medina might be.

◆

Medina tried giving the kinds of sounds that someone who was not panicked but wanted to talk would give—Muppet-like sounds, she realized. It worked as Ingersol said, what're you trying to say? Whisper now, okay?" Ingersol removed the tape.

"Margery," said Medina softly. "Litt is a problem, yes? You can't endanger your son with him—or yourself."

"Chad rescued my son—more than the FBI ever did."

"He's killed at least seven people so far. What makes you think you're impervious?"

"He cares for us. In another day, we'll be out of here."

"To a life of what? Always on the lookout? Fleeing? Paranoid? Is this what you want for your son?"

"I don't want to be in jail, I know that."

"You've got to make better choices than you've been doing. You owe it to Billy."

"Shut up," said Ingersol, now angry and reaching for the tape again. Medina had no choice but to shout, "Fire! Help! Billy, call 911!"Ingersol looked startled and slapped her, but Medina then shouted again, "Call 911!" Footsteps rushed in. Chat Litt didn't stop when he entered. His foot hit her hard on her head. Once again, she passed out.

A clackety noise was the first thing she heard. Medina opened her eyes to see she was outside in the dark. The outlines of trees were visible and moving. Litt carried her. The sound of a train on the tracks was loud. She was still bound and her mouth taped. It was so woodsy around her that even though Starbucks and main street Wayzata was on the other side, no one could see her. He must have waited for the train to do this—the sounds would mute out her struggle.

Litt smiled when he saw her eyes open. "Sorry, Babe. We can't let the kid know, and Margery agreed to let me do things my way."

Medina tried screaming again and wriggled hard, but her voice felt muted with the loud train, and Litt kept a tight grip. He started running. "The sooner you're in the drink the better." Something heavy was on her chest, a weight of some sort. She would sink quickly to the bottom.

The trees bounced by more quickly. The train clacked on, and in a few more seconds she'd be underwater. This was how her life would end? Alone, in the night, murdered? This fucking was it, and she screamed louder, wriggled harder, to no avail.

Before his second step on the dock, Litt blurted out a groan, and she flew out of his hands. He slipped? She bumped hard onto her butt and skidded down the dock. She twisted onto her stomach to give her more stopping power as she was now sliding off the dock. Even shallow water would kill her. She shoved the tips of her shoes against the dock to slow her down. She stopped right near the boat hoist, which held a speedboat out of the water.

She was almost halfway off the dock like a log teetering on the edge. She held herself as straight as she could to keep her weight in favor of the dock. She was safe for the moment, as long as she could keep this position. However, soon Litt would merely walk out and kick her in.

But that wasn't happening. Although she couldn't see clearly because of the darkness, it seemed Litt was on the ground, wrestling with someone. They were just shadows twisting as the train hammered on. Was that why Litt tripped? She needed to hold on. Was it the boy? Ingersol? Whomever it was screamed over the train, deep in pain.

Chapter Nineteen

Once in flight to Minnesota, Ian had stared into a cloud whose shadowed contours made him wonder why God would live on such nothingness. Ian then thought about what he was doing—perhaps the stupidest thing he'd ever done. Would he be able to explain this extravagance to his father? What if Medina wasn't at the same hotel or what if she didn't answer her cell phone? Then again, this felt like his last chance. He needed to follow this through.

He pulled out a blue gel pen in a metallic casing, which he'd bought at an airport newsstand along with a *Newsweek,* and he wrote on the back of his magazine. Things to do at landing:

Rent a car

Reserve room at Sheraton (maybe she's there, too)

Contact Medina

He drew circles around the last. He probably couldn't tell her at first that he needed her for more than just finishing the case. He could only tell her when the situation was right.

When he landed, it was just after sunset. He'd seen the last spit of the sun dive under the horizon while the plane was descending. Once in the airport terminal, he called Medina, but he only got her voice mail. He said, "It's me, Ian. I have some good news. Give me a call." He next had called the Sheraton where they had stayed before. He asked for her room, and the operator put him through, which told him he had her hotel—but she didn't answer. She was probably at work on something—a good sign. Hope surged in him.

But where might Medina be? She might interview Dottie again. Ian decided to go to the county jail first. If he didn't find Medina there, Dottie might know where she was. After all, Medina might have had to speak with her again.

Ian zoomed toward downtown Minneapolis in another rented Focus. He tuned his radio to the NPR station. His heart gave a start. Medina spoke. "The way I look at the world, nothing is perfect, but, rather, society is in a balance," she said on the radio. "On one side is the sense of peace and safety and people are inherently good."

What? This had to have been taped earlier. In L.A. He remembered her mentioning the interview. Now in his car she sounded so lively, so smart.

He listened to the rest of the interview smiling, pounding his steering wheel once. "Go Aleece! I get the subtext. Give it to Wexler!"

"I try to help keep things in balance," she said.

Ian was charged.

He found the county jail thanks to Google Maps on his phone. He learned at the jail that, while it was still visiting hours, Dottie would have to approve to meet him. He hoped she would.

Ten minutes later, Ian stepped though a metal detector, passed, and was led into a visitor's booth where Dottie was waiting on the other side of the glass. Ian picked up the phone.

"Actually, I'm glad you came," said Dottie.

"Why's that?"

"I'm truly sorry for what happened to you. Know that I never meant for you to be taken hostage." Dottie was doing what Ian had done with his parents, Pierra, and Cromley: apologizing.

"Thank you. I forgive you. Sorry if I sound hurried, but I'm in Minneapolis looking for Aleece Medina. Have you heard from her?"

Dottie explained she'd met Medina earlier, and Medina had been looking for Margery, who was now with Chad Litt and her son and in danger. Dottie had told her about the bakery and boathouse. "But that was hours ago," said Dottie. "If she caught them, there's been nothing said to me here." Ian asked a few questions and gleaned the necessary details of where the bakery and boathouse might be.

Now Ian worried about Medina and tried her cell phone yet again. He still only got her voice mail, which meant she was on the line or her phone was turned off. "It's me again," said Ian. "Now I'm starting to really worry. Are you okay? Call soon, please."

He rushed to Wayzata. There he found the Wuollet Bakery, but it wasn't next to the tracks. There was Starbucks, though, in a big old place. Could that be it? As he parked, he spotted a silver Volvo, the one Medina had rented before, and when he looked inside, there was Medina's briefcase on the floor. On the roof of the car stood a cup of coffee. He dipped his finger into the coffee. It was cold. So was the night air. He hadn't packed anything, and his long-sleeved shirt wasn't enough for this October evening. He rubbed his arms for warmth, then stepped up to the railroad tracks to see if he could spot a way through the hedge.

A huge horn sounded, and he looked down the tracks. A train was coming, its bright front light on. He had to make a decision—one side or the other. If it was a long freight train, it'd be many minutes until he could cross the tracks again.

He spotted a break in the hedge and jumped in. The train soon rumbled by, shaking the ground. The wheels created a loud clacking and screeching.

The interior of the bush was very dark, and he stumbled, disoriented. He emerged and saw the boathouse in the moonlight, but no lights were on. If they were hiding out in it without the owner's awareness, they wouldn't have any lights on.

A screen door slammed, and Ian moved behind a tree. A dark figure emerged from the boathouse carrying something. Was that Litt, and what was he carrying? A body? Medina? It was her size, and she wasn't moving, and Ian needed something to kill the bastard with. Litt hadn't heard Ian because of the train, so Ian still had surprise on his side. Ian glanced about for something he could use as a weapon. He needed one *now*.

He peered through the screening of the front porch, and in the dim light were a number of objects on the floor. He opened the door to the porch as the train clacked on, and he scanned over the items quickly—a lawnmower, two rakes, a gas can—and a shovel, which he grabbed. Litt was moving toward the lake with the body, but now the body wiggled violently. Medina? Whoever it was was *alive*.

With the loud train, Litt wouldn't hear him. Ian ran noiselessly toward the dock with the shovel and now saw Medina's face in the moonlight. It was her, duct tape over her mouth, and she struggled against her bonds. Ian gained ground. Just as Litt stepped onto the dock, Ian leaped and swung the flat blade of the shovel toward Litt's head but hit his shoulders. Litt grunted and immediately fell, dropping Medina on the dock. She slid toward the water. Stay on the dock, he willed, as Litt flipped around and clasped Ian's legs. Ian fell.

Litt stood up, grabbed the shovel and swung it toward Ian. Instinctively Ian threw up his right arm, and the shovel came down hard on his cast near his elbow, which, to Ian's surprise, didn't hurt. He gripped the shovel, yanked it away, and stood up, getting his bearings. They were on the shore, and Litt charged before Ian could lift the shovel. Litt was going to ram him into the water. Ian stepped to one side and smashed Litt in the neck hard with his cast. Litt fell again, and Ian screamed as he felt shooting pain in his wrist. Still, the cast had done the job. Litt gasped for breath, stood up once more, staggered, then forced ahead again. With the relentless rumbling of the train, all their sounds were swallowed. Litt with his huge fist smashed Ian in the chest, and Ian screamed in pain but did not fall.

He dies or I die, Ian knew. Litt's large hands came around Ian's neck. Litt squeezed. Ian struggled for breath and tried pounding Litt's arms, but Litt had the advantage. Ian jammed his good hand into his left pocket hoping to find car keys. His fingers found something better. His gel pen.

Ian yanked it out and jabbed Litt hard in the side. The shaft jammed through the T-shirt and slid in between ribs. Litt screamed and let go of Ian's neck. Gasping for air, Ian managed to grab the shovel handle. He swung hard with the edge, slicing Litt in the legs behind the knees. Litt crumpled once more.

Ian scrambled backward, stood, raised the shovel, shouted gutturally and lunged ahead as Litt moved onto his knees. Ian chopped at the man murderously, and with a side edge out, his blow caught Litt directly in the chest. Blood splattered, and Litt careened back hard. Litt held his own chest—surprise in his eyes. "You?" Litt fell backward.

The train passed into the distance, and soon its clacking quickly made way to silence. Ian raised his blade like a hatchet and aimed for the man's neck. Time to kill him. But Ian hesitated. He needed some slight movement from Litt, a suggestion of aggression, but Litt lay helpless. Ian heard Litt's desperate breathing and something more: a splash. Ian looked to the dock. Medina was no longer there.

It would only take another second or two to kill Litt, but he didn't. Ian ran. "Help! Police! Call the police! Help!" he shouted into the still air. Maybe no one would hear. He jumped in near the boat hoist into about four feet of water, and he pulled himself underwater feeling for Medina. It was too dark to see anything. The water was warmer than he expected. It was also murky black, but his good hand came down on what seemed to be an arm, and then he felt the rope. He grabbed the rope and stood, pulling her up. He quickly yanked her toward shore and into the air. He clasped her firmly and lifted, screaming at the effort of lifting her onto the dock. A light went on at the main house. Up on the lawn, he could see Litt still on the ground.

He checked her breath. Nothing. "Help!" he shouted. "She's not breathing!"

He ripped off the duct tape on Medina's mouth, scrambled onto the dock and put his mouth to hers the way it was done on TV. With one huge breath, he blew in. Instantly Medina gasped and, turning her head, threw up water.

Ian screamed "Yes!" with tears coming to his eyes.

Medina looked up at him. "Oh, fuck," she said. "Ian?"

"Yes! You're alive!"

"I thought I was dead."

"No, no." Ian began untying her, but his hands were shaking, he was so amazed she was still here. It was if all the gravity in the universe brought them here at this moment—and he felt so light. He found himself breathing quickly not in disbelief but the opposite: in utter belief. Once he had her arms unbound, she hugged him firmly and kept saying "Thank you."

He undid her legs and the weight plate that had been duct-taped onto her chest.

"How did you get here?"

"God is in the details."

The distant sound of a siren could be heard, and it was getting louder. The police were coming, he hoped.

"Let's get you up," he said, and as he lifted her, he could feel her shiver. "You need a blanket. Let's go to that house."

Medina stumbled.

"We don't have to walk fast," he said.

"Stop a second," she said, her voice cracking. "How did you find me? How are you here?"

Ian held her to keep her warm, then looked over at Litt, who was wheezing badly. "All I wanted for so many days was to have him dead," said Ian. "Now he'll probably bleed to death, and I feel sorry for him."

"It's not your worry."

He let her sit. Nearby, perhaps on the other side of the tracks, tires screeched and peeled away. "I wonder if that's Margery and her son?" he said.

"She's the Busty Bandit—why would she stick around?"

Ian nodded. A mother's love knew no laws.

He walked over to Litt, who stared upwards, shivering, looking helpless. Ian fully expected Litt to find the power to resist and make another attack, but the man merely lay there. The sirens kept approaching. Maybe Litt would make it to trial after all.

Ian returned to Medina.

"How'd you get here?" she asked again.

He told the story as the sirens approached more loudly. Soon lights flashed, throwing swirling red and blue through the trees. Men were running toward them, flashlights bouncing. He had to tell her what she needed to know.

"I am so amazed," he began.

"You should be in the FBI," she said.

"Remember when you told me about taking responsibility? Well, I did. My parents forgave me. My ex-girlfriend forgave me, as does my professor. Will you?"

"You saved my life."

"Yes, but I need more."

"I forgive you," she said. "But I don't think you came all the way here to ask me that."

"We work together well, don't you think? It just seems to me… I mean…"

A strong light flashed on them. A bearded man in a police uniform said, "You okay? What happened here? The people in that house said someone was shouting for help."

"I'm a special agent with the FBI," said Medina. "That man over there has been wanted in connection with bank robberies, interstate flight, and kidnapping."

"And murder," said Ian, pointing over to Litt. "He was trying to murder Agent Medina."

"He requires medical help," said Medina.

"So do you," Ian said.

"Gurneys!" the man shouted toward the light green fire trucks and ambulances next to the police cars. "Three people here. All need help."

"I'm probably okay," said Ian.

"We'll check you all out."

More lights shone on them. Soon the crime scene was abuzz with activity, including the arrival of ambulances. Litt was put in one and Medina in another.

A young officer, clean-shaven, asked Ian, "And who are who?"

"Just a guy—in love with her." He pointed to Medina who was talking to two paramedics inside her ambulance. She could not have heard what he'd said.

"I have her statement so let me get yours. What happened here?" the young officer asked. He had a pen in hand.

"This man over there, Chad Litt, had tried to kill her by throwing her in the lake tied up. I happened to come in time."

"And how is that?"

"The story is too long—starts with my being a hostage after a bank robbery in California. I'll tell you later, okay?"

"That's fine," said the officer, shutting his book. "Maybe at the hospital."

Ian looked over to the ambulance with Medina inside. A man was shutting a door. "Can I go with her?" Ian asked.

"Hold up, Juul. Take this guy, too."

They hurried over.

"Hey," Ian said to Medina when he entered the ambulance.

"Hey," she said back.

He sat next to her and took her hand. He knew the words but he had to get to them. He flubbed things far too often, and he just needed to say it well. "You see," he began.

"I heard what you said. I love you, too."

"You do?"

"I do, but—" said Medina.

"No 'buts'."

"I just kind of know where this is leading, and the fact is, you and I aren't normal people."

"What's wrong with that?" He took her shoulder gently. "Really."

The ambulance started up with its siren. They moved off quickly, and Ian felt jostled.

"It's not like I don't want you," Medina said. "But I also know that I tend to have strong ideas and opinions, and most guys seem to tire of that."

"You're a strong woman, you're saying."

"Yes."

"My type. And you seem to accept my occasional misunderstanding, which is good."

"Occasional?"

"I *know* you. We are alike. We're each romantics," he said. "We like the idea of destiny but are more determinists. We're alone more often than not because we have some twisted vision of a perfect relationship. You know what's normal? Imperfection. When I think about the last few days and look at the people in love, no one's normal. My parents are in love and abnormal. My high maintenance ex-girlfriend Pierra, not normal, but she's found her Preston. Would you consider Dottie and Catherine normal?"

"They're nice—and different, I'll agree. Dottie made me see a few things about relationships."

"I consider it in our favor that we're not normal." He smiled. He tried to read her face, but it was too dark. She nodded.

"Fact is," he continued, "I've adored directing in the theatre because I could make people behave the way I wanted—what I couldn't do in life. But now understand why David Mamet's hard edge has morphed into making him a gentler, funnier playwright. Fuck it, right? We have to enjoy what we have. Being around you, I learned I don't need so much control. Around you, everything is chaos—and it's not so bad."

"I don't know about that."

"I'm in the moment. And know what else I've learned? My life in theatre has given me a lot. It's helped me in our investigation. My studies haven't been wasted."

"That's true."

"And another thing—I heard you talk on NPR on the radio. It's about balance, right? When we're together, we have balance."

"Balance," she echoed.

"We've found it. I love and need you."

"You do?" she said.

"Will you at least go out with me? On a real date?"

She touched him tenderly near his ear. "Yes. But if you're thinking marriage, I'm not the marriage type."

"You're a handful," he said.

"And you aren't?"

Ian moved in to kiss her, but she put up her hand.

"My mouth," she said, "tastes funny."

"Monkeys don't use toothpaste, and they kiss."

"What?"

"Well then, no tongues."

But he lied. They used tongues. Lightning couldn't have stopped them.

And the siren screamed into the night.

Acknowledgments

Thank you to my wife, Ann Pibel, whose support, easy-going nature, and critical abilities mean a lot. Many thanks to FBI agent Stephanie Benitez and to former agent William J. Rehder, a thirty-three-year veteran of the FBI whose specialty had been bank robbery investigation in Los Angeles. I'm grateful to agent Eric Lasher for introducing me to Mr. Rehder. I'm in gratitude to editor Lynn Hightower, who saw the whole thing through and really helped me stay true to my original intentions while keeping it dramatic. I'm grateful to Carol Fuchs for being the first proofreader and an adept one, as well as others who joined in, including Ehrich Van Lowe, Allison Robbins, David Pibel, Sandi Holden, and those in the Meeks clan including George, Laura, Annie, and Zach.

About the Author

Christopher Meeks has had stories published in several literary journals, and he has two collections of stories, *Months and Seasons* and *The Middle-Aged Man and the Sea.* His novel *The Brightest Moon of the Century* made the list of three book critics' Ten Best Book of 2009. His novel *Love at Absolute Zero,* also made three Best Books lists of 2011, as well as earning a *ForeWord Reviews* Book of the Year Finalist award. He has had three full-length plays mounted in Los Angeles, and one, *Who Lives?* had been nominated for five Ovation Awards, Los Angeles' top theatre prize. Mr. Meeks teaches English at Santa Monica College, fiction writing at Southern New Hampshire University, and Children's Literature at the Art Center College of Design. To read more of his books visit his website at: www.chrismeeks.com.